Jennifer Matthews was raised as a privileged New York debutante of the mid-1880's. Following the deaths of her parents her Uncle, Julian Carlman, came to her rescue. Only it wasn't a rescue. When Julian attacks Jennifer with nefarious intent she strikes him dead and flees to parts west. There she meets and marries the man who could save her or be her worst nightmare.

Indentured Bride
Copyright © 2019 Regan Taylor
ISBN: 978-1-4874-2660-6
Cover art by Martine Jardin

Published by eXtasy Books Inc or
Devine Destinies, an imprint of eXtasy Books Inc

Look for us online at:
www.eXtasybooks.com or www.devinedestinies.com

Indentured Bride
The Bride Book 1

By

Regan Taylor

DEDICATION

To Rosemary Rogers, Kathleen Woodiwiss and Johanna Lindsay who introduced me to the wonderful worlds of historical romance.

PROLOGUE

1855 Adler Creek, Wyoming

"Marry you? You want me to marry you?" Christina Jeffers laughed without humor. "You don't seriously mean . . ." her laughter becoming hardier " . . . you think I'd *marry* you?"

"That's generally where a courtship leads, Christina." Brett Parker told her, how stunned he was at her rejection clear in his tone.

"Oh, Brett, you sweet man. Yes, generally it does, but I can't marry *you*."

"Why the hell not?" Brett Parker asked.

Stopping her laughter for only a moment, Christina told him, "Brett, look in the mirror . . . you're half Cheyenne. I couldn't possibly marry an *Indian* let alone a dirty half-breed."

Refusing to show the hurt he felt at her answer, Brett stood and pulled himself up to his full six feet four inches. Drawing in a deep breath, he looked down at the petite blond sitting before him. It took all his control not to wring her lily white neck when he answered, "And here I thought giving a whore a proper name was worth my time."

He caught Christina's hand a second before it would have connected with his jaw. "I am *not* a whore!"

"No? Then what do you call a woman who spreads her legs for any man who happens by?"

"I'm better than you, Brett Parker. I'm White, all *White*. You

1

can only try to pass. No self-respecting woman is going to marry you. Maybe I have slept with a few men here and there . . . it's not like a crime for a widow to take a lover, you know. But I'm no whore."

"No, Christina, you aren't better than me. You aren't better than anyone."

He stepped away from her. As he grabbed his coat, she called after him, "Brett, just because I won't marry you doesn't mean we can't carry on."

"What?" He knew his surprise at her statement showed clearly on his face.

"Well, until I find a decent White man to marry, I don't see why I can't have you in my bed . . . that's all any of the women want with you, Brett, your body and your money. I thought you knew that. You may as well give your body to me because I don't need your money."

Drawing on a lifetime of control, Brett walked out the door, taking care not to slam it lest the depraved woman on the other side know just how angry and hurt he was by her comments.

He controlled his gait, making sure his strides did not change from the length he normally took. Clenching his hands, he forced himself to lose the image of choking Christina with them and to let his arms hang loose. He knew he was half-White, half-Indian and so did the entire town of Adler Creek. Everyone accepted him for who he was—a Deputy Sheriff and because of his father's business acumen, a fairly well to do rancher—but most importantly, a self-made man. *Yeah, a self-made man who isn't good enough for any woman to marry.* Despite how his father fought for Brett to be treated as an equal, despite how hard Brett tried himself, it was clear the old prejudices were alive and well in Christina Jeffers. Vowing to never again become involved with a woman, especially a white woman, it took all his effort, but he strode past the saloon and walked on to the Sheriff's office where his lifelong friend and boss, Rick Hansen, sat behind his desk reading the local paper.

"Thought you wanted tonight off to take care of some personal business," the blond haired, green eyed Sheriff greeted his Deputy. His smile quickly faded when he saw Brett's face. "You want to tell me what happened?"

"No."

"You want me to buy you a drink?" he asked while opening a desk drawer and pulling out a bottle of whiskey.

"No."

"Okay, then we'll sit here and talk."

Brett ran his fingers through his collar-length black hair. He'd worn it long in his younger days, but now, as a Deputy Sheriff, he felt it important to be as White as possible. Drawing in a deep breath, he paced back and forth across the room while he exhaled, finally coming to stop in front of Rick's desk. "I asked Christina Jeffers to marry me."

"You did?" His surprise at Brett's actions evident in his tone. "And?"

"And she said no . . . she didn't just say no, she threw it in my face that I'm a half-breed. She said no self-respecting woman would ever want to marry me."

"Well that's just one stupid bitch's opinion." Rick slouched back in his chair, causing it to creak with the movement. His Nordic ancestry evident in his broad shoulders and heavily muscled body.

"No. No, it's not. She said some hateful things, but Rick, they were true. She said that women only bothered with me for my money . . . not because I'm someone they could . . . love . . ."

"Brett, she's just one woman . . . one woman who has slept with half the men in this town. You're better than her and if she can't see that, it's her problem, not yours."

"Yeah, well it will be a cold day in hell before I put myself out like that again."

CHAPTER ONE

March 1860

Twenty-one-year-old Jennifer Matthews stood at the entry to the parlor that held the coffin of her dear father. She needed to be strong today. She needed to withhold the tears that had flown so freely the last few days. The smell of the flowers and death barely registering through her grief. Today she'd cried no tears, but the rims of her eye lids showed the heartbreak she had endured the past few days. *Why Papa? Why did you take your life? Why did you leave me? And why did you leave me in Julian Carlman's hands?*

Oh, she knew the answer to her last question. Julian was her mother, Dorothy's, brother and when she was first born, he had persuaded her mother to make him little Jennifer's guardian should any thing happen to her and her husband, William. However, the news of this guardianship only became known to Jennifer with her father's passing. Why he killed himself, she would never know. Yes, there was a note that he could no longer live without his beloved wife. But it didn't add up because just days before he had told Jennifer he was considering courting Myra Holcolm, the widow of one of his associates. He seemed so young, so delighted at the prospect, especially when Jennifer told him she was pleased for him. And she genuinely was. More than anything Jennifer wanted her dear papa to be happy and for as happy as her parents were, her mother had been dead several years. It was time for her papa to find a new wife.

William Matthews had been a successful attorney in New York City, providing his beloved wife and daughter with not only a plush mansion to live in, but a staff of servants to provide whatever assistance they would require. He ensured Jennifer had the best education available to a young woman, even hiring tutors for the more advanced studies that most women did not indulge in.

Dorothy was a petite woman, delicate in stature and health. Jennifer was her greatest gift. After trying for many years to conceive and birth a healthy and living child, the Matthews had all but given up. It was much to their surprise and joy little Jennifer was born.

While not entirely certain of Julian's ethics and values, William could deny his wife nothing and agreed to allow her brother to stand in as godfather to their little bundle of joy. According to Dorothy, Julian just seemed to run into bad incident after bad incident, but he would truly care for little Jennifer should something befall them. At one time William thought he'd heard some discussion about Julian's business dealings and that he manipulated people to get his way with never a care of who got hurt in the process.

And, with their charmed life, what could happen? Hadn't she delivered Jennifer even though the doctors had said she would never carry a child to term? Having Julian made godfather was just a formality.

Growing up, Jennifer never doubted her parents' love. They doted on her like no child had ever been so doted on. Yet she was not spoiled and, at her father's insistence, she had been well-educated and taught to stand on her own two feet. While her mother ranted that Jennifer would never make a good wife with all her independent ways, William held firm in his belief that some independence would serve his beloved daughter well.

Standing now in the parlor, Jennifer reflected on how, as a

child, she had loved the parlor—with its comfy chairs, its pretty lamps, the crystal candy dish her mother had kept filled for her—but that only her father would let her have the yummy butterscotch candies from. The room's wide windows overlooked the park and had been a favorite place to sit and read and dream. But since her mother's death six years ago—had it really been six years—she hated the room.

Her mother had always been so full of life, or so that was what her father had told her. He would tell Jennifer how lucky she had been to have Dorothy as her mother. Then suddenly, without any warning, she was gone—a tragic carriage accident. What seemed so odd about it was that just a day or two before, her father had the carriage checked over and it was fine, in perfect condition.

Fortunately Dorothy had left Jennifer home that day or Jennifer herself may have died as well. From the day her mother was laid into the coffin and placed in the parlor, Jennifer hated the room. In fact, until today, she had not set foot in it since her mother's funeral. And now her father had joined her mother. With revulsion, Jennifer relived that horrid night three nights ago when she returned home to the quiet house and found her father dead, having taken his own life.

"Father? Father?" Jennifer rushed in, exhilarated with the news she had to share with him. Addison Hawthorne had proposed marriage and was going to arrange to talk to her father that very night, to ask for her hand.

"Father! Where are you?" She would normally find him in the library, but the room appeared dark. He usually returned home from work at his firm and would sequester himself in there till dinner, only to return for hours after the evening meal. Ever since her mother's death, he'd buried himself in there night after night. But tonight the room was dark and he didn't answer. Spying their housekeeper, Judith, she hurried over. "Did my father send word he would be late?"

"No, Jennifer dear, not a word."

Sighing she looked about the foyer. "I wonder what would keep him that he wouldn't at least send a note." She moved towards the library door and in the dim light cast from the hallway saw her father's form lying across the desk.

"Father? Father?" She approached with Judith close behind her. "Father?" As Judith turned the lights up, Jennifer first gasped and then screamed. Her father was indeed sitting in his chair, but his head lay on the desk not in repose, but in a pool of blood. When the doctor came, he advised it appeared to be a self-inflicted gunshot wound. He assured Jennifer that William had died instantly and felt no pain.

No pain? No pain? But what about my pain? Oh father!

A note had been found beneath his body. Amid ink and blood stains were incoherent words that spoke of her mother and how desperately he missed her. He missed his beloved wife so much he took his life and left Jennifer to fend for herself.

Her Uncle Julian came early the next day. He asserted that even though she was twenty-one, he still needed to stand in as her guardian. After all, he *had* promised her parents before God and man when he became her godfather that he would care for her as if she was his own.

Now she shuddered at the thought of the man. From her earliest memory of him she was revolted by his mere presence. There seemed something unclean about Julian. She would try to tell herself it was how he slicked back his dark hair, making it appear as if he wore oil, or that it was the dank smell of his clothes. Yet inside Jennifer knew it was the man himself the cringed from. How he could have been related to her mother was beyond comprehension. As a little girl she couldn't avoid his touches, done in the name of *loving* his little niece. She rejoiced as she grew older and managed to avoid even being in his company. And now, now with her father's death he'd been appointed her guardian. A chill moved through Jennifer that had nothing to do with her father's death or the weather. Like a premonition of horrors to come from that man . . . her uncle Julian.

Uncle Julian. Her stomach turned at the thought of him. He always seemed to her to be a disgusting, vile man who touched her in ways she did not want to be touched. In front of her parents he acted with proper decorum, but as soon as their backs were turned, he would pat her bum, her *boopie* as he called it. When she was older and her breasts began to develop, he'd grab her and whisper that she had *a lovely boopie and lovelier boobies* and would laugh his lewd laugh at his own sick humor. In front of her parents he would give her a proper kiss on the cheek and pat the top of her head. And again, when her parents would not see he would place his lips on hers. On her thirteenth birthday he tried to stick his tongue in her mouth. Even now the thought of such an invasion turned her stomach. When Addison kissed her it was short, sweet, on her cheek and only on occasion her lips. He never tried to use his tongue on her.

When she turned fourteen she tried to tell her mother, but Dorothy insisted her brother Julian would *never* behave so inappropriately. Jennifer redoubled her efforts to avoid the disgusting man. And now . . . now as her guardian he could control her life. Now she was being forced to go live with him. Somehow she'd manage to avoid his advances, somehow she'd maintain her dignity . . . and her virtue . . . around him.

What she didn't understand was the way he pushed her to sign papers, legal papers he said, almost as soon as he arrived. The man didn't give her a moment to grieve her lost parent. The way he rushed her through it, pushing page after page in front of her, telling her that her father wouldn't, couldn't, be properly buried unless every one of them were signed before the mortician arrived. The condescending way he had patted her on the head when she tried to ask about them . . . well better her head than any other part of her body. And now he was forcing her to go to his home in Maryland with him. They'd never visited there. Whenever Papa suggested they go, Julian would have a reason why it was not a good time. By the same token, when he visited, he would regale them with stories of all the treasures and riches in the house.

"Well, Jennifer my dear, I hope you have packed what you will need for the short term . . . until we can have the rest of your belongings sent for. I'll have my solicitors take care of putting this house and its contents on the market."

"No, Uncle Julian, I don't want to go with you or sell my home. I intend to remain here." She fought for calm and strength, telling herself if her words sounded strong they would be enough to protect her.

"I'm afraid that's not possible my dear, your father's Will specifically stated that should he pass before your twenty-fifth birthday I shall remain your guardian and administer your Trust. Your future is in my hands, so to speak, and I believe it best if I remove you from here and you put this all behind you."

Into his hands. He certainly had tried her entire life to get her in his hands. Living with him for the next four years would be a slice of the hell the minister spoke about every Sunday. There had to be another way, there just had to.

With her father barely cold and in the ground beside her mother, Julian rushed them to the train station. Jennifer hardly had a moment to say goodbye to the household staff before Julian practically dragged her out of the house. She'd wanted to assure them of good references and pensions, however Julian cut her off and whispered in her ear it had been taken care of. That in and of itself would have been fine, except the letch had stuck his tongue in her ear just as he finished speaking. He seemed to grow more disgusting with each passing day.

As the miles from New York to Maryland passed, Jennifer wondered how she would survive the next four years with the odious man. What could she do escape him and whatever nefarious plans he had in mind for her—and reprehensible plans they would be if she knew anything about her Uncle Julian. For all his smiles and pretended warmth, all one need do was look into his eyes and know there was not a sincere bone in his body.

CHAPTER TWO

Julian's House — Maryland

April 1860

Arriving in Maryland with her Uncle Julian three short days after her father's funeral, Jennifer Matthews looked forward to a respite to contemplate the changes her life had taken in such a short time. She'd hoped for some peace on the train to Maryland, but that was not meant to be. He'd procured a sleeper car for her which at first, she appreciated. She had just begun to slip into sleep's escape, the clickity clack of the train on the tracks, when Julian tried to enter the compartment. Fortunately she's tied a sash around the door knob, barring his entry. It took considerable effort on her part, but throughout the trip she'd managed to avoid Julian's constant attempts to touch her.

And it wasn't him just taking her arm like any gentleman would; no his arm would rub against her breast or his hand would stray to her fanny. His arm would snake around her shoulders, and her stomach would turn at the thought of his foul breath near her face. He was disgusting. From his oily black hair, to his smelly cigars, to his lewd actions, he was just intolerable. Jennifer had nowhere to turn, no one to turn to. Perhaps here, she thought, in his house, he would stop the constant attempts to paw at her . . . but it wasn't to be.

"I had the lavender room set up for you, my dear," he told her as he escorted her upstairs in his rather ostentatious house. "I hope you will be comfortable here and once we sell off your father's house, there will be plenty of money to change it any way you wish."

She gave him a sharp look at his reference to the sale of her home . . . her *home,* he changed his approach a bit. "What I meant, my dear, is that I have plenty of money available. I only thought that in your own bid for independence you would want to pay your own way where you can. You see? It would allow you to start taking responsibility for your financial situation. Of course, I will always be available to guide you." His hand lingered a bit too long and a bit too low on her back as he showed her into the room.

"It's lovely Uncle, it truly is a lovely room."

"Good! I'm glad you like it. And, my dear, should you need anything, my rooms are just through here." He walked to one of the doors in the room and pulled it open to reveal an opulent, yet garish bedroom. A red satin spread covered the massive, four-poster bed. Rich black carpets covered the room, and heavy, red velvet drapes covered the windows. Even though she had never been in one, Jennifer had heard descriptions, whispers from friends who knew someone who had been to one and as she looked at the room, the word *bordello* came to mind. Yes, her uncle's room looked like a bordello.

Despite her revulsion at sleeping so close to him, Jennifer managed to force out a "Thank you for your concern," before turning away and telling him, "I am a bit tired from the trip and would like to refresh myself and perhaps nap a bit if you don't mind?"

"Of course, my dear, I'll have Antoinette, the housemaid, come wake you in time for dinner. We dine at six-thirty here."

"Thank you." She waited for him to leave and when he continued to stand there, his lingering gaze directed mainly at her breasts, she was at a loss as to what to do. Finally the events of the past week came to the fore and she boldly told him, "If you would leave now Uncle, I'll take that nap."

Julian smiled, though the movement of his lips sliding back on his teeth more resembled a leer or a grimace, she wasn't sure which, and left the room.

Dinner was both a trying and tiring affair. Jennifer tried to tell herself that her father had not betrayed her by leaving Julian as her guardian, and being here with the odious man was for the best, but her uncle completely turned her stomach. He leered at her during dinner and under the table he continually pressed his knee against hers. When the meal finally ended Jennifer announced, "If you don't mind, I'd like to look through your library, see if a book catches my eye, and retire early. I'm quite tired and the past few days have worn me out."

"Of course, my dear." This was his favorite phrase, and he said it like he was going to eat her for his next meal.

One thing Jennifer could say about Julian's library — it was massive and one of the best she had ever seen. Better even than the one at home — or what had been her home. She quickly chose a volume, not because it appealed to her, but because she wanted to get away from Julian and have a moment's peace. She went up to her room and read for a short time before nodding off to sleep. But a peaceful night's sleep wasn't to be . . . it seemed she had only closed her eyes before a creak woke her. There, the sound again, like someone moving in her room . . . and a low light crept through the doorway . . . *the doorway to her uncle's room!*

"Uncle Julian?"

No answer.

"Uncle Julian, are you unwell?"

He approached the bed, and Jennifer saw a garish red velvet robe loosely belted and two skinny legs peeking out the bottom.

"Uncle Julian, if you are unwell tell me and I will send for the doctor."

"Oh I'm quite well my dear, quite well." His hand moved to caress her cheek as he slid to sit on the bed. "I just thought how sad for you to sleep alone on your first night here."

"I'm fine, Uncle, I've slept alone for years."

"Ah, but no more, my dear, no more. I know you will want to earn your keep in some way and show your appreciation to me for taking you in, and I believe I have found the ideal way." He climbed onto the bed and shifted to lie next to her. Jennifer gasped and tried to pull away from him but he anticipated her move and grabbed her.

"Oh no, my dear, no running now. Perhaps in time it will be a fun game to play, but not now, not tonight, I want this to be special for us both."

Afraid of what he meant and suspecting it was worse than she could imagine, she tried to shove away from him.

"Dear, dear Jennifer, I don't want to hurt you—the first time will hurt enough, but I will try to make it as pleasant as possible—for both of us."

His low laugh turned her stomach. *First time for what?* Jennifer began to struggle as Julian slid his hands up her arms. Suddenly, he grabbed her hair at the nape of her neck with one hand, holding her firmly in place while his other hand groped for her breast. The delight in his voice was evident in his chuckle as he squeezed the globe. "So firm, so plump. Yes, my dear, you will be an excellent bed partner and who knows, in time perhaps we can make other arrangements, with my friends, so you can pay your debt to me even faster."

Friends? Arrangements? What is Uncle Julian . . . He was going to rape her! Jennifer felt her mind shutting down as the realization of what this man—her uncle—the man her parents had blindly trusted to take care of her was going to rape her!

She had to distract him, she had to stop his assault. "Debt? What debt?"

"Why the one you owe me, Jennifer dear."

She continued shoving against him and through gritted teeth told him, "I don't know what you are talking about."

"Jennifer, Jennifer, taking a young woman into my home is no easy matter. I will need to hire you a personal maid, pay for your food, clothes . . ."

"I have plenty of clothes."

"Oh my dear, not the kind you need, not the kind *I* want to see you in." All the while his hands kept groping and grabbing at her, stroking her breasts until she squirmed away from him which prompted him to move to touching her derriere. It didn't take long until she realized her movements, her struggles to avoid him, excited him even more. His breathing changed from his attempt at whispered seduction to excited panting. His mouth seemed to have an over-abundance of moisture as he tried to kiss her.

Self-preservation took over and Jennifer began to struggle in earnest until she realized her continued struggles only excited him more. She had to do something — she had to get away.

Seeming to anticipate her rising panic, Julian laughed, "Now you can scream if you like, but the household won't answer — I've already told them you are both wild and demanding — and they certainly won't do anything to interfere with the master of the house. One of the advantages of indentured servants and slaves is they don't disagree with anything the master wants. Best you learn that, my dear, best you learn that, because you are little more than that. You belong to me now and I will care for you as I see fit."

His hands tore at her night shift, rending it in two. She felt something wet strike her breast and realize he had drooled on her. *My god, the man is so excited he's drooled on me!* Then suddenly his hands were everywhere, her breasts, her hair, between her legs, poking and prodding until she began to scream. Instead of causing the letch to stop his attack it served to increase his delight in forcing himself on her. *He is insane! Oh, Father what have you done to me?*

Panic overrode common sense and Jennifer began to grope around her, feeling for something, anything, to stop his assault. His excited panting increased and the smell from his mouth was worse than usual; his hands were cold and clammy as he groped her wherever he could. Somehow her hand fell on the bedside lamp. It was a good-sized lamp, but she managed to lift it and in a moment brought it down on his head. With a grunt he slumped and lay unmoving on the bed. She shoved him off her and stared in horror at the blood pouring from his head.

"Uncle Julian?" She reached to shake his shoulder and when she had no response, called to him again. "Uncle Julian?"

Jennifer stared in horror only a moment before scrambling to her feet and running to the armoire. *I have to get out of here! Oh my god, I've murdered him . . . I've got to get away before anyone knows what I've done.*

Jennifer stood staring in horror at the man's body lying before her. No, not just a man . . . it was her Uncle Julian, and she'd killed him. She knew no one would believe her. He was too well established here in Maryland, and no matter how badly he may have treated his staff, they would have no reason to support her side of the story. After all, hadn't he told them that she was a willing participant in whatever relationship he had planned for them? Mentally shaking herself she softly called out, "Uncle Julian?"

When there was no answer. She stepped closer to the bed and poked at his shoulder, "Uncle Julian, can you hear me?"

When he did not move . . . not that she had ever seen a corpse move . . . she whirled and rushed to the closet and hurriedly pulled out her clothes. Dressing quickly, she pulled on the traveling skirt and jacket she had worn the past two days, all the while glancing over her shoulder at her uncle. He still hadn't moved. "Oh my god, I've killed him!" She couldn't help but repeat the statement over and over beneath her breath. The growing fear of being blamed for his murder, and that no one would believe she'd struck him in self-defense spurred her to move faster. She grabbed her small satchel and shoved a few necessary items and articles of clothing in it before she quickly finished dressing. Still there was no movement on the bed, just blood that seemed to still be flowing from his head. He was dead. He was well and truly dead and Jennifer Matthews knew without a doubt she was a murderess. She had to get out of there and away as quickly as possible.

Jennifer ran down the stairs as quietly as she could, unlocked the front door, and stole out into the night. But where to go? She knew no one here in Maryland. She couldn't return to New York—the authorities here would know by morning what she had done and they would look for her—so where could she go?

She walked aimlessly down the street, towards the center of town, towards what she hoped was the rail yard. When she came upon it, she spied an open box car and climbed in, hoping that the train would soon leave and take her away from there and the horror she had just left behind. She moved to the furthest corner of the car and sat with her back to the wall yet able to keep an eye on the door.

Towards morning she was startled awake with the sound of the car's door slamming shut, followed shortly by the train's movement, hopefully leaving the station. *I'm getting away! I'm getting away. They haven't found me . . . but where do I go from here? Where will I be safe?*

With no light entering the car and only the sound of the wheels on the rails for company, Jennifer had no true idea of their direction or how long they traveled. The one thing she wished she had thought about in her flight the night before was food and water and now, in the heat of the car, she was becoming thirsty. What seemed like days later the train stopped and she waited a bit to see if anyone would come and open the door. When all was quiet she went to the door and tried it. To her relief it pushed open. Cool evening air greeted her. *Maybe my luck is changing.*

Looking around quickly and seeing no one, she jumped from the car and moved first away from the lights of the rail yard and then towards what appeared to be the lights of a town. Hungry and thirsty she kicked herself again for not thinking about taking money from her Uncle Julian. What difference would it make to be labeled a thief as well as a murderess? She stopped and felt in her purse and was relieved to find some coins in the bottom. At least she could buy a meal and a place to sleep until she found some work. She walked a short distance further before coming on a tavern. She'd never been in one before, decent young ladies didn't enter places like that. Well, maybe desperate ones did. *Here's hoping they won't object to letting a room to a lone woman.*

She entered the building and was surprised to find about twenty women of all sizes, shapes and style of dress sitting and standing about the room, chatting in small groups, almost all of them smiling and seeming to glow with anticipation.

A tall redheaded man approached her. "You here for the train west?"

"Uh, yes, yes I am." *Train west? Trains are going west? West is good, that will work. Yes, it will get me away from here, wherever here is.*

"Do you have a letter or telegram from your future husband or taking your chances?"

"Err, taking my chances." *Letter? Husband? Chances on what?*

"Okay, there's quite a few of you doin' that, but I think the men will be happy about that. So go ahead, take a seat and we'll be starting in a few minutes."

"Fine. Um, err, where might I buy a bit of dinner? I've been so excited I haven't eaten in a few hours."

"See the man at the bar. I think they're still serving."

Just as Jennifer returned to her seat with her meal, the red-headed man called for quiet.

"Well ladies, thank you for coming. My name is Dustin Hendricks, but you can call me Dusty. This here is Zeke . . ." A man with long blond hair and a closely trimmed beard stood and waved to the room in general, "and we've been hired to guide you on out to Adler Creek in the Wyoming territory and your grooms."

Wyoming Territory? Well Uncle Julian's solicitors or the authorities will never think to look for me there.

"They paid expenses for twenty-five so there's room for . . ." he stopped to count the women in the room " . . . three more so if you have any friends who have been thinking about coming along, they need to be ready to ship out tomorrow."

Tomorrow . . . good. Wherever I am now, it's still too close to Maryland. The sooner we start to wherever, the better.

Dusty continued, "Now before we get out on the trail, there's a couple of things you will need to know. While we have an escort leaving with us and will be met by some Army troops in St. Louis, you will be driving your own teams, cooking your own meals and you will need to know how to shoot a gun, preferably a rifle. Now I know that's not considered *lady like* to some of you, but the west is not your cultured city. Those of you who have messages from your future husbands, trust me they are eager to meet you."

Several of the women giggled, pleased smiles on their faces.

"Those of you who are planning on meeting your grooms there, I can tell you that you will have your pick — so not to worry that you won't be getting hitched. There's a passel of good-hearted, hard working men anxious for wives to share their lives with. So tomorrow morning I want to see you all down here by 6:00 AM and ready to start learning to drive the teams."

Jennifer finished her meal, feeling better than she had just a short time ago. A plan began forming in her mind that she would go as far as St. Louis and then, with a new name and a history she could create for herself, she could begin a new life. *I'm sure I can find some sort of acceptable work to do and no one should be able to find me.* In her headlong flight from Maryland she didn't let her thoughts linger long on the fact that she had killed a man. As the meeting broke up, two women approached her.

"Hello." One of the women from the group greeted her.

Jennifer's tentative *hello* in response was warmly returned when the woman continued, "This is Beatrice, or Bea as we call her, and I'm Maybelle, but my friends call me Belle."

"I'm . . . Jenna . . . Jenna Martin."

"Pleased to meet you, Jenna. We noticed you came in late and wondered if you had signed on with another wagon yet."

"Uh no, I hadn't, no, not yet."

"We need a third for ours — the way Dusty explained it is that we need three women to each wagon, to make the trip go smoothly. That we'd alternate one driving, one cooking, one to gather wood and clean each night. Would you be interested in sharing our wagon?"

"Oh yes, thank you. I would truly appreciate that. Thank you."

"Wonderful!" Belle beamed at the news. "So do you know who your husband is or are you taking your chances?"

"I'm taking my chances. And you?"

"We both have our husbands — or letters from our intendeds." Her wide smile put Jennifer or the new person she had chosen to become, Jenna, at a level of ease she hadn't felt since her parents died. "But from what I hear they are all handsome and . . . ardent." She giggled, a warm and friendly sound.

"Ardent, huh?"

"Yes. Definitely will be warm in the cold months, yes?"

"It would seem so."

"Well, we also have room in our room here if you haven't taken one yet."

"Oh yes, thank you. I arrived late, in fact, just before the meeting began and haven't gotten my bearings yet."

"Not a problem. So where are you from originally?"

Jennifer thought a moment . . . *I can't tell them New York, they might have heard of my family and Father's suicide. And I can't say Maryland because of Uncle Julian's . . . death . . .*" Connecticut. I'm from Connecticut. And where are you from?"

"Right here in Virginia."

Virginia, I made it to Virginia!

"Well, we'd best turn in, early start tomorrow you know."

Jennifer picked up her satchel, prompting Beatrice to ask, "Where's the rest of your luggage?"

"Oh, I wanted to travel light, you know, coming down by myself I didn't want to have to depend on anyone, if you understand me?"

"Oh, good thinking. You'll need to pick up a bonnet though if you don't have one."

"Thanks, I'll look into that tomorrow . . . we should have a little time before we pull out, shouldn't we?"

"Oh yes, we're learning to handle the teams tomorrow, shooting the next day and then we leave to join our intendeds!"

The women headed up the stairs to their room and Jennifer waited till Beatrice and Belle completed their ablutions before doing her own. She would have dearly loved a bath, but until she had a better lay of the land, she would follow what the others did. She felt relieved and fortunate that the two approached her. At least she could stay in their shadow until they pulled out. While she had never done anything dishonest, until she killed Julian that is, Jennifer was astute enough to know that if she paid close enough attention to the two women, she could construct a new identity for herself by time she arrived in St. Louis.

CHAPTER THREE

Jennifer didn't remember laying her head on the pillow and apparently slept a deep, dreamless sleep because Bea had to give her a good shake to wake her the next morning. The women dressed and headed on down to breakfast. When the meal ended, they headed on out to the yard and joined with the rest of the group for their first lesson in handling the ox teams. She eyed the two oxen skeptically since she had never been this close to such animals until Bea told her, "Actually, I've driven an ox team a few times at home on the farm so it won't be that bad. And they are actually pretty decent beasts, not mean at all."

For the next several hours Dusty coached, yelled, and then coached again on how to drive the teams. Round and round in circles they went, first straightening out and then back in a circle. He finally called a break for them to return to the inn and have their noon meal before another several hours working with the teams. When the meal was done, a bone-weary Jennifer approached the innkeeper and requested enough hot water for her and her two new friends to have hot baths that night. Unused to the physical exertion of managing the ox team and wagon, Jennifer was sure there wasn't a bone or muscle in her body that wasn't hurting. Once they were on the trail, it would be a long time before another hot bath was going to be available, and since her future *husband* was paying her way . . . at least to St. Louis . . . she felt she could afford to spend some of the coins she had.

And as to the money from the unknown husband? Well

somehow, some day, she'd find a way to find out who he was and pay him back. Bea and Belle were delighted when they entered the room and found the tub waiting for them. For Jennifer, after the past few days, even having grown up with every luxury imaginable, sitting in the small tin tub with the lukewarm water was truly the most pleasant bath in her life. She patted herself on the back for learning to handle the oxen as well as she did today and how she'd gotten this far despite her uncle's attempt to rape and do who knew what else to her. It bothered her that she'd killed a man, but she wouldn't let her mind go there . . . not to the blood pouring out of his head as he lay there dead on the very bed he planned to rape her in. She had to focus on her future and making a life for herself. She smiled as Bea and Belle talked about their soon-to-be husbands and read and re-read the letters they had received from those charming men.

Jennifer woke to Belle once again shaking her and calling her name. Coming out of a restless sleep, she looked around at the still dark room. "Is it time to get up already?"

"No Jenna, you were calling out something about *no* and *don't touch me.* You were having a bad nightmare."

"I'm so sorry."

"Not to worry. I think we all have moments of nervousness about this adventure. But really, from what I've heard and what my Henry, my groom to be, has said . . . all of these men, our future husbands, plan to treat us like princesses. But your nervousness is natural, really."

"Thank you, Belle, thank you. I appreciate your understanding."

They fell back to sleep and Jen was relieved when she woke easily in the morning with no real memory of the dream that had upset her the night before. Again after breakfast, they went out to the yard and Dusty taught them first how to clean and load the rifles and then began teaching them to shoot.

After lunch he showed them how to shoot the pistols that would be also provided to each wagon. At dinner that night he congratulated them on their progress in such a short time.

"Ladies, you have done really well. Not perfect, but you've done really well. I suggest the most experienced drivers take the reins tomorrow morning when we head out, the least experienced I'd suggest sitting up front to observe. If you all want to sit up front that's fine, but make sure the most experienced has the reins. The first few days should be easy going but we're going to push for ten to fifteen miles a day. By the end of the first week you should all be proficient with the teams. After dinner each night we'll go over cleaning and loading the guns and take a few practice shots. I want you all to be ready for what we may encounter once we pull out of St. Louis."

Jennifer considered that . . . St. Louis . . . where she would be leaving with her new friends and starting a new life. She was sure she would know what it felt like to be in love with someone when it was right, after all, she loved Addison, hadn't she? She wouldn't have accepted a proposal from a man she didn't love, so of course she loved him.

Addison. Someday she'd have to tell him what happened, but not any time soon.

On the other hand, there was Uncle Julian who showed her just how repulsive a man could be. There was no way she was going to marry a stranger and take her chances with an unknown man for a husband. She was sorry some man, who may turn out to be wonderful and kind, was going to be disappointed, but she couldn't get married, not to a stranger and not until she made peace with herself over killing Julian. Addison . . . she again considered sending word to him, but would he still want her after what had happened? Would he believe her that she was still untouched? Not that that would matter . . . after all, she would be in prison for murder if not hanged. No, Addison couldn't help her.

Jennifer had requested another hot bath for herself, Bea, and Belle — it was going to be her last *luxury* for a few weeks and she intended to enjoy and share it. Physically and mentally tired, she fell right asleep and, judging by the happy mood of her two friends the next morning, she hadn't had another bad dream.

The excitement of finally leaving was evident in all the chatter from the entire group the next morning, and Jennifer herself got caught up in the anticipation as the wagon train pulled out of the small Virginia town. She was on her way west. She was on her way to freedom and avoiding capture for murdering Julian Carlman.

CHAPTER FOUR

"So Brett, give, why didn't you put in for a bride?"
Brett looked over at his boss, peering at him through long, dark lashes, "Cause I don't need a wife."

Rick shot Brett an appraising look before continuing "Now that's bullshit, plain and simple bullshit."

"And why is it bullshit?"

"Cause out on that ranch of yours it gets plenty lonely, especially on a cold winter night."

"My ranch doesn't get any lonelier than your place here in town—I have Marta and Franco there to keep me company along with the other hands, and on a cold winter night I just throw another log on the fire and another blanket on the bed."

"Well, a lush female body is a lot more pleasant than another blanket."

"Now if that's so true, why didn't *you* buy yourself a wife?"

"Well now I just might. Dusty said he'd be bringing several more women who are looking for husbands, and I might just pick one of them."

"And break the hearts of half the women in the territory?"

"Never know, but how I see it, you didn't order a bride so you could have free pickins of all the women here."

"Yeah, yeah, sure . . ." Brett picked up his hat as he stood. "I'm headin' over to Mary's place to get a coffee, you interested?"

"Nah, not right now . . . Brett? Hang on a sec, would you?"

"Yeah?"

"The bride thing . . . Brett, we've known each other a lot of years and I know family is important to you . . ."

"And?"

Even if Rick couldn't see the look on Brett's face, he would have known his friend was not in the best of moods at the mention of the brides.

"Truth—why didn't you send off for a bride? Was it because of that business with Christina a few years ago?"

The Brides as they were being called were the brainchild of Henry Bascom. One winter evening over cards the men had been talking about how nice it would be to have a loving woman to go home to and snuggle under the covers with. As the conversation progressed, Henry, businessman that he was, suggested that maybe the postal service could bring them . . . and, after considerable ribbing said, "Fine, I'll arrange it."

Next day Henry put an ad in the Gazette that he was sending back east for a bride and if anyone else wanted to get himself a mail order bride to see him by the end of the week. Come the end of the week eighteen men sent in their notices that they would like to arrange for a bride, and Henry handled sending the information to several newspapers in the East. Surprise rippled through the town when twelve women wrote back they would like to move west and marry. A few exchanged letters, some telegrams and the brides were now on their way. Rick and Brett got a lot of teasing about not sending for brides for themselves—Rick bowing out gracefully, telling the men that it was his job to keep the law in town and getting married might distract him with so many new folks coming. He assured them he'd wait to for the next round. Brett was his usual quiet and stoic self about it and merely smiled when the subject came up.

With a heavy sigh Brett sat down and gave Rick a long sardonic look before speaking. "I've been thinking on it . . . but I can't seem to make up my mind. Do I want a local girl, one of those mail order women, a woman from my mother's tribe or another half-breed? You know how us *breeds* got to stick together."

"Brett . . ."

"I know, I know . . ."

"Well don't you think it's time to let it go?"

"I would if everyone else would."

Brett's father, Whitney Parker, was on his way to the California gold country when he got as far as Adler Creek and fell in love with the land. His wife, Clarissa, hadn't wanted to move west in the first place and was never very happy in the Wyoming territory. She took ill and died not long after giving birth to Brett's older brother, Kendrick. One of the neighbor women said it was from problems with the birth, but his pa said it was more like it was from how sad she was. It was only a year or so later Whitney met Brett's mother, Falling Leaf, and married her. His pa often said that Falling Leaf was really his one true love. Brett was born a year after their marriage, but his parents' love did not keep the reality of his being of mixed race from the other children. While most of the other children were like Rick—accepting and good friends, there were the ones who took on their parents' prejudices and Brett endured not only name calling, but a fair share of being beaten up by a few of the older boys. Fortunately for Brett he grew tall rather quickly and had no problem holding his own.

A few of the girls were curious about kissing him, but not one of them showed any interest in him beyond a few secret kisses. Of course, that was still when they were in school, but Brett hadn't done any courting since being rejected by Christina Jeffers six years ago. The skinny blonde wasn't really very attractive—she just thought she was, and most of the young men agreed with her only because they knew how easily she'd give away her favors. Sadly for Brett, he'd believed when she spread her legs for him it was out of love and not because she was only interested in his body and his money. When he was courting her, he thought she didn't want anyone to know she shared her bed with him so they would think it was a proper courtship . . . that she had class. He was too much of a gentleman for a bitch like Christina. When Christina told him she would never marry *some dirty half-breed*, the statement cut Brett more deeply than anyone except himself ever knew — not because of the lie that they had not slept together, but for her words. After that the only White women Brett associated with were those that worked at Ellie's Place . . . ladies of the night. He'd go out to his mother's people and his brother, Wolf, a few times a year, but never spoke much of the Indian women he'd see. On the occasions Rick would accompany him, he saw how virtually all of the single women eyed the dark-haired man, but Brett never returned their interest.

"Brett, Christina Jeffers was years ago, she's moved back east and I believe the last of her stink left with her. You have a lot to offer a woman, if you just gave one a chance."

"Yeah, well, maybe next time. We can get ourselves some brides at the same time." Wanting to end the discussion Brett asked again, "So that coffee?"

"Not right now, but check out the saloon while you're about though, would you? Thought I saw Tom McKendrick come into town earlier and I was hoping he could pull a few nights here at the jail this week."

"Sure enough."

Rick watched his friend leave, a feeling of sadness bubbling up. For all Brett's talk about not needing or wanting a wife, Rick knew there was a loneliness in the man. Or maybe it was his own loneliness that he was saying was Brett's. Most in the town had gotten over that his mother was an Indian, but the emotional scars of being treated like an outcast, being called *half-breed* for most of his life, still affected his friend. Yeah, he had women. Female companionship or rather sex, was not lacking in Brett's life. They liked his money and the ones who invited him to their beds only wanted the physical pleasure he could give them.

Not that Rick was a bad catch. Oh yeah, sure, he was the Sheriff, had some good acreage, but he had his own secrets. Secrets that Brett didn't even know.

Still, a wife would be good for Brett and one of those eastern women wouldn't know about the past or how some of the locals felt about Brett's mother. Well, they'd see what happened when the women arrived.

CHAPTER FIVE

Just as Dusty said, after a week out on the trail Jennifer began to feel completely at home handling the ox team as well as handling the rifle. That both surprised and pleased her. Growing up in New York, she had the best of everything and most everything labor related was done for her. She rode horses, of course. But a groom saddled them, she rode side-saddle like a lady and a groom took care of the horse when she was finished riding. This was entirely new for her and she was thrilled at what she was accomplishing.

The farther they went from Virginia and Maryland, the safer she felt. After the first few days Belle and Bea stopped asking her so many questions about her family, where she was from and what she was looking forward to in . . . where was it they were going? *Addison, Abner, ah! Adler Creek.* At first Belle was so inquisitive Jennifer considered screaming — and then she broke into tears and told her that both her parents were dead and that talking about them or having to leave her home in Connecticut was just too depressing. Fortunately the women seemed to understand that and stopped asking. Jennifer had also discovered that all of them were more than happy to talk about their pending nuptials and their dreams about their weddings. It was only in fleeting regret she lied about coming from Connecticut rather than New York.

"So Jen, what does your wedding dress look like?"

Oh no, how do I answer that? "Well to be honest, not knowing what my husband might like, I thought I'd wait till we arrived and then I'd see what his tastes are and buy or have one made."

"Oh that was good thinking. I have mine with me, but I might do the same, you know, see what he likes, but I hear that they plan to marry us as soon as we arrive. You know, off the wagon and down the aisle. Maybe you should look for something in St. Louis — I'm sure whoever you marry will like it."

"Well," Bea interjected, "I don't think it's the weddin' dress our grooms are going to be looking at . . . it's gonna be about taking those dresses off!"

"Bea Edwards! You lascivious woman you!" Belle's laughter carried away from the wagon causing several of the other women to turn, curious at what was so funny.

"You don't want a few days to settle in and look around the town?"

"Heavens no! Jen, I'm thirty years old and I feel lucky that Mr. Clive Gunnell wants to marry me at all. I'm afraid if I wait, if we wait, the wedding won't happen at all. And . . . I want children and he says he wants them, too, so we'll need to start on making a family quite soon, if you get my drift."

"I suppose. What about you, Bea, do you want to get married right away?"

"Definitely. I'm only twenty-six but no one was offering for me at home and when Calvin saw my tintype and asked me to come marry him, I knew I didn't want to wait. I plan on marrying him as soon as possible. Why would you want to wait, Jen?"

"Well I'd like to get to know him, whoever he is, a bit. Remember, you have both gotten letters and had a chance to correspond with your intendeds. I don't even know if anyone will want me."

"Oh, someone will. Not just because someone paid for a bride, but you're a beautiful woman . . ." With a gamin grin spreading on her lips, Bea continued, "Even with all that trail dust all over you."

"Isn't that the truth? I don't mind the cold streams for bathing, but that next hot bath I get you won't be moving me out of for six hours."

The three friends had a good laugh at that before Bea went on, "But, Jenna, don't you feel like you should marry the man who paid for you as soon as you arrive? After all, some man paid good money to marry you, why would you make him wait?"

Paid for her. The words reverberated in her mind. Being paid for, even as a bride, was no different than the slaves or indentured servants her Uncle Julian kept. No, Jenna affirmed to herself, she'd make her own way. No man was going to buy her.

"Jenna? Why would you make him wait?"

Shaking herself out of her reverie, she answered, "To make sure we're suited and if we're not, well then I'll find a way to pay him back."

"How are you going to do that? Are you an heiress or something?"

There was no malice in Belle's question—one thing Jennifer had learned was that both Bea and Belle were kind and considerate and neither seemed to have a mean bone in their bodies. *What would they say if they knew I killed a man? The way they talk about just giving themselves to a stranger, even if they are married to him, would they condemn me for not giving myself to Julian?*

Belle noticed the shiver go through Jennifer and she asked, "Jen, are you feeling alright?"

"What? Oh, yes, fine. The breeze just kind of chilled me for a moment. Nothing to worry about. And as to paying my intended back—well buying a bride, paying for a bride, it still feels a bit to me like buying, like buying a . . . ."

"You mean like the slave trade or an indenture?"

"Yes, exactly. But since I haven't a dowry or parents to pay for my wedding . . ."

Jenna was relieved a few moments later when Belle shifted the conversation to talking about their wedding nights.

Again Jennifer couldn't believe how easily the other two considered giving themselves to total strangers. Uncle Julian was no stranger and his touch revolted her from the time she was a child. They couldn't really think it was going to be easy, let alone pleasurable, to give themselves to total strangers.

"Well I don't care if he has a large or small wang, as long as he knows what to do with it."

"And how would you know about a man's wang, Bea Edwards?"

"Well, you remember Marabeth Andrews, don't you?"

"Of course." Turning to Jennifer, Belle explained, "we grew up with Marabeth and she got married about seven years ago, has four children, and she filled us in on the marriage bed and all."

"I see, and what did she say?"

"Well I don't know if she was telling the total truth or not, but she insists that her husband, John, has a *huge* wang . . ."

"By a *wang* do you mean his . . . his . . ."

"Penis. It's an affectionate way to say penis."

"I see."

"One?"

"One what?"

"One what what?" The three women burst into such loud laughter that the women in the wagons in front and behind them craned their necks to see what brought the laughter to such a peak. A woman called Millicent jumped down off the wagon ahead of them and walked back, her smile warm and open. "What has you the three of you laughing? All day today I hear you girls giggling. Tell, tell!"

"Oh," Bea started, "we're discussing the fine art of wang manipulation."

"Wang manipulation? Bea Edwards, you can't manipulate

a wang, it's a solid rod when a man is excited."

When Millicent jumped down, Bea saw Dusty start back towards them, clearly to see if there was a problem. She realized she embarrassed him no end when she turned to look up at him and asked, "Isn't that so, Mr. Hendricks?"

"Isn't what so?"

"When your wang is hard you can't bend it around."

Dusty coughed and turned abruptly on his horse and rode to the head of the line leaving a billowing cloud of dust in his wake.

"Well maybe he can't bend his." Once again their laughter was heard up the line and Millicent rushed back to her wagon and climbed aboard to tell her travel mates what had transpired.

By time they stopped for the evening every woman in the train had heard the story and even the shyest of the group, if not laughing outright, was chuckling to herself.

CHAPTER SIX

Day by day, Jen found herself more at home with the other women, especially Bea and Belle. And day by day she realized how hard it was going to be when she left them in St. Louis. While she'd had friends in New York, these women were more solid, more real in some ways. Or maybe for the first time in her life she was able to appreciate other women, people with substance. She listened eagerly to their stories and thought about which ones she might use to build her own new identity. She wasn't proud of planning to steal events from the other women's lives, but had little else to use. No part of Jennifer Matthews could remain because if there was they could find her and bring her back to stand trial for Julian's murder.

She also appreciated how neither Belle nor Bea asked about the nightmares that now came to her almost every night. They would wake her, ask her if she was alright, and when she would assure them she was, everyone would go back to sleep. After the first few times when Jenna would not respond or try to dismiss the dreams, they'd stopped asking. While there were a few times she wanted to confide the horrors she experienced each night — seeing again over and over in her dreams Julian attacking her followed by her killing him — she knew if she told them any part, they would ask more questions.

Finally, in mid-June, almost two months after beginning their journey, they rolled into St. Louis. Bigger and busier than she expected, the sights, sounds, and smells thrilled Jen. Clearly it was going to be easy to lose herself in this city.

Dusty led the train to a nearby inn that he'd used before when leading the wagon trains. "Alright ladies, let's get the oxen secure and we'll order up some hot baths and comfy feather beds for the next two nights. Being as we're traveling in summer we should make good time getting across the plains. You got letters you want to write back home, now would be a good time and we'll get them sent off. Any questions?"

"Yes, I do," Dahlia Verdun called.

"Yes, ma'am?"

"Will we have a little time to shop? Maybe pick up a few items?"

"Sure enough, tomorrow you'll have time, just make sure you can afford it and that there's room in your wagon for whatever it is."

A short time later, Jennifer luxuriated in a hot bath planning her next move. There wouldn't be time tonight, but tomorrow she'd go to the shops and hotels and see if she could hire on. There weren't many things she could do but she felt if she was determined enough she'd find something.

After a good night's sleep, the first in weeks because she was once again in a soft feather bed, she woke refreshed and ready to greet the day. Bea and Belle had already left the room so she ventured downstairs alone. While she would have preferred a quiet breakfast by herself, Dahlia and a couple of the other women called her over. Why Dahlia was going to Wyoming to find a husband puzzled Jen—she was attractive, funny, and came from a well-to-do family. She was very much like what Jen had been before her father killed himself and Jen would never have considered moving away to marry.

After finishing breakfast she begged off the shopping excursion and pretended to have something to attend to upstairs but instead she dashed into the kitchen and out the back door. Hoping to go the opposite way of the other women, Jenna ventured into two shops. At each she was told there were no openings and no need for help. The nearest hotel was her next stop and just as she entered she heard her name. Or rather, Jenna's name. When she didn't turn or respond, Dusty walked quickly up to her and took her arm. "Miss Martin?"

She gasped and Dusty would have had to be blind not to see the panic in her eyes as she pulled away from him.

"I'm sorry, Miss Martin. Really I am. I called you several times but you didn't seem to answer."

"Oh I'm sorry, Mr. Hendricks, I guess I'm more pre-occupied than I thought." *I have to remember my name, I have to remember I'm now Jenna Martin.*

"Well, from what I heard back at Pauline's Millinery you sure do have a lot on your mind."

Trying to keep her surprise to herself several questions went through Jenna's mind. *Whatever is the man doing in a millinery? How much has he heard? And why does he care?*

Her blush, while endearing, told him indeed more was going on than he originally thought.

"Yes, well I guess I do. Have a lot on my mind that is."

"This trip kinda' sudden for you?"

"Yes, that and, well, I didn't think to pack for different weather and well, conditions and . . ."

"And you thought you'd take a job for a day and make enough to cover those expenses."

There was nothing she could say. Clearly the man had heard something . . . how much she couldn't guess, but he'd heard something. When she didn't answer Dusty continued, "Why don't we grab ourselves a cup of coffee and see if'n I can't help you figure things out?"

"All right. Yes, that would be nice." She'd have the coffee and then try to find a way to ditch him, put the job hunt aside for the day and hopefully manage to stay hidden until the wagon train left tomorrow. After all, if she managed to avoid authorities looking for a murderess in Virginia, she could certainly hide from a wagon master with a timetable.

He guided her into the restaurant and they placed their orders for their coffees. Dusty studied Jen for a moment before speaking. "I'm not the smartest or wisest man in the world, but I do know people and what's normal and what's not. There was no Jenna Martin on the manifest and no letters or telegrams have been exchanged for one. Now that's not really much to say because there's several women who heard about the bride search from friends and decided to take their chances. But there's no one else from Connecticut and while you could have heard from a friend, you didn't know anyone when you joined up. And before you tell me you saw an ad, there were none in Connecticut. So I don't know how you found your way to us and I don't care. What I do care about are those men, hardworking, decent men. Men who paid the way for their brides and expect me to deliver them safe and sound.

"Now let me tell you about these men, Miss Martin. Most of them do all right financially, have ranches or decent businesses, but saving up to basically buy a bride didn't come easy. They had to save and trust someone with that money to pay their way and provide for them once they arrive in Wyoming. These men put their hearts and lives on the line hoping for a good marriage. Each one of you cost a bit of money to transport.

"Now beings you're among strangers and gonna be around more strangers, I can understand a body, especially a woman, being nervous."

He paused a moment, took a sip of his coffee, as if to give her time to respond. When Jennifer did not, he continued, "In a few weeks you're gonna be laying beside a man you never met before and sharing every aspect of his life with him. I can understand you being afraid and having second thoughts, but if one of you were to decide that you were going to stay here in St. Louis, that wouldn't be right. It wouldn't be fair to the man, who, in essence, paid for you to be his wife."

"That's slavery Mr. Hendricks."

"No, not it's not. It ain't slavery, but some man paid for you and unless you have the money to pay him back, now, today, you best be prepared to go on to Adler Creek and marry the man who is paying your way. Is that understood Miss Martin?"

Jenna was quiet for a moment before answering. The man was certainly plain spoken and he certainly had expressed her very own thoughts on being a mail order — paid for — bride. "Yes Mr. Hendricks, I do understand. And you are right. I am afraid and was afraid to say I was afraid. I will not give you any more concern on our way to Wyoming."

"I'm glad to hear that Miss Martin, I'm glad to hear it. Now whatever it is you are running from I don't care. That will be between you and your husband. And he may not care himself. But just be sure you are in your wagon and ready to go in the morning."

"I will. I promise. And, Mr. Hendricks, I'm sorry if I caused you concern. I'll find a way to put my fear aside."

"Good. Now, did you need some money to maybe buy yourself a few things?"

"No, I'm fine, really."

"It's there if you need it. Some of the men knew their betrotheds may not have enough money to outfit themselves."

"No, really, I'm fine."

They finished their coffee and Jennifer went back to the inn and up to her room. It was clear she wasn't going to be able to stay in St. Louis . . . she was going to Wyoming. *Well maybe no one will want me and I'll be able to get a job there and pay back whoever paid my way.*

When Bea and Belle returned, they tore open their packages, showing a few new dresses to Jenna, excited by what they had found. Over dinner, if she was more quiet than usual neither Belle nor Bea seemed to notice and while not obvious, she felt Dusty's eyes on her more than once. As they moved to retire for the night she stopped by his table. "As I said this afternoon, Mr. Hendricks, I won't give you any cause for concern."

"Miss Martin, like *I* said, I don't much care why you joined up with us, but you are with us and you'll see, when you get to Adler Creek, there'll be a fine man waiting for you."

The next morning Jennifer was there with the others, ready to go. As they gathered, Dusty announced that in addition to their military escort they would also have a photographer joining them. "Mr. Webster has one of those newfangled camera things—a tin type they call it and he will be . . . What is it you call what you want to do, Mr. Webster?"

"Mornin', ladies. Pleased to be joining you. What Mr. Hendricks was referring to is I'm going to do what I call a *photojournal*. I'll be takin' pictures along the trail and then at your weddings so you'll always be able to remember the big day."

Many of the women ooohh'd and ahh'd, clearly indicating their delight in having Mr. Webster along. Bea hurried over to him and asked if he wouldn't mind taking a picture of her, Belle, and Jenna together telling him they were her two best friends in the world and she wanted to remember this trip with them always. Jenna tried to dissuade her. "Oh, Bea, I'm sure Mr. Webster is quite busy getting settled to join us and . . ."

"Not at all, Miss."

He was almost relieved when Belle stepped in, telling Webster, "I'm Maybelle Kline and this is Bea Edwards and this is Jenna, Jenna?" She looked around and Jenna seemed to have disappeared. It seemed Dusty noticed her move off, and was obviously curious about what she was up to . . . and somehow wasn't all that relieved when she called from their wagon.

"Over here! I want our picture to be taken with Ding-ding." She stood behind one of the oxen, patting her on the head. "After all, she and Bingo are part of this, too, aren't they?"

Bea squealed as she rushed over. "Oh, Jenna, what a fun idea! Yes, Ding-ding and Bingo *are* part of our adventure. Mr. Webster?"

Dusty was a bit curious about what Jenna was doing until he saw the way she stood beside Ding-ding so as you couldn't really see it was her standing there. The lady was clearly hiding from something. But he gave her credit, she was going to do what she could to make her friends happy.

Dusty tipped his hat to her as he ordered they move out, leaving Jenna to wonder just what Dusty knew.

CHAPTER SEVEN

The wagons wound their way across the plains and the scouts commented how lucky they were that no Indians were to be seen. It was, amazingly, a peaceful journey. In September, towards the end of their travels Dusty had Zeke and one of the scouts moved on ahead to let the men know their brides would be arriving shortly. While on the trail Jennifer felt relatively safe and secure despite the dreams, which had fortunately began to come farther apart. Sometimes she'd go a night or two without one, but once they got to their destination, well, she'd just have to find a way to avoid getting married. Along the way she'd looked for places where she could disembark and leave the train, but Dusty always seemed to be nearby, watching.

At one stop she was sure she was going to succeed, having told Bea she was going to nap and Belle she needed to use the privy and then was going to take a nap herself. She disappeared into some bushes and settled down to wait for the train to leave. Just about the time the last wagon began to roll out Dusty appeared behind her. "We're about fifteen miles from the nearest way station and without water, how were you planning on making it alive?"

When Jenna refused to answer, he took her by the arm and led her to his horse. He deposited her none too gently on the big stallion and told her to hang on.

"Mr. Hendricks, I assure you, I can walk fast enough to catch the last wagon."

"Miss Martin . . . I'm afraid I don't trust you to do that. I don't know what's going on with you and frankly I don't care. But those two women you're traveling with, they would care. How do you think they would feel knowing you had just disappeared?"

When she didn't answer, Dusty pressed, "I asked you a question, Miss Jenna Martin, if that is in fact who you are. How do you think those nice women who took you in, would have felt?"

"I have no desire to discuss my personal life with you, Mr. Hendricks."

"We're not discussing your personal life, Miss Martin. We're discussing Miss Bea and Miss Belle and how it would hurt them something awful if something happened to you."

He paused a moment and Jenna's hope he was done was quickly dashed when he spoke again, "Unless, of course, you've told *them* what you're running from."

"I'm not running from anything. I . . . I just. Well I changed my mind and just don't feel I can marry a stranger."

"Oh, you're running, Miss Martin. You are definitely running from something. Fortunately for you the west is full of people, mostly men though, that are running from something. I just hope if it's a husband who hurt you, you come clean to your new husband.

"I assure you, Mr. Hendricks, I have no prior husband."

"No matter to me."

They rode in silence a bit, the other women casting curious glances as Dusty rode by their wagons with Jenna planted firmly before him. A few whispered to themselves they had thought all along Dusty was smitten with Jenna with how he spent time with her in St. Louis and kept an eye on her on the trail. Speculation ran rampant that maybe he had finally declared himself to her. The response was generally to the effect that they did make a sweet looking couple.

A short time later Dusty rode back down the line to Bea

and Belle's wagon and helped Jenna off the horse onto the wagon's seat. As he tipped his hat, he told her, "Have a nice rest of the day, Miss Martin, and we'll talk again later."

Red faced, Jenna mumbled to herself, "Not if I can help it."

Belle was all atwitter. "What happened, Jenna? Did he propose to you? Did he kiss you?"

"Oh, yes," Bea broke in. "What happened with you two? I've noticed he looks at you a lot, always seems to be watching where you go and if you need help or anything. Are you going to marry him?"

"Marry Dusty Hendricks? Oh goodness, Bea, Belle, oh, goodness no. I can barely stand the man!"

"Well if that's true, why did you hang back with him and then ride with him for so long?"

If Jenna thought she was uncomfortable with Dusty, she was even more so with Bea and Belle because she liked them. She genuinely liked the two women whom she considered better friends than any she had grown up with. How could she tell them what happened without lying even more than she already had?

She swallowed before speaking. "I got nervous, scared actually. What I'm doing, where we're going, suddenly hit me and I got scared. I know it was foolish, but I was going to try to go back . . . by myself."

"Oh, Jenna." Belle pulled her into an embrace and patted her head much the way Jenna's mother had when she was a child. "We're all a little nervous. You've just been so quiet about it we thought you weren't worried. This is new for all of us, and we're all wondering just what we're going to find. It will be okay, Jenna, I promise, it will be okay."

"Yes it will, Jenna," Bea added. "And most of all we have each other. Right?"

Later that night, after the dishes were done and the animals bedded down for the night, Jenna sought Dusty out. "Can I speak with you for a minute?"

"If it's to convince me to send you back . . ."

"No. I need to apologize. You were right today. I was thinking only of my own fears and concerns and not how badly it would hurt Bea and Belle. They were a little worried . . . but apparently mostly thought you and I . . . well, they thought . . ."

"They thought I was courting you?"

"Yes."

"And?"

"I told them no, not at all."

"That's good. Because, Miss Martin . . . pretty as you are, I sure don't want a wife that is going to try to wander off at every turn. I want a woman who is steady and doesn't have any dark secrets in her past."

"Well, I'm sorry for any trouble I gave you today."

"Apology accepted. Now, I suggest you get on back to your wagon and get some sleep."

Now, here they were, just a few days away from their final destination. Just a few days from meeting the man who was going to marry her. Dusty said these men were decent, good men and the last thing one of them needed was to be saddled with a murderess. Or worse, what if she was forced to marry one and he demanded outright she share his bed? No one would deny a man his rights to his wife. It could be worse than Julian's attempted rape because a man could bed his wife whether she was willing or not. And what was the difference between what Julian wanted to do her and some man buying a bride? Yes, she'd have to figure something out.

"Riders! Riders!" Edgar Samuels called out. Several other men joined him on the street as the Zeke and the scout dismounted in front of the Sheriff's office. Rick stepped out to greet them.

"Gentlemen?"

"The Bride Train's on its way, your intendeds should arrive in about four days."

"That's good news, very good news. You eaten yet?"

"Nope, rode almost straight through."

"Well, let's get you a meal and a room and bring us up to date. Brett, you coming?"

"You buyin'?"

"Yeah, I'll buy."

"Then I'm coming." He lifted himself out of his chair and moved away from the paperwork he'd been working at and headed down the street with the Sheriff, the scouts and the growing group of men anxious to hear about their future wives. Looking at his excited neighbors it occurred to Brett that maybe he should have sent for one as well. Well, if there was an extra, maybe he'd take her . . . maybe. At least some stranger woman wouldn't know about his past . . . that he wasn't really White. That no decent woman in the territory had wanted him. Not that he'd courted anyone after Christina. He just knew how they'd react.

"So, Edgar," one of the men, barely able to contain his excitement, demanded, "fill us in. They're really coming? Did my Dahlia get my letter?"

"And my Belle?"

"What about my Sarah?"

"Gentlemen, gentlemen, these men just arrived after a hard ride, let's let them have a bit of a drink and order our meals before we bombard them with questions, okay?" Rick laughingly asked.

Amid the grumbles, the rest agreed it would be okay to wait . . . but just a bit. The group headed off to Lilly's, the local saloon. The townsmen gathered around tables closest to Zeke's and sat as patiently as they could while the first round was bought for the scouts and meals ordered. Finally Rick asked the question burning on all their minds, "So the brides are really coming."

"Yup," Zeke answered. "I figure they're four days out about now, there's twenty-three of them and all lookin' forward to marryin' ya'll."

"How'd they look?"

"Dang, Edgar, how do you think they look after traveling cross country for almost twelve weeks?"

"What I meant . . ." asked Harris Stephens, " . . . is are they pretty?"

"Sure enough are. Except that Miss Millicent."

"My Millicent?"

"Yeah . . . pity that."

Edgar's face fell a moment before he brightened. "Well who cares, I got me a wife and we're gonna have a family and it don't matter what she looks like."

"I was joshin' you, Edgar. They're all right pretty, even with all the trail dust on 'em."

The questions came fast and free as Zeke, his partner, Graham, and a few of the others ate and drank.

"Well, I'm thinking, I'd like to ride on out with you tomorrow to meet the ladies."

"I'm not sure that'd be a good idea, Edgar," one of the others spoke up. "Being if they're trail tired and all, they might not want to meet their new husbands without a chance to gussy up."

Conversation resumed about whether or not Edgar would go until Rick cut in, "Actually I think it would be a good idea—Edgar put this whole idea together, got you men writing letters and taking care of all the arrangements. It would only be fittin' if he went back out with Zeke and Graham to meet them."

"Well, then I'm gonna go, too," George Culver announced.

"Me, too," came from Harry Myers.

"Count me in," declared another.

"Okay, okay, looks like you're all eager to meet up with the bride train. We don't want the town closing up while you're out so I'd say to make sure your businesses are covered and the ladies would probably appreciate the chance to meet you. It will make 'em feel pretty welcome I think."

"Sounds good to me," Zeke added. "We'll be headin' out first light so be ready. I figure, by time we meet up with them they'll be maybe three days most out and eager to get here to town and get a hot bath and settle in."

"I'll go speak to the reverend and let him know that there's gonna be a passel of weddings in the next week or two."

"Thanks, Sheriff, that's good of you."

Zeke stood to leave and motioned Rick and Brett over to him.

"What's up, Zeke?"

He glanced around to be sure no one heard before speaking. "Seems there's one lady that Dusty's not so sure about. Didn't have a letter or telegram like most of the others. She sez she came from Connecticut, but I didn't place no ads up that far north and she doesn't talk too much about getting married. She may be bride shy or maybe something else going on, but he was a bit concerned about her."

"Like what kind of *something else*?" Rick asked.

Before Zeke could answer Brett spoke, "She a little thing, long hair?"

"Yeah, long brown hair, looks like it's got spun gold running through it. Yup, that would be Jenna."

"Oh, there's no problem then."

"There's not?" Rick's surprise evident in his voice.

"No, that's my bride. Yeah, Jenna has long brown hair and, well, she's a little shy."

"*Your* bride?"

Brett turned to his boss and, looking him hard in the eye, answered, "Yeah, Jenna is my bride, you got a problem with that?" His own lie bothered him, but maybe this was his chance, his chance to meet someone who could eventually care for him.

"Nope, not a one, not a one." Rick's grin lit up his whole face and Brett knew there would be a lot of ribbing once they were alone. That was after Rick grilled him on just why, in a matter of a couple of weeks he had suddenly decided to get married. Brett didn't take to falsehoods and he'd just told a whopper, but there was something about this Jenna's story that drew him. Even if all he knew, after pumping Zeke for the bit of information he had, was she was small, had long dark hair. If Dusty was right and she was hiding something, his gut told him to speak up for her, marry her and make her his own. And maybe, just maybe, his parentage wouldn't matter to her . . . maybe.

"Well that's good to hear, she's pretty reserved, and well, Dusty thought she was chickening out in St. Louis," Zeke filled them in.

"Well that was probably 'cause she didn't get my letter and thought she had to have it. I'm sure she was going to write me to be sure—you know, that last letter everyone sent firming up the details."

"Yeah, sure."

"So if it's all right with you, Rick, I'm gonna ride out with the men, I'd like to meet my bride, too."

"Sure 'nuf, Brett, sure 'nuf. In fact, I'll ask Tom McKendrick to keep an eye on things and I'll ride on out with ya'll, too." Brett's displeasure at Rick's plan was quickly hidden, but not before Rick saw it and grinned at his friend.

"Well, Zeke, glad we solved that situation with Brett's . . . bride. See ya in the morning. Brett, you wanna walk to the Reverend with me so we can tell him 'bout the pending nuptials?"

Knowing Rick was going to pump him for information one way or the other, especially since he had said he wasn't planning on marrying, it was easier to just go and get it over with. Thing was, how little could he say without adding another outright lie? Whatever had possessed him to say that this Jenna woman was his bride was beyond him, but what was done was done. He was getting married.

Neither said anything as they walked towards the church, but before he knocked at the preacher's house attached to the church, Rick turned to his friend.

"So, you wanna tell me what's going on?"

"Nope."

"Well, I'd like to know."

"Rick, you're my boss and you've been my friend my whole life, but this is something I'm not of a mind to talk about."

"Yeah, I got that . . . but you know, when a man you've known for thirty years, a man who you hunted with, fought side by side with, protected a town with and sat down to a good meal with says he's not getting married one day and then the next says he is, a body's gotta wonder."

"So I changed my mind."

"In an hour or two? Just happened to have written . . . and sent a letter no one else knew about? Brett, when I asked you a few weeks ago and then today, you said you weren't interested, not even a bit. Now I hear you tell Zeke you've been writing this woman and that she was supposed to have your letter saying to come on out — a woman from a state we didn't send an ad to. Well, something's not right."

Brett sighed and looked up at the sky, "Rick, I didn't want to say anything in case she changed her mind. After the crap I've been through with some of the women in this town, the last thing I wanted was for people to know I'd been thrown over again. So I didn't say anything."

"It was one woman, a stupid woman that no one in his right mind would want. And even Zeke was surprised that you *suddenly* wrote a letter."

"Look, it's my decision, mine and Jenna's, and while I'd like your support and good wishes, if you aren't inclined to give them, that's fine. I'm still your friend and I'm still your deputy."

"Well, then I wish you the best and I hope you two will be very happy."

After they spoke with the reverend and Rick headed off to his place to sleep, Brett opted to stay at the jail rather than riding out to his ranch. It wasn't unusual for him to stay in town and Marta tended not to worry unless he was gone for more than a day or so. He'd have someone ride out and tell her and Franco that he'd be back in a few days . . . with a wife.

Rick looked out the bedroom window of his place lost in thought. Brett may have really put his foot in it good this time. They'd grown up together and Brett's dad always made sure to include Rick, whose own family was pretty troubled — his mother leaving when he was quite young, his father rather abusive, in whatever the Parker family did. His dad loved Falling Leaf, his second wife to distraction. Now theirs was a marriage to aspire to. In fact, Brett's parentage was about love being passed from one to another.

Brett's dad had been married when he arrived in Adler Creek, to a White woman. Rick remembered when Clarissa Parker, his wife died shortly after giving birth to Kendrick who was now a Deputy U.S. Marshal. After grieving Clarissa for a time, Whitney met and married Falling Leaf who gave birth to Brett. While he'd heard how much Whitney had loved Clarissa, there was nothing that was ever going to convince him that there ever was a love as strong as Whitney and Falling Leaf had. When Whitney died, most everyone thought Falling Leaf would soon pass over with him. Instead she went on to marry a man from her tribe and had several years with him before she, too, died. While neither Brett nor his younger brother, Wolf, saw Kendrick often, the brothers were still close, something that, Rick believed, came from Whitney and Falling Leaf's teachings.

Brett's dad was a smart man, he knew that Brett would grow up to have a foot in both worlds — his dad's White world and his mother's Indian and that Kendrick would also be exposed to the issues that would come up so he made sure the boys learned about both worlds and Rick was included. Rick knew Brett thought the women in the Indian village were sweet, honest, kind, but there were none there he wanted to spend his life with. The women here in Adler Creek were pretty decent, Christina Jeffers had seemed like a dream until she showed her true colors . . . the bitch. She liked Brett's money, but when he brought up marriage her response was cold and heartless. Even though she had taken him to her bed . . . often she wanted their relationship hidden and refused to marry his friend. After she rejected him she made sure the entire town knew how she'd set him down. The bitch broke Brett's heart and for a time Rick worried over how reckless the man became — that was when he offered him a job as deputy. At first Brett declined, saying he didn't want to compete with Kendrick and was happy on his ranch. It wasn't long before Brett changed his mind and took the job. Now here Brett went, getting himself a mail-order bride, except something didn't ring true about it. *I sure hope you know what you are doing, partner.*

A wife . . . only now, alone in the dark with sleep evading him did Brett wonder at just what had possessed him. He'd sworn off getting married and now he'd up and said he'd sent for a bride. It hurt him to lie to his friend, but when he saw how enthused the other men were, he wondered if he should have looked into finding someone as well. Someone who would live with a half-breed, a successful man, but a half-breed just the same. When Dusty spoke about the woman, Jenna — he liked the sound of her name, it rolled off his tongue — and how something seemed to trouble her, he knew he had to have her. He knew she was meant for him. Bluffing his way about her looks and where she came from was easy thanks to Zeke's talkative nature. How hard was it to describe most women — long hair and a slight build. If she went along with it, only Rick would wonder what the true story was. But, his friend would, he had no doubt, stand beside him on this.

Next morning Zeke and Graham set out with Rick, Brett, and just about all the men who had sent for their brides. Those who stayed behind had offered to do so for what Henry Bascom called the *important part* — arranging the wedding dates with the reverend. That and getting rooms in the hotel for the ladies, making sure there were enough tubs so they could have those hot baths Zeke said they'd been missing, the Emporium to have flowers and other doo-dahs that they would need for their weddings. And Miss Effie's place needed to be ready with twenty-three wedding cakes! In light of all that, riding out to meet them was easy work.

They rode hard and came upon the wagon train towards evening on the second day. Brett rode in the lead with Zeke and as soon as they spotted the wagons, he looked for his Jenna. His Jenna — when had he begun to really think of her as *his*? And what if she wouldn't go along with his plan to marry her? Well they'd figure it out, him and his Jenna, they'd work it out. If his gut was right, there was something that had the woman worried and if he offered his protection maybe it would be okay and she would be content to marry him.

As they neared the train, some of the women stopped what they were doing and stood looking. Noting the preparation for the evening meal stopping one by one, the others joined them standing, staring almost hungrily. All but one.

Brett noticed one lone woman turned abruptly and was heading off towards the stream. That had to be Jenna. Her step sure and quick, almost running away drew him to her. To her credit, she didn't look back to see if anyone followed. As the men pulled up, a few of the women started to clap and in seconds names were being called: Belle? Calvin? Dahlia? Martin? Rosalie? Adam? One by one the couples who had exchanged letters found each other. Those that didn't, looked over the remaining men while Zeke assured them, "There's plenty more eligible bachelors back in Adler Creek, so if you don't see what you like or your groom's not here . . ." Leaving the couples sharing laughter all around Brett head off towards the lone woman.

"Jenna?"

She gasped, clearly startled by the sound of his voice.

"I thought I was alone."

"You are, Jenna, aren't you?"

"Yes, how . . . how . . ."

"I'm your husband to be, Brett."

"Wha . . ." Her hand moved to her chest just a moment before she fell in a heap at his feet.

CHAPTER EIGHT

"Jenna? Darlin? Can you hear me? Jenna?"

One of the women saw Jenna fall and several began running towards her and Brett. Jenna stirred slightly and through the fog she heard someone — a man — say, "Jenna, listen to me, my name is Brett and I told Zeke you were my intended, just agree with me on that, all right?"

Jenna looked up at the man supporting her. He was clearly the most handsome man she had ever seen in her life. His hair, just cresting his collar was the blackest, silkiest looking hair she had ever seen. His eyes were a rich blue, so blue they rivaled the most precious sapphire, and they were fanned by the longest lashes she'd ever seen. Her gaze took in an almost too perfect nose sitting above a pair of lips that were so full and sensuous that to her surprise she felt moisture beginning to moisten her bloomers. Between her legs she felt an unfamiliar feeling yet one that was so pleasant. She nodded just as the other women reached them.

"Jenna, are you well?"

"Did this man hurt you?"

"What did you do to our friend?"

"Ladies, ladies, its okay, I'm Brett Parker, Jenna's fiancé, she just didn't expect to see me this soon."

"Oh, all right." Belle stood a moment looking at the man who held her friend like a delicate piece of china. She started to walk away, hesitated and turned back to Jenna, "Are you sure, Jenna?"

"Y-y-yes. Oh yes."

"You were going to . . ." She glanced at Brett and back to Jenna, her last thought unfinished although Jenna was pretty certain her friend was going to ask why she had said she would be taking her chances once she arrived.

Jenna pushed away from Brett as she told Belle, "I'm fine, really, M . . . Mmm, Mr. Parker just startled me." As Belle headed back to the chattering crowd, Jenna turned to Brett. "Mr. Parker,"

"Brett."

"Mr. Parker . . . what would possess you to say I'm going to marry you? I don't know you, I've never heard of you, and I have no intention of marrying anyone."

"Because, Miss Jenna, I *am* going to marry you, none of the men or women here have met before and your intention to marry anyone of us was made clear when you joined the wagon train. Every woman on that train came west intending to marry. And, since I've already announced you will be marrying me, it appears to be true."

The man was too smug to suit her. If he thought his good looks alone were going to win her over, he had another thing coming. As she went to push him back so she could stand, her hand connected with something cold and sharp. Moving her hand away, her eyes focused on his badge. "D-d-deputy?" *Good lord, they found me already! He's here to arrest and hang me for Julian's murder.*

"Yes, Deputy Brett Parker at your service. I promise you won't be in safer hands."

"Deputy." She said it in a voice that she was sure made her sound like an idiot. "You're a deputy."

"Yes, ma'am."

"Well, Deputy, you need to understand, I have no plans to marry anyone. Now if you spent money to bring me here I understand you would like to recoup your loss and I'm happy to do that. As soon as we arrive in town, I will find a job and begin paying you back immediately."

"I don't think so."

"You don't think so?"

"Nope, I want a bride and from what I've already told everyone, it's you."

"Don't you understand? I don't *want* to be married. Not just not married to you, but to anyone."

"I don't think *you* understand, you will marry me."

"Brett, you gonna bring the lady to back to camp for some dinner?"

Rick's voice startled the two of them. If he'd heard Jenna's refusal to marry Brett, he didn't let on.

"Yeah, we'll be along in a minute."

"Right, Ma'am." He tipped his hat and strolled back to the wagons.

"Miss, Miss Jenna . . ."

"It's Martin, Jenna Martin."

"Fine, Miss Martin, I want you to listen and listen carefully 'cause I don't think we'll be able to talk very privately again before we get to town. When Zeke arrived in Adler Creek he told Rick, that was Rick who was here just now . . . the Sheriff, that there was a woman who seemed kinda troubled."

He glanced over at the couples seeming to get to know each other, almost hesitating when he continued, "I wasn't planning on a bride myself, but when he mentioned you, I spoke up and said you were my bride. I said that the reason you were probably kinda skittish and holding back was because you probably hadn't received my last letter that included the information you'd need to get here. Now I went round and round with Rick after that and I told him that I hadn't said anything because I didn't want to make a big deal about it but that I was pleased you agreed to marry me.

"Ma'am, it's too bad if you don't want to be married 'cause if you don't marry me I doubt it will take very long for whatever secret you want to keep to come out. I will protect you, care for you. I will never beat or strike you and will do what I can to be a good husband. If it puts you at ease, I will also promise you, once we're wed, you will share my home and I will court you within those four walls until you feel comfortable coming to my bed. I will not touch you until you are ready. But marry me, share my home and eventually my bed you will do. Agreed?"

"You promise me you won't try to force me?"

"I promise."

"You will court me?"

"I will."

"Then what harm in courting me and then if we suit maybe in a year or two . . ."

"No."

"No?"

"No. By the end of the week you will be Mrs. Brett Parker and living in my home as my wife."

Jenna only swallowed and again tried to push away from him to stand. He stood first and helped her up, she noted her head barely came as high as his chest. At some point he'd accept that while she might be a little thing, she knew her mind and would give him a run for his money on stubbornness.

"If you don't mind, I would like to wash up a bit."

"No, don't mind at all."

She waited a moment and when he didn't leave or even turn around, she said, "Mr. Parker, if you could kindly leave."

"Nope. I plan to wash up a bit myself."

With a huff, she turned and went to the water's edge. The irony of being forced to marry a deputy, a man of the law, and basically being imprisoned in his home was not lost on Jenna. She'd escaped the law only to run right into it.

CHAPTER NINE

The remainder of the trip passed too quickly for Jenna. She had two days to convince Brett Parker that marrying her was the worst thing he could do. Thing was, how to convince him since if she told him the truth, he'd have to arrest her for murder.

Worse than the feeling of lost companionship with Bea and Belle, Brett Parker—make that the breathtakingly handsome Deputy Brett Parker—was by her side almost all day, every day. She couldn't help but wonder if he knew about Uncle Julian and was just being nice by not arresting her in front of everyone. It wasn't like she could run anywhere.

Sneaking little peeks at him, she admired his broad chest, the way his buckskin shirt fit like a glove over his chest muscles. When he walked, she enjoyed taking in his posterior . . . how his muscles would bunch and stretch when he bent over. His thighs as they gripped his horse. Oh yes, he was a fine-looking man until he smiled. *That* made him devastatingly handsome. And when he smiled and looked at her with those blue eyes of his—the same shade of blue she remembered from a mountain lake she'd been to with her parents shortly before her mother died. A rich, deep blue that a body just felt like it belonged in. When he looked into her eyes and smiled that smile, the strangest thing happened in her belly and between her legs. Her panties would become damp and she had no idea why, but since it was accompanied by such other delightful feelings Jenna felt it was of no concern.

It seemed the only time he wasn't nearby was at night

when she climbed into the wagon to sleep or when they'd stop and she'd need to use privy facilities. The man didn't say much, which was fine with her. As long as she stuck with the story he concocted, which actually supported hers, he seemed content to let her be. When she drove the team or simply sat with Belle or Bea, he'd ride alongside. Whenever she'd chance a look up at him, he'd be looking straight ahead, ramrod straight yet seemingly relaxed in the saddle. When they pulled to a stop at night, he'd be right there to assist her off the seat, holding on to her waist just a beat too long before releasing her. He didn't do anything improper and the only time she had alone with him, if it could be called alone, was when he'd escort her to wherever they had designated a privy for the night. Both nights when they stopped, she tried to once again persuade him not to marry her. Both times, as soon as she started to tell him what she wanted, he'd stopped her. Now, by nightfall they would be in Adler Creek. She had one more chance to stop this fiasco before they arrived.

It was clear to Jenna from the way the other men interacted with Brett they respected him. When they made camp each night Brett, and his friend Rick as well, took the time it stop and visit with each of the couples, joke a bit with the men. First though, Brett took the time to see to his horse. He clearly cared for the big stallion, making sure he was fed and watered before being bedded down for the night. A man who was that concerned about his horse and friends couldn't be all bad, could he?

After the evening meal he would escort Jenna a short distance from the campsite, not saying much. It seemed he mostly just wanted the time with her, just the two of them. He said little, which was fine because to Jenna it meant he did not expect her to speak much either. She was relieved when he asked her little about her home. It was almost as if he was more concerned of what learning about her past would do to them than she was. When he smiled though, oh that smile, sent ripples of delight and anticipation down her body. He was incredibly handsome and seemed so kind. It seemed he would keep his promise to protect and care for her. But what of when he found out she was a murderess? What then?

Despite almost everyone being eager to arrive, the travelers stopped for the last night on the trail. Brett sat next to her, his arm just shy of brushing hers as they sat. The other couples murmured conversation back and forth and the other brides chatted with them or each other.

"Mr. Parker, would you walk a bit with me?"

Though softly spoken, her voice was sweet, clear, and did something to his insides he never thought to feel. It seemed to go right from his ear and, like a fine whiskey, flowed down in a fiery path to his groin. But it wasn't just sex. With this woman, it wasn't just a pretty face or easy sex. He thought he had loved Christina, but what he felt for her was nothing compared to what he as beginning to feel for Jenna. There was something about her that went to his heart and he wasn't about to question why he felt this way about someone he'd just met. That would be the White side of him talking. In this he would trust the Indian side . . . the side that told him there was more to see than what he saw with his eyes.

"I'd be pleased, Jenna."

He stood quickly and offered her his hand. He watched her closely and saw that as much as she wanted to be rude and ignore it, she couldn't, she just couldn't in front of the other women who had become her friends. Brett Parker knew he hadn't done anything *to* her and she certainly didn't know anything about him. He just wanted a wife. They walked a few paces, out of hearing of the rest before she turned to him.

"Mr. Parker."

"Brett."

"Mr. Parker."

"Do you plan on calling out *Mr. Parker* when we're intimate in bed at night?" He kept his smile to himself when Jenna's mouth flew open in shock and her face turned beat red.

"*Mr. Parker,* that is the *rudest* thing I have ever had a man say to me and I will thank you to keep your lewd and dirty thoughts to yourself."

"Nothing lewd or dirty about it, Jenna . . . I told you, I will court you and when you are ready, I will bed you. When I bed you, Jenna, I believe you will regret the time you could have spent being pleasured by me and pleasure you I will."

He kicked himself when, in her shock and upset at his statement, her hand connected with his cheek in what had to have been the loudest crack he had ever heard. Admittedly, he deserved it. A bride probably didn't want to hear that her husband had considerable experience in bed and his words were said with little consideration for her sensibilities. The women in Adler Creek may be used to a plain-spoken man. That may not be so true for an Eastern woman.

He saw he stunned and perhaps even upset her, when she gasped and, seeing heads turn in their direction, she spun and ran away from the wagons, back the way they'd come. Brett was hot on her heels, while behind him women yelled to stop him before he killed their dear Jenna.

Before anyone could move, Rick put a stop to any pursuit. "Let them work it out. You know Brett would never hurt a woman so let them work it out."

Brett's longer legs quickly ate what little distance separated them.

Before she knew what happened Jenna was swept up in his

arms. As soon as she felt her legs leave the ground she began to struggle, screaming at him to put her down.

"I will, I will, as soon as you stop struggling and talk to me."

She struggled a moment or two more and the painful realization that he was not only bigger and stronger than her but no one was going to come to her aid made her settle down.

Brett set her on her feet, but his hands held her firmly in their grip.

"You can let me go now."

"And let you hit me again? I don't think so."

"You have no right."

"I have every right . . . I bought a bride . . . you . . . I have every right."

All of a sudden it all came crashing down on her. Her father's death, losing her home, Julian forcing her to leave, his attack, his death, her head long flight to escape, the sleepless nights, meeting new people, having to pretend she was someone else, being caught trying to escape. And now, now, being forced to marry this man, this handsome, compelling man that did things to her belly and lower, this man who didn't deserve someone as horrid as she was. It all hit her and she crumbled in a ball in the dirt, tears streaming from her eyes, her body shaking with the fear and grief that had built inside of her the last three months. "I can't take it, I can't take it, I just can't take anymore."

Brett was instantly aware of Rick's quiet approach. "It's fine, she's fine, just a little trail weary."

A sense of preservation overtook Jenna's need to run from Brett and she turned to Rick. "Please, Sheriff, I just, I'm just exhausted . . . I . . . ."

"She's all right Rick, and I don't think she'll be hitting me or anyone else anymore."

Brett continued to hold her as she sobbed out her pain and fear, finally falling asleep in his arms. A short time later he rose and carried her back towards the wagons and lifted her into her wagon. After a brief word to Belle and Bea, he left her for the night. Taking a plate of food, he moved off to think by himself.

"You all right there, Brett?"

"Yeah, Henry, she's just tired, just trail tired and worn, she'll be feeling much better when she's had a hot bath and a good night's sleep in a bed."

Some of the men grumbled their agreement and went back to quiet conversation before turning in.

The next morning Brett walked Jenna over to the stream and saw she was still a bit shaken. When Rick approached to see if he could help, Brett told him, "Move on out, she's still a bit upset to go ahead right now, leave my horse and we'll follow in a bit."

Feeling rather than seeing his friend leave, Brett knelt down beside Jenna and pulled her into his arms and held her. She wasn't going to hit him again and even if she did, it would be okay. From what Dusty had said there was something that upset the woman. Whatever was eating at her was coming out and the sooner she faced her demons the sooner she'd be content, if not happy with him.

The wagons had left and were a distant spec when she finally raised her head, her eyes still red from the tears, her cheeks stained from their trail through the dirt, her throat raw from the long cry. "I'm sorry, I'm so sorry. I've never meant to strike another person, I'm so sorry."

"Shhhh, it's okay, darlin', it's okay."

"No, no it's not," she sobbed, the tears starting again. "You didn't deserve that last night. It was thoughtless and mean spirited. I don't know what happened to me and I'm so sorry."

"Better me than someone else."

"Mr. Parker, please, you have to understand, you deserve a better person than me, I'm not a good person."

"Good or bad, Jenna, you're stuck with me."

"You need to listen to me, you need to believe me — you don't want me." She grabbed the front of his shirt and held on to him as if her life depended on it. Her knuckles were ghostly white against the tan buckskin, and her body shook from her tears and the anguish that he heard in her voice. "You really don't. Please, just let me take a job and I'll pay you back every penny and I'll help you find a wife who deserves you — someone who is decent and kind and who . . . who . . ."

"Who what, Jenna?"

"Who isn't me."

"I can't do that. Jenna, we have an agreement."

"No, no we don't, don't you see? *You* said what you wanted. You said you sent for a bride, and maybe you did, but it wasn't me. And when you came up with this plan, it was *your* plan. You didn't ask me, you told me and you have to listen . . . I don't want to get married, not to anyone."

"I want you, Jenna." He knew the Indian side of him was speaking when he uttered the words and a part of him knew that if he persisted in that train, he would lose her. So he forced the White side to the surface. "You'll marry me, Jenna. You'll marry me and accept it. I told you, I'll protect and care for you, I will court you and when you are ready and only when you are ready, will I come to your bed. But you will marry me."

"I can't."

"Why?"

"I just can't."

"Are you married to someone else?"

Her head popped up. It hadn't occurred to her that that was the perfect excuse for not getting married.

"Because if you are, it isn't a concern, not out here. If you're a runaway wife, I'd guess you have a good reason for running away and I'll still protect you. Out here, well there are couples who left bad situations and decide that a common law marriage is better than what they had. But if there is a husband going to come looking for you, you'd best tell me now."

Jenna took in the earnest look in his eyes. She wanted to lie to save herself, but there he was, so honest, so plain spoken, so compelling. The falsehood that ventured from her mind never made it past her lips.

"So is there a husband?"

"No, there's no husband. I'm not running from a husband."

But you are running, Jenna. It's plain you are running from something. I only hope you'll tell me before its too late. "Then there's nothing to concern ourselves with."

"But there is. Why won't you listen? *I – don't – want – to – marry – anyone.*"

In a heartbeat his voice went from warm and comforting to cold and orderly. Evidence of his job as a deputy was clear in his tone. "This discussion is over. We're going to get on my horse and we're going to ride into Adler Creek, and you will have a choice. I will put you up in a hotel room and make sure you have a hot bath and a soft bed or I'll put you in the jail for the night. Your choice."

The edge in his voice didn't match the sadness Jenna saw in his eyes. For a fleeting moment it seemed to her all his hopes and dreams were wrapped up her answer. "Why would you put me in the jail?"

"To make sure you can be found for our wedding tomorrow."

"Tomorrow? Are you mad?" Fear that he knew what happened came back to the surface. Was he trying to trap her with the marriage offer, trying to see if she'd marry him and add more charges, of maybe stealing his money, to murdering her uncle? That was the only thing that made sense.

"Nope. I just think the sooner we say our vows, the sooner you'll settle to the idea that you are going to be my wife."

Brett stood, helped Jenna to her feet, and walked her over to where Rick had left his horse tethered. He pulled a handkerchief from his pocket and, reaching for one of the canteens, moistened it before gently washing her tear-stained face. "It'll be okay, Jenna, I promise you, it will be okay."

No it won't, Brett Parker. No it won't. I don't deserve a man like you and I shudder to think what happens when your feelings of kindness turn to hate for me.

"You ever ridden?"

"Side saddle, a bit."

"Well today you are going to learn to ride astride." He lifted her into the saddle and she made the mistake of looking down from the high perch. Seeing the fear in her eyes, he quickly climbed up behind her and pulled her back against his chest. She was tense as they started out, but once Jenna realized he was going to hold her and not let her fall she began to relax. So much so she even told him that from the view atop the horse she saw what a truly beautiful country she had come to. After a few hours Brett thought perhaps she had fallen asleep in his arms because of how relaxed she had become in his embrace. It was only her soft sigh of pleasure that told him she was still awake.

"Doin' okay, Jenna?"

His deep voice, a voice that would melt butter with its smooth tone, startled her. "Oh yes, I'm fine, I've just been enjoying the scenery. It really is beautiful out here."

"Glad you like it. I think you'll enjoy the sunsets at the ranch."

"Ranch?"

"Yup."

"What ranch?"

"Mine."

"Are you always so quiet? Do you ever say much except when you are insisting I'm going to marry you?"

"Yup."

Well that wouldn't do, if she was going to be stuck with this man she wanted to hear that voice of his. If it were possible she'd fall in love with him just for that voice alone. But right now she wanted to hear him talk just to distract her because sitting for so long between his thighs, thighs that held her in a powerful grip, leaning back against his broad chest was taking her mind to places it hadn't gone before. She found it was stirring up those feelings she didn't quite understand but knew it didn't bode well for her plans to avoid marriage to him.

"I thought you were a deputy."

"I am."

"So is your ranch close to town?"

"Nope." At that she heard the chuckle in his voice and it annoyed her.

"Mr. Parker, if you aren't going to have a civilized conversation with me, I'd like you to stop this horse and let me get down and walk."

"You might want to call me Brett and as to letting you down to walk, I don't think so, Jenna, I find I like holding you and look forward to spending some long nights holding you close . . . after we make love." He pulled her tighter in his grip . . . remembering how the last time he spoke so intimately it had ended badly he changed the direction of this thoughts. "My ranch, *our* ranch, is about five miles outside of town. Most nights I go home, but one, maybe two nights a week I stay in town so Rick can relax a bit. Adler Creek is a pretty mellow town but we do have our moments. I used to stay in town just because there was nothing to go home to, but now that is going to change.

"Mr. Parker, it's *your* ranch so I fail to see why you insist on calling it *our*. Unless you have other family . . ."

Ignoring her interruption, he continued, "*We*, and I *do* mean *we*, Jenna, you and I, have two folks that help out, Marta and Franco. I think you'll like them. I have no doubt Marta will fuss over you no end and I ask only you let her do that. She's a kind woman with a big heart. I don't care what you think or say about me, but Marta has a kind heart and I won't take it kindly if you hurt her feelings."

"I'm not a bitch, Mr. Parker."

"You are plain spoken, I'll give you that. For the record, I didn't say you were . . . just asking you to be nice to her."

"As long as I don't have to be nice to you."

"Didn't say that either."

They rode into town shortly before sun down to find a festive crowd gathered. "Looks like one big engagement party going on."

"I suppose."

"Jenna, the men of this town are excited to be getting married and it appears so are the ladies. I know you say you aren't keen on this, but if I were you, I'd think on enjoying myself. These are nice people, friendly people, and you are going to be living with them a long, long time. You'll find yourself pretty lonely if you push them away early on."

"There they are!" Belle's voice carried over the crowd. She rushed up to the couple, her smile infectious. "Jenna! You're here! It was so romantic of your Mr. Parker here to stay behind so he could ride in with you like this. And on horseback . . . it's like something out of a penny novel."

"Belle, you *are* a romantic," Jenna told her.

Brett dismounted and reached up to help Jenna down. His hands continued to hold her firmly about her waist as her feet touched the ground. Holding her a moment longer, he leaned in to place a kiss on her lips. The lightest feathering that she felt not only on her lips but it seemed to travel down to her belly. There was something about this man that made her feel things she'd never felt before — and she'd only known him a few days. Even though it was only a light kiss on her lips, her mouth tingled for long moments after, leaving Jenna wonder what a deeper kiss would feel like. Before she could let those thoughts take root, Belle cleared her throat which caused Brett to recall himself and loosen his embrace. Not letting go, but giving Jenna a bit of room to move. As the couple turned, the flash of the photographer's camera temporarily blinded her. In reaction she reached out to grasp Brett's arm, *so warm, so solid.*

"Mr. Parker, please, don't let him develop that picture."

"Why, Jenna?"

"I hate having my picture taken. Please, he's dogged me since we left St. Louis, please, stop him."

"I'll see what I can do, darlin'." He gave her a puzzled look before dropping his arm around her waist and leading her over to the crowd. As soon as he was assured she was feeling comfortable in Belle's capable hands, he moved off to secure his horse.

When it was full dark the crowd moved into Lilly's to continue the celebration.

Jenna kept to the background, feeling like an intruder

because she knew that her marriage would not be a real one. And, as soon as she could convince Brett that this was a mistake she'd be gone. She jumped when he came up behind her, placing his arm around her and whispering in her ear. "I got you a room at the boarding house, and ordered a hot bath for you whenever you're ready."

Surprised at his kindness and consideration, she smiled as she thanked him. "I appreciate that, Mr. Parker. I believe that is one of the nicest things anyone has done for me. I'm ready now."

"The let me escort you over." He offered his arm and she gladly took it. Before they cleared the door, Bea's voice carried to them over the crowd. "Jenna, Jenna!"

They stopped as the bubbly woman approached them. "Jenna, Belle and I are going to be wed the day after tomorrow, a double ceremony. We thought maybe you'd like to make it a triple ceremony."

Before Jenna could respond, Brett spoke. "That's a wonderful gesture, Bea, we'd love to. We had talked about saying our vows tomorrow, but I think your idea is better. Thank you for thinking of us."

When he didn't deign to look at Jenna, she found her foot coming down rather firmly on his instep. His only reaction was to glance down at her, eyebrow raised and merely continued, "Isn't that thoughtful of them to ask us, darling?"

"Yes. Yes, Bea, that's very thoughtful."

"Are you sure, Jenna? You don't sound too excited about it."

"I am, Bea, really. I'm just tired and Mr. Parker arranged a bath for me—a *hot* bath and I . . . I . . . I just . . ."

"Oh, I understand, Jenna. No problem. I completely understand. I guess that even though riding on the horse looked so romantic and that you and Mr. Parker look so much in love, you must be tired. I thought about a nap earlier, but it's just too grand and exciting to finally be here that I don't think I'll even sleep tonight."

Jenna broke from Brett's embrace to reach for Bea and hugged the other woman. "I'm so relieved you understand, Bea. I am looking forward to the weddings."

"Great! I'll tell Belle, and I'll ask my Calvin to arrange it."

"Thank you again, Bea, I'll see you tomorrow."

Brett escorted her out into the warm September night and guided her towards the boarding house, just a short distance up the street. "Jenna . . ."

"I can't believe you did that."

"Did what?"

"Agreed to get married with them the day after tomorrow. She's my friend and she was asking me."

"And what would you have told her, Jenna?"

"That we wanted more time."

"No. And, if you recall, I had told you I planned to marry you tomorrow — so you do have more time."

"More time? A day is *not* more time, it's nothing."

"You want me to tell Calvin that we're getting married tomorrow?"

"I won't let you bully me. I'll tell you right now, Mr. Parker, I will not abide by you bullying me."

"Not bullying you, Jenna. Just setting the rules . . . you came here to be married and the sooner we're married the sooner you'll feel at home with things."

"Mr. Parker, why won't . . ."

"Jenna . . ." There was a warning in his voice and there was a hardness in his eyes she hadn't seen before.

"Mr. Parker, you have to see, this can't work. I told you . . . I don't want to get married. Not to you, not to anyone."

"Jenna, we've been through this. And we've been through the fact that my name is Brett and that, as my intended and soon to be wife it would be highly appreciated if you called me by my name."

"But you still don't understand. I . . . I . . . I don't even like you."

"Doesn't matter."

"And that's part of why I don't like you. You don't care about me, I'm just a thing to you, just a . . . a . . . piece of meat. Why don't you pick a woman who actually can stand you?"

So caught up in her own feelings she missed the look that momentarily crossed Brett's face when she told him to choose someone who could stand him. The pain of the reminder shot through him, making his response more gruff than he intended, "Because I want *you*. You will marry me, Jenna Martin, and I don't care if you don't like me or glare at me in hate night after night. In the dark one woman doesn't look any different than another."

She stopped and turned to him, and before she knew what she was doing, her hand came up to strike him again. This time, however, he was prepared and caught it, bringing her hard against him. "I'd give some thought to not doing that again. Once, I don't mind letting it go by, but I won't abide by having my wife strike me whenever the fancy takes her. And come to think of it, I seem to recall you promising you wouldn't be doing that as well."

What is wrong with me? I've never struck another person in my life and now I've struck two men, killed one and was going to hit this man again, this man who hasn't done anything to me, nothing but been kind and offer to marry me.

Hanging her head, Jenna fought the tears that welled up in her eyes. "I'm sorry, Mr. Parker, I'm truly sorry. I don't understand myself, I really don't. I've never done anything so uncivilized, and it appears I've done it to you or tried to twice now."

"Just so it doesn't happen a third time. I understand your upset, darlin' . . . it's been a long trip and you're finding yourself about to marry someone you don't know. Just try to trust me. I told you, I'll protect you. I'll care for you . . . you just need to give us a chance."

"Can we go to the boarding house, please? I am so tired."

As he continued to escort her down the street, her mutinous thoughts continued. *Fine, I'll marry him . . . and as soon as he sees we don't suit, he'll give me an annulment and I'll move on.*

Brett was lost in his own thoughts. He silently berated himself for his harsh tone, for the crudeness of his words. *How am I going to win her over if I threaten her and say things like I did about women in the dark? How can I already be so attached to her that the thought of losing her is like a knife in my gut?*

Walking through the door of the boarding house, Brett raised his hand in greeting to the man at the counter and escorted Jenna upstairs. He pushed open the door and stood aside for Jenna to enter ahead of him. She spied the hot bath as soon as they entered, as well as her satchel, which had already been moved into the room.

"Enjoy the bath, Jenna."

"Thank you, Mr. Parker." She stood there a moment, chewing lightly on her lower lip, unaware of the simple gesture affected the man standing in front of her. "Um, well, good night."

She felt his gaze on her lips, the intensity making her feel like he'd actually kissed her. She resisted running her fingers over them, instead turning towards the door. "Oh, Mr. Parker, Brett?"

"Yes?" Suspicion creeped into his voice.

"The photographer, did you stop him from taking that picture?"

"Want to tell me why it was so important?"

"I did, I don't like having my photograph taken. Did you stop him?"

"Yeah, I did."

"Thank you. Thank you." She reached out towards his arm, catching herself just before she put her hand on it.

Taking note of her movement Brett drew into himself, "I'll fetch you in the morning for breakfast. And, Jenna?"

She looked up at him.

"Don't even think about trying to run off tonight . . . I'll find you and bring you back."

She nodded, resigned to marrying this man and then hoping soon he'd seek an annulment. As she turned to close the door, his arms came around her and she tilted her head up to question his intent, but before she could utter a word, his lips descended to hers. His lips nibbled on hers, plying little kisses along the upper and lower while his hands massaged her back. Pressed firmly against his chest, she felt her nipples begin to harden and, without volition, her lips parted to welcome his tongue into her mouth. Without thought, Jenna gave herself to the sensations this man evoked in her. She couldn't stop herself if she wanted to . . . *I do want to, I want to stop him, I want to, I want to . . .* the moan that escaped her lips seemed to startle them both into awareness.

"I'll be by around eight to take you to breakfast. Sleep well, Jenna." He closed the door.

"Sleep well. He says to sleep well, after that kiss." She paced to the window and looked out, catching a glimpse of the man she was doomed to marry as he walked down the street. The kiss caught her completely off guard. It wasn't like the gentle, courting ones Addison had given her. No, far from it. In form it was like what Julian tried to do, but with Brett it was like fresh honey, warm, pliant, a sweetness all its own. His kiss shook her to the core, leaving her wanting more, and that was dangerous, oh so dangerous for her.

True to his word, Brett was at her door promptly at eight. If he was surprised to not only find Jenna there, let alone that she was ready, he didn't let on. Over breakfast he asked her if there was anything she needed for their wedding the next afternoon.

"No, I don't think so."

"Well, we'll go on by the Emporium and see if there's anything that catches your eye and pick it up for you. Rick said he'd stand up for me and that he'd also walk you down the aisle unless there's someone else you would like."

"Rick, the Sheriff?"

"Yeah."

"That would be fine. I'd like that."

If he noticed her tone was flat and disinterested he didn't let on. "Good, he's a good man. Our ceremony is at one, so he'll be by about noontime to get you. I've paid for your room and board till tomorrow night so you won't have to worry about a meal."

"And then?"

If he noticed the fear creeping into her voice he didn't let on. "I figured we'd go on out to the ranch and settle in."

"You have enough room there for me?"

"At the ranch? Jenna, it's gonna be your home. There's enough rooms for you to have your own . . . for a bit . . . unless you decide you want to share my bed . . ."

"No, I told you no, that I don't even . . ."

"That discussion is closed."

"Well then, at your ranch, I mean, to keep your promise, that you won't . . . that I won't . . . that we won't . . ."

"If you are still of a mind to wait to share my bed, yes. There's plenty of room . . . and more for our children when the time comes."

Children? He's already thinking of children? Why doesn't he understand that this isn't going to work? That I'm going to leave?

They finished their meal in silence, Jenna concentrating on each bite, Brett watching the woman who would soon be his wife. Breakfast done, Brett walked Jenna down to the Emporium. Several of the other women were already perusing the wares, picking out ribbons and other trinkets for their weddings. When nothing seemed to catch Jenna's eye, Brett asked if there really wasn't anything she wanted or needed.

"No. I'm fine, really."

"No girly doo-dahs catch your eye?"

"No . . . really, I'm not comfortable spending any more of your money than I already have."

"Jenna, I can provide for you. If there's something, anything you want, we'll get it."

"Well, I err, I don't need them, but there *is* a pair of gloves that would go well with the dress I plan to wear tomorrow."

Brett quickly retrieved them and purchased them for her. His enthusiasm in buying her even one small item was clear. The man might be a barbarian with his refusing to listen to her, but there was something endearing about his desire to please her. Jenna had to grudgingly admit he really was trying to make her feel comfortable, welcome, and wanted. He touched her often but not in an inappropriate way. He'd rest his hand on her arm or on her waist, taking her hand to guide her where he wanted them to go.

They spent the rest of the morning walking along the main street, Brett pointing out different people and aspects of the town. A few of the townsfolk came up to congratulate their deputy on his pending nuptials. They stopped for lunch at a café that charmed Jenna.

"You know, back home, when we hear about the west or *out west* we hear that it's rough, that its uncivilized, but it's not that way at all, is it?"

"Some towns are a bit rough, and things do happen here, but Rick is a good Sheriff and we're pretty peaceable."

After lunch they'd started back to the boarding house when Brett suggested they stop by the jail. "So you can see where I work . . ."

Jenna was instantly nervous, thinking that this was it, he'd thought she'd fight being arrested and wanted to make her comfortable so he could make slipping her into a cell easy. Well, she decided, she wouldn't fight it. "Yes, that would be good."

Rick was sitting at his desk looking over some letters that had come in for him on the wagon train. As Brett spoke with him about a few of them, Jenna moved to look at some of the posters on the wall. She knew that she'd been right to avoid the photographer on the trip. If she wasn't careful, she'd end up on one of those posters. In her mind she could see the headline: *The Uncle Killer*. She was relieved when Brett offered to escort her to back to Lilly's where the women were going over wedding arrangements. Leaving her at the door, he bent to give her a quick kiss. She fought the disappointment that he didn't kiss her like he did the night before. Jenna lay down for a short nap and woke what only felt like a short time later to a knock on the door.

She wasn't surprised when Brett appeared at the door as the sun was setting and offered to escort her to dinner. Rather than get into another argument with him, she agreed, telling herself that sharing a meal with a man wasn't a lifetime commitment. If she was honest with herself, there was something pleasant about being in his company. Taking an even longer look at herself, she realized she was hoping he'd also kiss her again . . . not the sweet little peck on her lips like this afternoon . . . but the toe curling, belly tightening kiss he'd given her last night.

They shared their meal with Bea and Calvin with Bea chatting excitedly about the wedding plans. If Calvin thought it odd that Bea not only did most of the talking but seemed to have planned the entire wedding, he certainly didn't show his feelings. It seemed to Jenna that Calvin had waited a long time to find a wife and would be happy with Bea no matter what she did.

Again, at the door to her room Brett took Jenna in his arms. She knew she shouldn't encourage his attentions, but his kisses felt so good. When his lips met hers she couldn't help the pleased sigh that escaped her and without thought, she found her arms around his neck. As long as they just kissed it would be ok, right?

"I'll see you tomorrow . . . I'm looking forward to it."

"Good night, Mr. Parker."

She could see from his look he considered provoking her, demanding again she call him by his name, but instead all he did was tell her, Sleep well, Jenna."

CHAPTER TEN

Jenna woke to an insistent knocking on the door. It took her a moment to get her bearings before moving to answer it. "Who is it?"

"It's Mrs. Nelson, dear. Deputy Parker ordered a bath for you this morning and it's ready for you."

"Oh, oh, of course." As she opened the door the proprietor and her helper brought in the tub and buckets of hot water.

As she was leaving, she turned to Jenna. "Deputy Parker also left this for you. He thought maybe you'd like it."

"Thank you." When the woman left, Jenna picked up the little box Brett had sent. Inside was a perfectly formed cameo. It was exquisite and was exactly the thing for the dress she planned to wear. She'd bought the white eyelet cotton dress on a whim, a few weeks before her father died. Despite having credit at all the major shops Jenna was a careful shopper, but when she saw the dress she had to have it. How Brett knew she would love the pin was beyond her, but it was a perfect piece. The cameo was just the right size for the collar portion of the dress. It drew attention to the area above the V-neckline, showing that plunged just deep enough to hint at the tops of her breasts. The collar connected to the shoulders which gave way to form fitting sleeves. As much as she hated to admit it, Jenna knew she looked beautiful in the dress. It was exactly the kind of dress she would have chosen had she been marrying a man of her choosing, not one who had bought a bride and that she had every intention of leaving.

Right on time, Rick was at the door to fetch her. His low

whistle told her that she hadn't been purely egotistical in her assessment of how the dress looked on her.

"Miss Martin, you are indeed a vision."

"Thank you, Sheriff. You look quite dashing yourself."

"I did want a moment to speak with you, privately, if I could?"

"Of course, what is it, Sheriff?" *Please don't tell me the authorities found me, please not yet.*

Leaving the door open, for propriety's sake, he entered the room and sat down. "Miss Martin, Brett Parker is a good man, a decent man. I've known him my whole life. He's like a brother to me and I'd lay down my own life for him."

Jenna nodded in understanding.

"It surprised and even shocked me when he said he was getting married, and that the woman he was marrying was a mail-order bride . . . one that Zeke said seemed to have had a little problem."

If it surprised him that Jenna just sat listening, to her relief he didn't let on. "Now I don't know what happened or why, and I don't care. All I care about is my friend. He's set on marryin' you and he says that for all the fussin' I saw it would seem that you are committed to marryin' him. I hope that's so because it won't please me any if you hurt him."

She had her chance, right there, right then, to end it. All she had to do was tell the Sheriff that it was a mistake, that Brett was forcing her into this marriage and that she didn't want it. All she had to do was say *I don't want to marry him* and it would be over.

But what if he wanted to know why? What if that opened the door for him to ask questions she didn't want to answer? What if her refusal to marry Brett led the Sheriff to look into what she was running from? Did she really want to risk that?

The answer was no, she didn't. It was safer with Brett. He said he'd protect her, and that included from prying questions about her past, didn't it? Just marry him, accept his protection and when he got tired of pursuing her and realized it wouldn't work he'd annul the marriage. Right?

"Sheriff, I'm committed to marrying Mr. Parker. I assure you, I have no intention of hurting him in any way. What you saw at the camp, when I struck him, it was a childish reaction to being tired from traveling and not being used to his sense of humor. I assure you, I'm not a violent person and such behavior will never happen again."

"I wasn't thinking about you hitting him, Miss Martin. I was thinking about you breaking his heart. Like I said, he's a good man and while he may not show it, he's been hurt a lot in the past. Some women took advantage of him, hurt him. He probably wouldn't take kindly to me telling you, so I hope this stays purely between you and me. Like I said, he's like a brother to me and while it may not be my business, I won't take too kindly to his wife hurting him, understood?"

"I understand, Sheriff. I told you, I have no intention of hurting him in anyway. I will do my best to be the wife he deserves."

"Then fine. We'd best be off before he thinks I've run off with his bride."

If Jenna thought the walk to the church was the longest she'd ever taken, then the one up the aisle was the shortest. She just couldn't get over the feeling that she was like a lamb being led to the slaughter. If not for Belle and Bea's enthusiasm for their weddings she may well have run from the church despite her promise to Rick. Entering the foyer, the three women arranged their skirts. Millicent produced bouquets of fresh flowers for each of them. One of the local girls walked ahead of them scattering petals of the local flora and the organist began the wedding march. Not surprisingly Belle practically skipped up the aisle. She'd waited a long time for her Henry and today she was finally going to marry him. Bea was a bit more sedate on her walk up the aisle, Calvin's smile broad and warm at seeing her.

When Rick offered his arm to Jenna, she looked up at him, the nervousness clear in her eyes, but she felt somehow reassured at his smile. As the walk began, she saw Brett standing tall and proud at the altar, so handsome, serious and intent and here she was with butterflies in her stomach. Before they were halfway up the aisle, Brett stepped towards them and met them almost halfway. Taking Jenna's arm in his and walking her the rest of the way, he told her, "I can't help myself, darlin', I can't wait to make you my wife."

She answered with a tentative smile and walked beside him with an assurance she didn't really feel. Suddenly they were before the minister and the ceremony began. Despite Brett's impatience, as if he knew she would run if she could, Belle and Henry were married first, followed by Bea and Calvin. When it came time for Brett and Jenna to exchange their vows, his voice was strong and sure, hers soft, yet with a sureness that surprised her.

"Brett Parker, do you take this woman, whose right hand you now hold, to be your wife? Do you promise before God and these witnesses that you will be her true and devoted husband, in sickness and health, joy and sorrow, in prosperity and adversity and forsaking all others will you keep yourself to her and only to her until death do you part?"

"I do." Brett's confirmation was offered in a firm and determined voice.

Turning to Jenna, the reverend then asked, "Do you take this man, whose right hand you now hold, to be your husband? Do you promise before God and these witnesses that you will be his true and devoted wife, in sickness and health, joy and sorrow, in prosperity and adversity and forsaking all others will you keep yourself to him and only to him until death do you part?"

Jenna stood silent, staring straight ahead, seemingly unable to respond.

Brett felt the slight tremble course through her body as he bent his head near her ear. "Jenna, darling, can you answer?"

She looked up at him, blinked and gave a short nod. "I do." Her confirmation was a soft whisper that Brett barely heard as he pulled her closer, offering her his strength and leaning to her ear, he said, "It's alright, Jenna, it will be alright."

Her look moved back towards the reverend and again, a bit louder, with more strength she said, "I do."

With the vows exchanged, the minister asked the traditional, "If there is anyone present who has just cause or knowledge why any of these couples should not be married, speak now or forever hold your peace." While Bea and Belle giggled, Jenna wondered if Rick was going to object. If he did, what would Brett do? Would he accept his friend's decision and let her go? She was oddly relieved when no one spoke up.

Then the minister's already wide smile grew even wider. "And now for the part you gentleman have been waiting for, you may kiss your brides!" While Belle and Henry hugged more than kissed, Bea giggled, Brett put his hands on Jenna's shoulders. His sapphire blue eyes intent, so intent she found herself getting lost in them, mesmerized and felt like she was falling into a warm, soft and inviting cocoon. Her lips parted ever so slightly has he lowered his own to her. Her mind told her to breathe, but she could barely take in air. It wasn't air she needed, it was his lips on hers, like a life-giving gift, his lips finally meeting with hers. His lips grazed hers slightly before his tongue sought its place within the warm cavern of her mouth.

She was sure Brett was surprised when she responded, not in the lukewarm way she had the night before, but with a passion that seemed to come from her very soul. It was a like a part of her soul knew his, that they were two parts of the same whole that had finally come together again. Each kiss she shared with him became sweeter and sweeter.

So lost in the kiss they were both startled when, after the minister had cleared his throat several times, Rick tapped Brett on the shoulder. "I think some of us would like to be moving on to the reception about now." While Jenna blushed a bright shade of red, Brett merely smiled the broadest smile she had ever seen on a man. It made him even more handsome than she already found him. If she wasn't careful, she was going to fall in love with him.

The townsfolk and other brides had prepared an outdoor reception. Jenna felt a bit overwhelmed by all the good wishes coming towards her and Brett, so much so she didn't see the constantly-present photographer snap their picture. It appeared the entire town had come to wish them well and were looking forward to the remaining weddings. Through the entire party, Brett never took his hand from Jenna — either holding her hand or his arm around her, he held on to her. At one point, she placed her hand around his neck and pulled him towards her. She reduced the bite of her telling him, "I promise you, if you let go of me I won't run away," with a quick kiss on his lips. The surprise of her kissing him without him prompting it first clearly delighted him, bringing another of those smiles she was quickly falling in love with. Before he could move to kiss her back they heard someone clear their throat.

"Ah, Marta! Franco! You made it! Jenna, this is Marta and Franco Fuentes." He turned her to face the older couple before continuing. "Marta is my . . . *our* housekeeper and Franco is her husband and ranch foreman. Marta, Franco, my wife,

Jenna." Even if she wanted to, Jenna couldn't miss the pride in Brett's voice when he called her his wife. It was evident he was committed to this marriage and determined to make it work. The warm and friendly smiles of the Fuentes made her feel both at home and yet so sad because she knew she would leave. As soon as she could, she would leave. There was no way she could stay. Her promise to Rick aside, she told herself it would hurt Brett more to find out the truth about her. Better the little hurt of her leaving than having to hang his own wife for murder. Someday she knew the authorities would find her and she would stand trial for killing Uncle Julian. She couldn't bring that shame to a man as decent and good as Brett Parker.

With the reception over, folks started heading towards their homes. The next weddings wouldn't be for two more days. As Brett walked Jenna to the wagon, the Fuentes drove to town in, he asked her, "Did I remember to tell you just how beautiful you looked today?" His voice held a slight tremor that surprised her.

"If you did, I wouldn't mind hearing it again."

"Mrs. Parker, you are the most breathtakingly beautiful woman I have ever laid eyes on."

Jenna looked up at him, searching his eyes before telling him, "Thank you, Mr. Parker. And may I say, today you were the most handsome man I've ever seen?"

"You certainly may."

"Well then, Mr. Parker, you were very, very handsome to-day."

"You ready to go home, Mrs. Parker?"

Mrs. Parker . . . she was Mrs. Brett Parker. A hint of sadness entered her eyes as she looked around. She was married. Jennifer Matthews was now married and her name was Mrs.

Brett Parker. "I am. Where are the Fuentes?"

"They'll be staying in town tonight. I thought you might like the privacy."

"Mr. Parker . . ."

"Brett."

"Brett, you promised me, you said if I married you that . . . that—"

"I mean to keep that promise, Jenna, but it is our first night as a married couple. And I thought . . ."

"No. No. You promised that you wouldn't force me, that you'd wait . . . you said nothing about bedding me and then waiting, you pro . . ." Though whispered, her panic was clear in her face and how she stammered.

His lips came down on hers hard and hot, silencing her. His arms held her close in an iron embrace and it only took a moment of struggling before she felt him harden against her. Against her belly, that part of him that made him a man, that part that the women talked about with such humor. Her mind screamed that this couldn't be happening, he couldn't want her, while her lips and tongue responded to his intense kiss. When he finally broke it, she was breathless and shaken by the depth of the passion he evoked in her.

Taking advantage of her momentary silence he told her, "I meant what I said . . . I will not force you or bed you until you are ready. But it is our wedding night and I thought you'd prefer some privacy. That you wouldn't want to air our arrangement in public and to have a little time to settle in and get acclimated before Marta and Franco returned home."

"Oh . . . I'm sorry, Mr. Parker. I'm just . . . it's been a long day and you know that I . . ."

"Brett."

"What?"

He sighed in a combination of resignation and frustration. "It's alright, Jenna, we'll figure it out. We'll figure it out."

He helped her into the wagon and left her to her own thoughts as he drove the team home. What could he say to put her at ease? How could he break through that barrier that kept her from committing to their marriage? Was it because of his heritage? Did she already know? And if she didn't, what would she do when she learned his mother was Indian. A short while later he felt her shiver and instinctively put his arm around her, surprised when she snuggled up to him. "I'm sorry, Brett, I'm sorry I'm not what you want or need."

"It's alright, Jenna. It's not easy leaving your home and just starting a life with a stranger."

He wasn't sure if she was awake or asleep when they pulled up to the house some time later; she just felt so good lying against him, held close in his arm. If they could stay like that all night it would suit him fine, but it wouldn't exactly be prudent. And, he was still hopeful she would rethink their wedding night.

"Jenna? Darlin'? Wake up, sweetheart."

She stirred against him and at the moment she blinked at him, it took every ounce of Brett's strength not to kiss her senseless then and there. He climbed down and moved to the other side to help her down. His hand on her lower back, he walked her to the door of the house. He knew that in the darkness Jenna couldn't see much of the large, two story structure so he told her, "I'll give you the grand tour in the morning, but real quick, the house is spread out on both sides, two wings so to speak. My daddy always wanted a large family and built the house to be ready for it."

When she didn't respond, he guided her to the stairs to the second floor where they stopped before a door before he told her, "Like I said, I'll show you the whole house tomorrow. Right now let me show you to your room and let you start to settle in. I'll be up to see how you're doing as soon as I bed the horses down for the night."

Jenna only nodded and then gasped as the door was opened. The room was beautiful. The walls were done in a soft green. A slightly darker shade of green curtains adorned the windows and what appeared to be a balcony door. Flowers stood on several tables, an armoire that appeared to be inlaid with pearl stood on one wall. A writing table and comfortable chair sat near one of the windows overlooking what she thought was the front of the house. She finally let her eyes rest on the very large four poster bed that was the centerpiece of the room. She swallowed. "It's beautiful. Thank you . . . where is your room?"

"Did you want to see it now?"

"All right."

He walked towards one of the other two doors in the room and pulled it open. "Right through here, I'll be in easy reach when you want me." The emphasis on the *when* told her he was still set on having a true marriage with her. Somehow there had to be a way to dissuade him from his purpose. "Unless you want to join me in there now?"

"No. No, I don't. And I'm sure when you meet a woman who you truly want to spend your life with, a woman who will love you, she'll make good use of this door."

He said nothing, only bent his head to place a kiss on her lips before walking out the door. "I'll be back in a bit."

Jenna sighed as he left. "Stubborn man." She opened her satchel and pulled out the few dresses she'd brought and hung them in the closet despite deciding that tomorrow no matter what, she was going to give them a proper cleaning. She tried the door opposite the one leading to *his* room and found a bathing chamber. The few toiletries she had she laid out on the counter and then began to pull the pins from her hair, luxuriating in pulling a brush through her long brown locks. What seemed all too short a time later Brett was back at the door to her room. It surprised her when he knocked and she hurried out. From the look on his face it seemed he'd been watching her for a time. There was a warmth in his eyes coupled with a look of longing.

Pulling a strand of her hair through his fingers he told her, "It's been a long day, it's late and I know you'd probably like to get to sleep, so why don't I show you the kitchen so if you need or want something during the night you know where it is."

"That would be nice. Thank you."

He escorted her downstairs, his hand again on her lower back. It seemed the man couldn't keep from touching her in one way or another. At the foot of the stairs he moved to the right and down a short hallway into the very large kitchen. "My mother, when she was here, liked the extra room so my daddy built the kitchen nice and big for her."

When she was here? Dare she ask? Jenna only answered, "I see."

"So here is the larder, the pantry . . . are you hungry, Jenna? Did you want a little something now?"

"Actually, if I could have one of these apples?" She gestured towards a bowl of ripe apples on the wooden table.

"That all you want?"

She nodded as she waited for him to tell her it was all right to take one.

"Well I don't know about you but I didn't get much to eat today and since I was with you pretty much the whole time after the ceremony I don't recall you having anything much, you sure?" He pulled out some bread and some meat before reaching for a knife and beginning to slice the meat. Jenna's mouth watered. She hadn't eaten all day, not even breakfast.

Her stomach was just too knotted up to eat.

"Well actually, yes, that would be nice." She looked around the room and moved to one of the cabinets on the wall. She looked in one or two before locating the plates. It was on the tip of Brett's tongue to tell her where they were, but held back feeling Jenna would feel more at home, that it *was* her home, if he left her to find her way as she wished. She brought the plates to the table and tentatively asked, "Would there maybe be some milk?"

"Yup—in the larder."

She walked over and brought out a pitcher and then opened a few other cabinets until she found the glasses. By the time she poured the milk, Brett had sandwiches made and they sat to eat. They ate in companionable silence, both lost in their own thoughts. When their meal was done, Jenna was barely able to stifle a yawn as she gathered up the plates and glasses and moved to the sink to wash them.

"Leave 'em till morning, sweetheart."

"It'll only take a moment."

Brett went to stop her, to tell her they were going to bed, but again stopped himself. She needed to feel at home, that this was her home and if she wanted to clean her kitchen, so be it.

When she'd finished the dishes, she turned and smiled. "Thank you. I was hungry."

"No need to thank me, Jenna, I told you this is your home and I'm not about to let my wife go hungry."

"Well, it was still a welcome meal."

They headed upstairs where Brett lingered at her door. "You sure you don't want to join me?"

"I'm sure."

"There's plenty of room."

"Mr. Parker."

"Brett."

"Brett, you promised me, you said you wouldn't push, please, I married you because I believed you."

He didn't answer her, what she hadn't said evident in the silence surrounding them . . . she married him because she believed him *and* he hadn't given her a choice.

Instead of answering, he pulled her into his embrace, with one arm around her waist, the other cupped her head and lifted her face to him. His gaze bored into hers, his eyes unreadable as he seemed to look into her soul. Slowly, so slowly, almost imperceptibly so it seemed time stood still, he lowered his head until his lips found their target. At first planting light kisses on her lips, his tongue finally ventured out to caress the soft parting of her own. Still moving slowly, as if time no longer existed, his tongue moved to stroke hers, gently searching every nuance of her mouth before joining with her tongue in a drugging kiss. Jenna gave herself into the kiss, wholly, passionately.

What harm in a kiss? It feels so good, so very good, a kiss doesn't mean it will be more . . . it's just a kiss. Something to remember when he annuls this farce of a marriage and I move on.

When he finally raised his head, Jenna could only stand and stare wide eyed.

"I'm just next door if you need anything . . . if you . . . want anything. Sleep well and I'll see you in the morning."

"Goodnight . . . Brett . . . sleep well."

She closed the door as he moved towards his room. Her hand came to her lips, touching where his had been. She'd kissed a few of the young men she'd known at home, but it was nothing like the kisses Brett gave her. She couldn't kiss him, not again, because if she did, she'd never want to leave him.

CHAPTER ELEVEN

Jenna slept so hard and solid it surprised her. It seemed to her the past few nights she had been sleeping more deeply and soundly than she had slept in a long time . . .she was sure since before her father died. She awoke just as the sun peaked over the horizon and she slipped out of bed, washed her face, combed out her hair, pulled on the cleanest of the dresses she'd brought, and headed downstairs. If she was going to be living here the least she could do was make breakfast for Brett. She wandered into the kitchen and began to pull fixings from the larder and pantry. Marta kept the kitchen clean and well organized so it was easy to find the griddle and frying pan. First she started up some coffee and then cooked some of the bacon she'd found, broke the eggs into a bowl and started to mix them and sliced up some bread to warm. Just as the bacon was about done she turned to go wake Brett up only to find him standing in the doorway, a grin lighting up his face.

"Didn't tell me you could cook."

"I'm not so sure you'd call this cooking, but I think it'll be a passable breakfast. Sit down and I'll finish up the eggs."

Instead Brett headed to the cabinet and pulled out plates and mugs, setting them on the table.

"So when we're done, how about I show you the rest of the house and see what we need to do to help you settle in? And then this afternoon I'll take you on out to the barn and show you a bit of the range?"

"Okay. Umm, well, I'd also like to clean up my dresses,

especially with another wedding tomorrow. I did the best I could on the trail, but they really need a good cleaning."

"Marta should be back after lunch, she'll take care of it."

"I can wash my own clothes."

"I'm sure you can . . . but why don't you at least check with Marta. For all her nagging for years about me getting a wife, I have a feeling she just wanted someone else to fuss over. Give her a chance to get to know you and then if you still want to do cleaning and such . . ."

"I see. I'm sorry, I forgot that this is her home."

"It's yours, too, Jenna. And if you aren't comfortable with Marta and Franco, I'll help them find another position."

"What?" She was clearly horrified at his words. "How could you say such a thing? I'd never send someone from their home. No, I hope she'll like me and please, if I can do anything to help her or for her to be comfortable with me, please tell me."

Her reaction warmed him. Whatever her secret was, whatever it was she was hiding from didn't include avoiding people who were different than her. Maybe she would even, eventually, accept him.

"Well let's take a look around, shall we?"

"Dishes first."

"Bossy, aren't you?"

"When you let me, I am." He resisted reaching out to grab her and kiss her. In time, in time she'd be ready to kiss him . . . yes, in time.

With the dishes done, they moved through the house — the formal dining room, sitting room, library, den and into the wing opposite from where their bedrooms were. "My dad wanted a passel of kids, but his first wife, Clarissa, died after my brother Kendrick was born. My mom only had me. With him anyway. When she remarried she had my brother with . . ."

He stopped short, catching himself before revealing Wolf's paternity. " . . . her second marriage, after my pa died. But while my pa was alive, in the hopes that there would have been more kids, he added a bunch of bedrooms . . . kids, nannies, friends for sleepovers."

She appreciated that he didn't add his own desire to fill those rooms. From the look in his eyes before he shuttered them, she knew it crossed his mind, but he didn't push her. As the headed back towards their rooms, Marta's softly accented voice filtered up to them.

"Hello? *Hola? Senor* Brett?"

"Up here, Marta."

"Ah, *yo ver*. Do you speak Spanish, Mrs. Parker?"

"Oh, Marta, please, call me Jenna. And no, I don't but if you could teach me some I'd very much appreciate it."

Marta beamed at Brett. "You chose a good wife. She be a wonderful mother."

If the older woman thought it odd that both Jenna's and Brett's beds had been slept in she didn't let on. Jenna didn't want to ask Brett what he had told the other woman because she didn't want to open *that* discussion again.

"Jenna wanted to collect a few of her dresses to wash up and then we were going to have some lunch."

"Ah, well let me have those dresses. You two continue your tour and I'll start these and some lunch for you, yes?"

"Thank you, Marta. That would be great," Brett answered for her.

As she trundled off with the dresses Brett showed Jenna the rest of their wing. Heading downstairs, Jenna saw Marta heading towards the family eating room with some dishes.

"Oh, Marta—we can eat in the kitchen."

"The kitchen?"

"Yes, it's warmer and so cozy in there. Would you mind?"

"No, not at all."

Seeing that Marta only put two plates on the table, Jenna looked first at Brett and then towards Marta. "Have you and Franco already eaten Marta?"

"No, we'll eat later."

"But why? Aren't you hungry now?" As she spoke she was heading towards the cabinet with the plates and taking down two more. Even though she had grown up with servants and other household help, Jenna often ate with the kitchen help when her parents were out for the evening. There was something about Adler Creek that class structure seemed non-existent. It was something that made Jenna feel more at home than she ever had in New York.

Brett chuckled to himself. *Even if they aren't hungry looks like they'll be eating.* But he was also pleased Jenna thought of them as family and people she wanted to be with. And that was how it felt, that she thought of them as family and not that they were a buffer against him.

After lunch Marta persuaded Jenna that it would really be just fine to leave the dresses for her to wash. "After all Jenna, you are a newlywed and should relax with your husband." Before she could reply, Brett had taken her by the arm and led her out. For the next few hours he showed her the stable and barn, and they walked out to the fields enjoying the warm late-summer day. Brett noted she was clearly impressed with the ranch. *If nothing else maybe she'll stay because of the people and things that are here.* He didn't begin to understand it, but from the moment he'd heard about her he knew, deep in his soul, he knew that she was the one woman who would make his life complete. His mother often spoke of there being one person for each other person and how he would know when he met that special person. He couldn't put his finger on it. In fact, it didn't make any sense that he would feel this connection to Jenna. Maybe it was the way Dusty described her, that there was something that had her skittish. There was no doubt in his mind, that person was Jenna.

As the afternoon waned, they strolled back to the house. "It's so big. I feel like I need to ask you for a map to find my way around."

"I think you'll get used to it."

"I suppose. You don't think Marta will mind us going to the wedding tomorrow, do you?"

"Why would she mind?"

"Well surely she'll appreciate some help around the house, won't she?"

"Help?"

"Yes, I'm here, I'm capable, why wouldn't I help?"

"Maybe because she sees you as the mistress of the house and she works for us."

"That's nonsense, Brett, and it would be rude if I didn't and I expect you to tell her that. Unless, do *you* have a problem with me helping, of me trying to earn my keep?"

"You do have your feisty moments, don't you?"

"Yes, well I'd have more if you weren't so stubborn."

"Jenna . . ."

"I'm not starting again, I'm not bringing it up. It's just if you expect me to feel comfortable here you're going to have to let me help, somehow, around the house."

"I'll speak to her—after the rest of your friends are married—think of the time as our honeymoon, alright?"

"Fine."

Entering the house, Jenna went to wash up and then went into the kitchen to help Marta with dinner. The older woman was a bit surprised at Jenna's offer yet when she saw the sadness enter Jenna's eyes, she suggested maybe she could set the table. When Jenna again took down four plates Marta went to stop her but caught herself. The younger woman was now mistress of the house and if she wanted to include herself and Franco and if Brett didn't disapprove then she would go along with it. She had seen the pride in Brett's eyes when Jenna reached out to herself and Franco earlier to include them in their meal. She wasn't sure about their sleeping arrangements. It was certainly odd for a bride to sleep alone, but if Mr. Brett was okay with it, then who was she to interfere?

When Brett came down for dinner, he raised a surprised brow at the four settings for dinner but said nothing as Jenna bustled in carrying a large bowl of potatoes. If it made her happy, settled in their home, he wasn't going to say anything. At the end of the meal he went to take Jenna's hand to lead her upstairs, telling Marta and Franco that they needed an early start in the morning because of the next group of weddings.

"I'll be up in a bit, Brett, I'll just help Marta with the dishes and . . ."

"I think Marta can handle it."

"But it would be ru . . ."

"Jenna . . ." Though softly spoken, the warning in his voice was clear.

Not wanting the newlyweds to get into a spat over something as stupid as dinner dishes, Marta spoke up. "I thank you for the help today, Mrs. Brett, but you must still be tired from the trip and you are, after all, newlyweds. Go and enjoy your husband."

Reluctantly she stood and followed Brett out of the room, dreading his anger at her stall tactics just then. She was surprised when all he said was, "I think she may be on to you." Jenna had only a moment to stand there and stare open mouthed before Brett stepped towards her and quickly took her lips in a kiss. One of his warm, sweet and so compelling kisses. It occurred to her that he hadn't tried to kiss her all day and, in a way, she missed those lips of his on hers. It was quickly becoming so easy to *enjoy* her husband. His kisses did something to her no one had ever done before and made her want something more. But what that something more was she wasn't sure . . . but she was sure it had something to do with those feelings in her belly and lower . . . between her legs. At her door he again took her in his arms and kissed her, enjoying her immediate response.

"Would you like to invite me in?"

"No, not really. You . . ."

"I know, I know, I promised. But, Jenna, I gotta tell you, you are the most attractive woman I have ever laid eyes on and when you kiss, well a man just starts to think with more than his brain."

"Then maybe we need to not kiss."

"I think, my dear wife, you need more kissing, lots more kissing." Before she could protest he'd pinned her to the wall, his body hard and hot against hers, with his tongue giving no ground as he explored the sweet warmth of her mouth. She felt just how strong his desire was as he pressed into her. She felt his manhood pressed hard and hot against her belly and the simple knowledge she had made him that hard caused a surprising wetness between her legs. A part of her mind wondered what it was about him, about his touch, that caused her nipples to pebble to such hardness and that delicious feeling between her legs. Only when she was well and truly breathless and he knew her lips would show the sweet swelling of his kiss the next day, did he release her.

Lying in his bed later, sleep eluding him, Brett questioned his own actions. Could he really wait for her to come to him? They'd only been married a day and already his body demanded he take her and make her truly his. How was he going to keep his promise not to touch her until she was ready?

Just has he was on the brink of sleep he heard a scream from the next room.

"Noooo! No, please no!"

Before the second scream left her lips Brett, pistol in hand, was through the door between their rooms.

"Don't, please don't . . . let me go."

Brett took in the room, checking the windows and door, making sure Jenna truly was alone before moving over to the bed.

Quickly laying his pistol on the nightstand he felt a clenching in his chest he'd never felt before. Not a pain, but something very close to it, as he saw her thrashing and struggling in her sleep against some unknown assailant. Her low moans and occasional sharp cry made him hurt for her. Sitting on the bed, he pulled her into his arms, "Jenna? Sweetheart? It's okay, Jenna, wake up sweetheart, you're safe, I'm here."

She moaned. Coming half away she began to struggle not only against her dream but Brett as well. Pushing against his chest her, "No, please, don't hurt me, don't do this," coming out in an anguished moan.

"It's me, Jenna. It's Brett. Come on, sweetheart, wake up for me."

She came fully awake while at the same time struggling to push him away and disengage herself from the blankets in which she'd gotten herself tangled. "Wha-what are you doing in here?"

"You were crying out, sweetheart, more than crying. You screamed a couple of times."

"I did? Oh, oh, Mr. Parker, I am . . . I'm sorry, I am so sorry."

"No reason to be sorry, Jenna. I told you I'd protect you and if someone was hurting you, I wouldn't be keeping my promise."

Unaware of what caused her latest round of movement, Brett reached to pull her back into his embrace. When, in an effort to comfort her, he felt how hot her cheek had gotten, he shifted so he could hold her by the shoulders and take as good a look at her as he could in the moonlit room.

"Oh, Mr. Parker . . . I am sorry." She'd managed to sit up and move a slight distance away from him. As she went to pull the covers up a bit higher, she noticed he was completely nude!

What he didn't realize, but Jenna certainly did, was the movement parted his thighs, revealing much more of him than she'd ever seen of any man. Even the other women's descriptions hadn't quite prepared her for the site that now greeted her. Swallowing before trying to speak, she managed to squeak out, "You see, that's another reason why marrying me wasn't such a good idea."

"Are you prone to bad dreams, Jenna?"

"Yes, yes I am and . . . and Belle mentioned on the trail that I often do call out in my sleep."

"Then that's even more reason for you to be married to me, sweetheart. If you are having bad dreams, you need someone to hold and comfort you when you wake up."

"But you need a good night's sleep, don't you? I mean, with a ranch to run and having to maintain the law here, you can't be being woken up every night or so to . . ."

"Even more reason you should be married, Jenna. To me. I understand how people can have fears and concerns and not just in waking life. Give us a chance, Jenna . . . you may be pleasantly surprised. Now, you want to tell me what that dream was about?"

"No."

He noted her answer was firm, without any hesitation. Clearly she was determined to build up some pretty strong walls to keep them apart. Well, it would be interesting to see who was faster . . . her building them up or him tearing them down.

"Sure? It may make you feel a little better to talk about it?"

"No, really. You know how dreams are . . . we have them and then they fade and are just a memory."

"I suppose. Just so you know, if you want to talk about them, you just need to tell me."

"Well, thank you. I appreciate that. Well . . . um, I guess I'll say goodnight again?" There was so much hope in her voice. He chuckled to himself that while she tried to dismiss him with her *saying goodnight again,* it came out like a question.

"You want me to stay with you tonight, Jenna?"

He noticed her quick glance down at his still exposed lap and groin before she hurriedly told him, "No!" His gaze moved to her throat and even the slight movement of her swallowing after her curt response aroused him. He wasn't sure if she saw just how big he got when he was full hard would make her want him or scare her even more. What he did know was he wanted to kiss her along the vein that pulsed in her neck, especially when she did those nervous swallows of hers, and from there kiss her down to her breasts, suckle on them while his hands moved to her nether lips and . . . *better stop that now, Brett . . . because she isn't going to take you beneath her sheets with her tonight.*

"I meant, no thank you. I'm still, you understand, tired and it's been a full few days and I didn't mean to sound so sharp."

"Not a problem, Jenna. I understand. I'll see you in the morning then?"

At her nod he debated whether or not to kiss her again. After the earlier kiss it had taken him a good couple of hours for his cock to relax. Did he really want to lay there all hard and aroused again? His lips somehow didn't hear his heart say *no* and before he knew what he was doing, he leaned in to kiss her.

He expected her initial hesitation and was rewarded by her ardent response. The feel of her arms coming around his neck encouraged him to slide his hand along her arm, its silky smoothness sending shots of pure arousal to his cock . . . but it was when his hand came to rest on her breast, lightly sliding over her nipple that he grew harder than he'd ever thought he'd been in his life.

Her nipple responded to his touch by immediately joining in the rock hardness he felt in his cock. Her soft sigh turning quickly into a moan roused him even more, and his body demanded he forget his promise and take her then and there. To his delighted surprise he felt her hand rest on his forearm and glide up over his biceps, resting there long enough for her to feel his strength before she began to explore down his torso. Brett felt himself holding his breath as her hand settled briefly on his chest . . . so involved with her exploration he forgot his own hand resting on her breast, stopping the gentle kneading he'd begun.

His tongue moved in her mouth of its own violation, the dance becoming more enticing when her hand slid to his lap. Telling himself to breathe, to act natural, he silently ordered his thumb to stroke her nipple . . . if her arousal grew, perhaps he would be joining her in bed tonight, consummating his marriage, making her his.

She moaned as his thumb rubbed a bit harder against her nipple, and she leaned further into him when he resumed the gentle kneading of her breast. Her own hand moved to his lap, her fingers entwining in the crisp hair of his groin while her palm settled on his cock . . . his hot and so very hard cock, and she jumped back as if she had been stung.

Jenna pulled out of his embrace and away from him so fast it took him a few breaths to realize she had done so.

Finally feeling like he could breathe again, he was surprised at the slight shake to his voice. "Jenna?"

"You are naked, Mr. Parker!"

"Naked?" He looked down as if just discovering he was without clothing. "Yes, I am, I sleep nude."

"Well, I . . . I don't and I, could we please say good night, Mr. Parker?"

Deciding she was probably more frightened by the passionate encounter they had both just shared than her dream and that leaving now would endear him to her more than forcing any issue he simply said, "Call me Brett and you have a deal."

"Yes, Brett, thank you for checking on me. I really do appreciate it. I'm tired and looking forward to tomorrow. Good night."

"Good night, Jenna, sleep well." He placed a kiss on the top of her head and strode out of the room. He felt her eyes on him as he walked.

It wasn't until she saw the last of his posterior and heard the click of the door that Jenna realized she was holding her breath. The man was just too sure of himself and much too virile. No, sure of himself wasn't the right word . . . he was comfortable with himself, comfortable in his own skin. And what skin he had! Jenna felt her face flame with the rush of an embarrassed blush as she thought about how his skin felt when she touched him — satin soft, except when her fingers would brush against a scar . . . nothing big . . . just what a man's man would have. Beneath that skin that she wanted to touch from head to toe were muscles, the likes of which she had seen on statues in the museum, but didn't think real, living men had.

He was beautiful. His body was perfect . . . based on what she had seen in those statues. And his . . . his . . . Jenna felt her cheeks glow even redder and was glad she was alone in the darkened room. Fanning herself, she knew the heat she felt coursing through her body wasn't just from the covers she had drawn up to her chin when he rose to leave. Oh no, it was from the thoughts she was having about him. Brett Parker. Her husband. She had *not* been prepared for the sight of his exposed groin, when he shifted to take her by the shoulders and she looked down and saw his manhood. Curious as to how touching him would feel, it was all she could do not to reach out and touch him. She desperately wanted to reach down and cup his balls, to feel how they felt in her hands, to savor their weight as she held them. The ones she had seen on the statue in the museum were nowhere near as fascinating as this man's . . . her husband's. And his cock. Lord above, he was huge. From the pool of moisture that gathered between her legs, she knew for the first time for certain where he would put that huge cock when he consummated their marriage.

No, no, it would not be consummated. There is no way I can let that happen, she told herself. Still, the temptation to touch him almost overwhelmed her. Self-preservation had taken over. The need to not be his wife moved to the fore and she resisted. Jenna knew without a doubt, had she reached out and cupped his balls or even gave the slightest touch to his cock, she would have been lost. There would have been no stopping him.

There was no doubt in Jenna's mind Brett was a good man, a decent man and he was so incredibly handsome. Undoubtedly the most handsome man she had ever laid eyes on. From those blue eyes of his that would go from the blue of a raging storm lit sky when something—she—angered him, to the crystal blue of a mountain lake in the sun shine when something pleased him, to the lush sapphire blue of his desire when she allowed the burgeoning passion between them show. Oh yes, his eyes and his mouth—those brilliant white teeth in a devastating smile. Oh, he was definitely the most handsome man she had ever seen.

He was so much more than that, though. His beauty went beyond his physical attractiveness. He was handsome as well on the inside. Brett Parker was decent, kind, courteous, considerate . . . he could make her laugh if she let him. He would make her feel many good things, if she would let him.

Brett Parker. Her husband. The man who would probably one day, one day very soon if she didn't leave, didn't run away, would arrest her.

I can't allow any more kisses. Many more of them, any more touches, I'll give in and I'll never be able to leave. He deserves better than a murderess for a wife. Brett Parker deserves someone wonderful and good and that's not me.

Brett turned as he closed the door of Jenna's room as softly as he could. Standing there, facing it with one hand on the knob and the other on the wood panel, he talked himself out of going back in to her and demanding if not his marital rights, at least that she at least tell him what troubled her. After several long moments and deep breaths he talked himself out of doing either.

Moving towards the window, he looked out into the moonlit night, drinking in the mountain vista that lay beyond his ranch lands. Rich and lush land, wonderful for cattle and growing a variety of crops. Land he wanted to raise his children on.

"What are you hiding, Jenna?" he asked the night sky. "Don't you feel it? Don't you feel that we belong together?"

Brett let his mind wander back to his childhood, to the love between his mother and father. He couldn't begin to count the number of times he and his older brother, Kendrick, stumbled on his parents in a loving embrace. It seemed they always hugged and kissed each other.

Once, as he sat alone with his mother, he asked her about the physical love between she and his dad. He told her about how his friends' parents never seemed to even touch, barely their hands to each other when they'd pass a bowl of food at the table. His parents though always seemed to touch, lingering touches and kisses. His father kissed his mother when he left in the morning, when he returned at night, sometimes it seemed he did it just because.

Seeing her son was ready to begin to learn about love between a man and a woman she'd sat him down. To this day, twenty something years later, he remembered her words.

"Brett," she'd said, "a man is not whole without a woman and a woman is not whole without her man. We are meant to be part of each other. Many men and women, like those of your friends, marry because they need to be part of a whole. They care for each other. I have seen this between them."

In retrospect Brett knew she was trying to be kind in talking about his friends' parents. Making it seem that they had real feelings for each other, if not love.

"They work hard to have their marriages and some couples, they like to keep their cuddling to themselves, not to share. Your father and I, we cannot help ourselves. It is as if we feel we must touch each other. So many men and many women meet and marry because they need to be whole. They care for each other. My people believe that for each man there is one special woman and for each woman there is one special man. This other person is a part of the other's soul. Their love goes beyond a human love. It is as if they are the same soul. Those that are lucky enough to find this person know it. They know the moment they see that person . . . sometimes even before. I knew of the man I would marry many years before I met your father. In my dreams as a young girl I would see a man with light hair and eyes bluer than the sky. When your father came to the territory I knew it was he I was destined for.

"He was married to Kendrick's mother when he came. She was a good woman, a kind woman. There was no doubt about that. And they both loved Kendrick. So when I met them, I thought first that my dreams were wrong or that I had offended the gods in some way and that my punishment was to see the man who was my other self live his life with another. When the fever took Clarissa, I mourned for her and Whitney and Kendrick. It was so hard on him as a little boy to lose his mother.

"Because Kendrick was, is, Whitney's son and I knew in my heart and soul your father was my destiny, I loved Kendrick. It was with great joy when your father asked me to care for Kendrick. I had even greater joy when your father came to me and asked me to be his wife. He told me that from the moment he met me, he felt drawn to me, that there was a special bond between us. A bond that would never die. So I married your father. He is the only man who can ever make me complete.

When his father died, Brett remembered confusion at Fallen Leaf's actions. Now he knew, she grieved in the Indian way. He was devastated when Fallen Leaf married Black Elk, a warrior from her tribe. In his pain, in what young Brett saw at her betrayal of his father, he ran away. Not that he got very far, but he tried to run. When he was returned home, Fallen Leaf sat him down again and told him that now she was the same as many of his friends' parents. A woman needs a man to care for her and that Black Elk was a good man and he would care for her and would raise Brett as his own. He was relieved when she told him that the love for his father would never die, but that he would want this — a strong man to guide Brett into adulthood.

"What about Kendrick?" Brett asked.

Kendrick was going to be sent back east to live with his mother's family. Brett didn't understand then what he knew now — that Kendrick's mother never liked the west and her family liked it even less. His grandparents would have done anything to have their White grandson grow up among Whites. While he missed Kendrick, Brett understood and accepted he would never see his brother again. Fate or destiny intervened and Kendrick became a Deputy U.S. Marshal and often worked the Wyoming territory. He never forgot his childhood and the happiness he felt in Adler Creek. As soon as he could, he returned to what he thought of as his home.

It wasn't long before Fallen Leaf gave birth to Brett's younger brother, Wolf. When Kendrick came west again, the three spent time together — blond haired, blue-eyed Kendrick, black-haired, blue-eyed Brett, and black-haired, brown-eyed Wolf. Each looked so different, but all were so handsome.

Falling Leaf had been gentle when talking about Kendrick's grandparents. Now, as an adult, Brett appreciated how she had tried so hard to raise him not to see a person's color, but the person inside.

Now it was the person inside Jenna he wanted to get to know. He knew, just as his mother had told him he would know, the moment he heard about her that she was his other half. When he saw her on the trail, walking away, trying to escape the crowd, he knew with a certainly unlike any other he'd ever had before she was the one he had spent a lifetime waiting for. Now he was glad Christina had rejected him — because if he had married Christina, he would not have Jenna. He would have been married just because he needed a wife, not because she was a part of his soul.

Jenna . . . his wife . . . the woman in the other room he wanted more than anything to be with.

Sighing, he moved to the bed, stopping a moment to look again at the door before climbing into his own bed. "Soon Jenna, soon you'll be my wife in all ways. Soon you will know as well as I do we belong together."

He could take on any man or beast, but her inner demons were beyond his reach until she trusted him to tell him what they were.

CHAPTER TWELVE

The weddings the next day went off well, as did the rest the following week. Even with so many, each was special and memorable in its own way. The ubiquitous photographer, Mr. Webster, was present for all of them. If Brett noticed Jenna's constant avoidance of him, he gave no mention of it. As the couples entered into their own wedded bliss those that hadn't found brides talked about another mail order bride venture.

At home, Jenna and Brett fell into an amiable routine where they would wake — each in their own room, and she would eat breakfast with him before he either left for town to his duties as deputy or work on the ranch. Each night, except the two each week he stayed in town to cover his shift, he'd walk her upstairs and kiss her at the door. With each kiss she felt her resolve grow weaker and weaker until she knew she was falling irrevocably in love with Brett Parker. Each night he'd lean into her, his hard, well-muscled body pressed against hers, showing her with his body what she wouldn't let him say — that he wanted her and only her. When he left on the mornings he would be staying in town, he'd tell her, "I hope my wife will want me as much as I want her when I come home."

She was relieved both because the recurring nightmares of Uncle Julian attacking her and her killing him seemed to have ended and Brett asked no questions about either the dream or what came before. Jenna wondered what kind of person she was becoming that she could put the memory of killing Julian and his dead body lying on the very bed he meant to violate her on aside and replace it, seemingly so quickly, with thoughts of how she felt when Brett held and kissed her. It was with effort she kept herself from dwelling on how those kisses of his made her so very hot, during the day and from giving into what her body began to more and more demand she share with him each night.

She had no idea why Brett never asked about the dream that shattered her first night in his house or why he never asked about her past. In fact, she was glad he seemed to want to go on without knowing anything that happened before he met her. Maybe it was because she never asked him about his past that he didn't want to know hers. Whatever the reason, Jenna was glad he didn't want to know.

When Brett was at work, Jenna spent most of her day with Marta, helping the older woman cook and clean. It reminded her of being home with her parents and growing up in New York except then she would have to sneak into the kitchen to try to help cook. Proper young ladies didn't cook or clean at home. She never felt comfortable having people wait on her. Now, for the first time in her life, Jenna knew what is felt like to be useful and honestly, she enjoyed it. Not that she was all that much help for Marta, but at least she felt like she contributed something.

Jenna learned quickly there were several year-round hands that lived on the ranch and some came for seasonal work such as branding or the spring planting of the crops they used to feed themselves. Brett was generous to a fault, often coming home with a new dress or other item of clothing for Jenna. She never asked to go to town or for any of the gifts he brought her. With nothing to give him in exchange . . . or nothing she wanted to give, it just did not seem right to take the things he offered. But when she would wear one of the new dresses or trinkets he bought her and she saw the smile on his face, the joy in his eyes when she gave into her own enjoyment of the new things.

Content on the ranch, seeming to live in her own cocoon of safety, Jenna gave no thought to visiting any of her friends from the bride train . . . only how and when she would be able to go away. Brett surprised her almost three weeks after their wedding when he broached the subject of her going to town with him.

"Jenna, why don't you come in to town with me today? Belle and Bea ask after you all the time. You could have lunch with them, do some shopping. I heard there was a new catalog from back east at the Emporium and I've been hoping you'd want to do some decorating of your own around here."

"Decorating?"

"Yeah, you know, add your own touch, things you like, make it your home."

"You have a nice home as it is, Brett. I can't see as anything would need to change."

She knew he was disappointed that she had no inclination to redecorate his home. As much as he tried to hide the sadness in his eyes or the temporary slump of his shoulders, Jenna could see the unhappiness he felt. At least she called him Brett now. That seemed to cheer him, that and those searing goodnight kisses.

Trying to soften the blow of not wanting to redecorate his house, Jenna suggested, "I was thinking though, Brett, maybe we could have dinner in town? Nothing fancy, just a nice meal together in Adler Creek?"

"You'd like that?"

"Yes, I would. If . . . if . . . well if you would."

She couldn't miss the excitement in his voice when he answered, "I'd like that very much, Jenna. You can see Belle and Bea during the day—it'd make them happy and you could catch up on the news. Then we can go to Mary's Café for dinner."

The news—from back east—maybe there would be word of

Julian's death and if they were looking for his killer. If they stopped
looking, she'd be able to stay here, give herself to Brett and he'd never
know about her past. There would be no reason to leave him. And
hours alone with Brett . . . how do I make it through that?

"Yes, I'd like to go. Give me a moment to get my hat and a
shawl."

Brett's smile was so warm when she returned, she felt the
same butterflies in her tummy she felt when he kissed her
goodnight. It didn't take much to make the man happy, that
was certain. But if she did too many things to make him
happy, when she left . . .

"Give me just another minute to see if Marta needs anything, ok?" Jenna said as she turned towards the kitchen.

"Sure, no problem."

Coming back in a bit, she had a shopping list of things the
other woman needed, and the couple left. To Jenna's surprise
it was easy to talk to Brett about everyday things. He seemed
to respect her need for privacy about her past and didn't ask
much if anything at all. Maybe her non-committal, one-word
answers dissuaded him. By the same token, he didn't say
much about his life and Jenna refrained from asking because
if she asked, it would open the door for him to ask about hers.
So she talked about funny incidents on the trail out and he
talked about incidents on the ranch.

When they pulled into town, Jenna quickly spotted Belle
coming out of the bank—probably there to see her Henry.
Jenna called out to her and waved as she simultaneously tried
to jump off the wagon. Brett stopped the team before she leapt
out and quickly dismounted and came around to help Jenna
down. Belle was over in a second, arms flailing as the women
rushed to hug each other.

"Jenna, I'm so glad you came! What's taken you so long to
come visit? I know it can't be because of you loving that man
of yours because we see him here at work all the time. Isn't
married life grand? Especially, you know . . ."

"Belle, we have a crowd here — let's go talk somewhere private, yes?"

"Oh sure, sure."

They linked arms and turned to start down the street as Brett's voice reached her ears. "Jenna?"

A blush quickly covered her face as she stepped back to him, his hands going quickly to her shoulders and drawing her into his embrace. The kiss he gave her not only curled her toes and embarrassed her like nothing else ever had, it was a message to every man in town that she belonged to him and only him. Finally releasing her, he held on to her just a moment longer to settle her. Reaching into his pocket, he pulled out some money, telling her, "Buy anything that looks appealing to you or just tell the Emporium or wherever shop you go to put it on my account."

"I will, and where do you want to meet me for dinner?"

"Come on by the jail."

"All right." Feeling impish despite her embarrassment, she stood up on tip toe and brushed a quick kiss on his cheek.

The two women wandered down the street chatting like it had only been yesterday they'd seen each other. "So how is Bea? Do you see her often?"

"Oh yes, she and Calvin have had us to dinner a few times and we've had them. I've been after Brett to bring you to town so we could have you to dinner. When can you come? And when do we get to see that ranch you live on?"

"I'll check with Brett, but why don't we plan for maybe the weekend? Say Sunday after church?"

"I'll ask Henry, I'm sure it will be fine."

They shopped, had a wonderful meal at the café and shopped some more along with stopping to visit with some of the other women who were in town.

At the bank's closing time, Jenna joined Belle going to meet Henry and she immediately told him about the proposed dinner. When Henry quickly agreed to the plan it was very clear to Jenna that two were in love and already doted on each other.

The couple escorted Jenna to the jail and before Jenna could say a word, Belle's effervescence crested. "Brett, I'm so excited to come to see your ranch, Jenna suggested Sunday for dinner, does that fit for you?"

Brett's smile was for Jenna as he reached for her. "Whatever my wife wants she will have. Sunday would be fine."

Bidding the Bascoms goodnight, Jenna turned to Brett. "Did you mean it?"

"What, that dinner Sunday would be fine?"

"That whatever your wife wants . . ."

"As long as she *is* my wife and my wife you *will* stay Jenna. Make no mistake, you will remain my wife." Seeing the sadness cross her eyes he instantly felt contrite. At a loss to explain, even to himself what possessed him Brett told her, "That was rude of me, I apologize. Forgive me?"

"I suppose."

Seeking to bring back her good humor, he asked what she had bought in her travels during the day. Jenna assured him she had gotten all of the items on Marta's list and then pulled out a pretty red silk scarf. "I saw this and immediately thought of Marta—it will look so good with her coloring, don't you think?"

"You bought Marta a gift?"

"Yes—was that wrong? Oh, Brett, she's been so kind to me, so helpful with me bumbling around the house, and I wanted to thank her."

"She'll love it, I'm sure of it. I have one more thing to do before dinner, do you mind?"

Remembering one of the reasons she agreed to come to town, she assured him there would be no problem and wandered over to the wanted posters, hoping her picture or likeness was not among them and looking for anything that would assure her Julian Carlman's killer was no longer sought. Reassured there were no pictures of herself, disappointed that she could find nothing that showed Julian was truly gone from her life forever, she still felt content when Brett took her arm to go to dinner who was his usual sweet, attentive self at dinner. Almost romantic to a fault.

It would be so easy to just be his wife, so easy. But how will he feel when they finally catch up with me and my own husband has to arrest me?

The dinner with Belle and Henry the next weekend went off well. Although she had served as hostess for several of her father's dinners, Jenna was nervous about the dinner with the Bascoms and how Brett would see it. Even though she knew she would eventually leave him, she still wanted him to be proud he'd married her. She confused even herself.

When the Bascoms left they made plans to have Brett and Jenna join them for dinner at their house the next week. Waving goodbye, Jenna realized Marta and Franco were already in their quarters

"Join me for a night cap?" His voice sent a pleasant thrill through her body. *I need to stop letting him affect me this way, I have to.*

"I'd like one, yes. A sherry would be nice after that fine dinner."

His fingers were warm as he brushed against her hand when she took the drink. With a silent toast and a smile, Jenna walked over to the window. "I do like to look out and see nothing but the land, the green, the rolling hills, just not seeing another house or building except for yours."

"Ours."

Brett had come up behind her, his presence warm and reassuring even though it seemed he would not give up his hope for a true marriage with her. It was getting harder and harder not to give in and be his wife in every sense of the word. *How much longer can I hold him at a distance before he gives in and grants me an annulment? Or . . . until I succumb to him and this growing feeling I have not only when he's near, but even when I think about him.*

Almost as if he could read her thoughts, Brett reached over and took the glass from her hand before placing his hands on her shoulders. She barely heard his whisper of her name before his lips claimed hers. Holding her close to him, he didn't even try to hide the evidence of his desire for her. Feeling drugged from his kiss, Jenna was barely aware of his increased intent. Always before he would just hold her, but now his hand moved from her shoulder to her breast. At first stroking over its peak, so gently, so lightly she barely noticed it except for the hardening of her nipple. By the time she was aware of the slow, sensuous stimulation of her breast it was almost too late. Her own desire evident in her hardened nipples and moan of pleasure from her lips. Pressing his suit he rubbed his groin over her mound while those long, warm fingers of his moved to pinch her pert nipple. Her other breast felt almost cold compared to the firm but gentle stimulation of the first.

"Jenna, Jenna, let me love you. Let me be a true husband to you. No more waiting." His body spoke louder than his words, his breath becoming harsh as his body moved more ardently against hers. His hands began to move not just over her breasts, but her waist, hips, into her hair, pulling the pins out with one hand while the other palmed her breast. His pursuit of her so ardent he wasn't aware that Jenna's movements were not meant as encouragement, but in panic, not ardor but struggle.

121

"No, no." Her voice was at first a terrified whisper. "Please, no, please, stop, stop." With sanity pricking at the edge of his consciousness, he became vaguely aware of the strained terror in her voice. "Don't do this, please, just let me go." The growing panic she felt became more clear in her words and struggles.

His hands slowed, but still roved over her body, his own needs wrestling with hers to be free of him. She finally managed to twist her hand into his hair and pulled back hard while her knee moved upward. Had her skirts not been tangled between both their legs her knee would have found its goal. "Please, don't make me scream for help."

"Jenna." His voice was a groan, a plea for understanding, an entreaty for release of the passion that had grown day by day for her.

She finally broke free from him, from his roving hands and she ran as fast as she could, his steps clear behind her. She hesitated a moment, debating if she would be safer upstairs or outside. Without another thought she bolted for the door and ran into the cool night air.

"Jenna! Come back. Come back in here."

"No, no, I won't let you do it. I won't let you force me, I won't." Memories of Uncle Julian attacking her propelled her forward. She could swear the man had returned from hell and pursued her over the grounds. Visions of his dead body lying on her bed returned to her mind, making her scream as she ran,

Brett's long legs quickly ate up the distance between the two, her struggles more fervent as she tried to break away.

"Jenna, you're my wife."

"No, you promised. You said you wouldn't force me . . . please, Brett, no, no, I can't. You can't mean to rape me just to prove your rights."

That stopped him, cold. Ice cold. "Jenna, a husband cannot rape his wife."

"But I'm *not* your wife . . ."

"Yes, you are, you exchanged vows with me."

"I want an annulment. We haven't consummated it and we can annul it. You can let me go now. Please, don't do this."

The tears she fought to keep back began to roll freely down her cheeks, making Brett realize she was terrified, and not just of him . . . not just whatever it was she was running from. Someone had hurt her, physically.

"Jenna, were you raped, before? Were you? Is that why you don't want to share my bed?"

The tears that had sat so firmly in her eyes spilled over her lashes. "No, but he tried, he tried to. Don't you see? You need to let me go." She sank to the ground, her sobs wracking her body, all strength gone from her. Brett slid downward with her, holding her, not in the passion that had overridden his sense, but with a gentle caring embrace.

"I'm sorry, Jenna, so sorry. Forgive me? I didn't know, I didn't know." His soft kisses on her forehead were caring, compassionate, not with the raw passion that had so shortly before consumed him.

"Do you want to tell me about it?"

"No." Her anguish was clear in her whispered denial.

"It might help you, might make you feel better."

"No, Brett, please don't ask me about it."

"If you want to, ever want to . . ."

"I know, I know. I just want to forget it. I just want to leave it in the past. Will you let me go now, please?"

"No Jenna, no. The marriage stands. There will be no annulment. I'm sorry, I can't let you go."

Too drained to fight any longer, she rested her head on his shoulder and her sobs softened to light whimpers. Brett stood and then leaned down to pick her up and carry her inside. He carried her upstairs and into her room, gently setting her on the bed. "Do you want me to ask Marta to come up?"

"Noooo, I just want to be alone. Please, just can't you leave me alone?"

"All right, but Jenna, I'll be next door, just right next door. Okay? If you need me I'll be just in there."

She nodded but didn't look at him. The pain of her rejection was made more tangible by her refusal to even look at him. *At least it was someone else who had created her demons. At least it's not because of my mother — that I'm mixed. But how do I reach her? How?*

Realizing that it would only estrange her further if he even offered to help her undress, he exited into the hallway, walked to his room, and made enough noise to make it sound as if he had retired for the night. Then he quietly crept out his door and into the hallway across from her room. As much as the thought hurt, he feared she would try to leave him in the night. He had a sense that sneaking out into the night was something that she'd done before . . . and would do again.

Much to his surprise the following morning she hadn't left. When he peeked into the room, he saw her lying on the bed, still in her clothes from the day before; she hadn't moved from where he'd left her. *Did I do the right thing leaving her be? Should I have stayed with her last night? Did I do the right thing marrying her?* He watched her another few moments and then knew without a doubt, marrying her *was* the right thing. There was no cogent reason he could define, but in his heart he knew he'd done the right thing. And somehow, some day, she would commit to her marriage with him. He backed out of the room, into his own and dressed for the day. Still not hearing any sounds from Jenna's room, he headed downstairs.

"Marta?"

"Mr. Brett?"

"Mrs. Parker may be feeling a bit poorly today. She had a little upset last night and may just not feel right. If you could, well if you think of it . . ."

"Don't worry, Mr. Brett, I'll check on her through the day and I see the way she looks at you. That woman cares for you, she may threaten to leave now and again, but she won't."

"She tells you that?"

"No, she doesn't say much and certainly not that she would leave you, but I see it in how you look at her, how you follow her with your eyes that you think maybe she will."

"Marta, does she ever talk to you about where she came from? Her home? Her people?"

"No, nothing. She asks about things here or talks about the ladies she came west with, but nothing much else."

"She ever talk about something . . . well something bad that happened to her?"

"No." She paused, assessing him before speaking again. "If you think something bad happened to her, you need to ask her."

"I have, Marta . . . I have . . . but she won't talk about it."

"Then you need to leave her be. She'll tell you when she's ready. Don't you give up on her, though. Don't you give up on her."

Brett left for town shortly after. It was going to be a long day. But at least if she tried to leave, it would be through town. And, maybe it was time to talk to Rick about Jenna and what was going on with her. Maybe he needed to go out to the village and talk to his brother. Oh he knew what his brother would say — that a warrior would not put up with his wife's refusal to share his bed. But Jenna was White and a part of him was, too. He'd talk to Rick and in a day or two go out to the village and talk to his brother.

After arriving in town he did just that. Grabbing a cup of coffee, he sat in the chair across from Rick's desk. "You got a minute?"

"For you? Anytime, what's up?"

"Jenna."

"Figured you'd be needing to talk about her long before this. Wanna tell me the truth about your relationship with her?"

Brett sighed, looked around the jail area, gazing at anything besides his friend.

Drawing attention to himself, Rick softly told him, "Brett, we've known each other since we were kids. You never lied to me before this woman came along."

Brett moved to protest, and Rick put up his hand to stop him. "I know, I know, you haven't lied, you just kinda omitted some things that might lead one to conclude it wasn't a love match."

The dark-haired man blew out a long breath. "Rick, ahh gees, I don't know where to begin."

"The beginning might be a good place."

"When we were kids, my mom would talk to me about how we all have someone special, someone we're meant to be with. That you just know or that there will be a sign that its time. Here, with my dad's people, I'd think I'd met someone special now and again . . . the one. But things would be out of place. I'd like 'em well enough, I'd enjoy bedding the ones who wanted that . . . but it felt empty. Even Christina, when I asked her to marry me I half hoped she wouldn't. When Zeke talked about the woman who seemed kind of out of place, Jenna, I felt something I'd never felt before. Sight unseen I knew, I just knew that she was the woman I was meant to be with. I knew that however she got here, she was the one. So I spoke up, before anyone else could step up I knew I had to say something and so I did."

"So there were no letters." Rick stated the fact, not asked the question.

"Nope. But I ask that you don't tell anyone that. For Jenna's sake more than anything."

Despite his feeling on Brett's wedding day Rick tried to assure him, "Not a word . . . but she seemed to be agreeable about marryin' you and all." He'd never said a word to Brett about the talk he'd had with Jenna before the wedding. Now he wondered if maybe that was the wrong thing, that he should have told him.

"Yeah . . . agreeable . . . starting with that smack she gave me out at the wash."

Rick got up and paced the room, as if he were considering what to say. "Are you asking me how to save your marriage or if it's okay to end it?"

"I want this marriage . . . I want a real marriage."

"What do you mean by a *real marriage*?" I don't like to see you hurt my friend.

"I haven't bedded her. It's a marriage in name only. Her body wants mine, but her mind won't let it happen . . ." Brett raised his hand to stop the comment he knew was on Rick's tongue. "I don't think it's me . . . I don't think it's because my mother was Indian because I've never told her, and I don't think anyone else has. I think it's because something happened to her, something bad."

"Tell me."

"She's always been a bit skittish around me, closing into herself for almost no reason. But when I kiss her, especially since the wedding, she responds. She returns my kisses. I feel the changes in her body. Then all of a sudden, she closes up. It's like a door in her mind closes and seals me out. Last night things were moving along, she kissed me back with more passion that I've ever felt in any woman. Always before I'd just hold her but last night I wanted to, Rick I *needed* to touch her, all of her and I let my hands move over her and at first, she was ok, eager even. Then all of a sudden, she was telling me no and, Rick, she tried to say I was trying to rape her. How do you rape your own wife?"

"I suppose if you force her to your bed and she doesn't want it, it could be like rape. Brett, I gotta tell you . . . I may have made a mistake, a big one."

"How?"

That decided him, "Your wedding day. I spoke to her . . . I told her I wouldn't take it too kindly if she hurt you and if she didn't make the marriage work."

"No, you didn't do anything wrong . . . it was no different than what I had told her . . . shit. I told her that all I'd do was protect and care for her and that I wouldn't take her to my bed until she was ready. Last night I thought she wanted me as much as I wanted her . . . but it fell apart. It just went to pieces. Now I don't think she'll ever trust me again."

"You know, it may not be that bad . . . maybe she just needed something to wake her up and make her see just what a good man you are. Give her a little more time, see what happens."

"Seems to be about the best thing to do . . .'cause I can't think of anything else."

As Brett left the office, Rick turned back to his paperwork. Or at least he appeared to. After staring at the page before him a bit longer without doing anything about it, he got up and paced the length of the office several times before going to look in the mirror that hung on the door to their kitchenette. He studied himself for a long moment, taking in his blond hair and green eyes, wondering if women saw him as handsome.

"Not that it would make a difference, no one would want you any way." He told his reflection.

That had been one silent bond between he and Brett . . . both handsome, rugged, successful men that seemed so unlucky at love.

Scrubbing his face with his hand, Rick turned to walk out of the office. He'd hoped Brett's marriage would work, because if it did, it meant there was someone out there for Rick as well.

Brett stayed away for two days before finally returning home. He asked Marta to send up water for a bath and after checking the downstairs for Jenna, went to her room. Even though he knew Marta would have told him if she had left, he still dreaded finding her gone. Seeing her sitting in there, holding a piece of embroidery in her hands — holding it, not even moving — he knocked on the door. The sound seemed to startle her out of a trance. "So you've come home. Was there a problem in town?"

"No, there was a problem in my home. I have a wife who has no desire to be a wife."

"You knew that when you forced me to marry you."

"I didn't force you . . ."

"No? And what choice did you give me?"

A long, hard sigh unwittingly escaped his lips. "I'm too tired to argue with you about this yet again, Jenna. I'll see you at dinner." With that he walked to his room and removed the clothes he'd worn the past three days. He hadn't felt that battered since the last cattle drive he'd done several years earlier. Even Christina Jeffers's rejection didn't beat him this badly. Looking in the mirror, he tried to see what Jenna saw, or rather didn't see. What could he change, what could he do to win her over?

It occurred to him that there was someone who could answer that question . . . but would she? Would Jenna tell him what would need to change to win her over? For now though, he was too tired, too hurt to go to her. He could not take another blow to his heart.

The next few days they said little to each other. Marta was none too pleased with either of them. But without knowing if it was Brett or Jenna that started the coldness between the newlyweds, she couldn't decide which one to yell at. Disgusted with both of them, she had Franco and herself take their meals in the kitchen. Jenna seemed beaten, defeated and said nothing when Marta snubbed both her and Brett. Something had gone out of both newlyweds and the older woman knew they would have to work it out for themselves.

A few days later, over breakfast which was yet another awkwardly quiet and uncomfortable affair, Brett told Jenna he'd be in town again for the next few days telling her "Jenna . . ."

"Yes?"

"Don't get any ideas. I expect to find you here when I get back. Understand?"

"Of course. And where do you think I would go? Brett, I want an annulment, you know that. I can't get one if I just up and leave."

His sigh seemed to carry the weight of the world in it. No answer came, just a tired shake of his head. He couldn't even bring himself to say goodbye when he left.

If he wants me to stay, why doesn't he act like it? Why didn't he even say goodbye?

Instead of heading towards town, he headed to his brother's village. He missed his mother. There wasn't a day he didn't at least think of her, often missing her wise counsel. But since he'd met Jenna it seemed he missed her more than ever. He had no doubt Falling Leaf would have liked Jenna, liked her spunk and smile. And he had no doubt she would have known what to tell him to help Jenna accept their marriage. But she was gone . . . yet he knew there would be someone there to speak with.

Arriving at the village, he was quickly surrounded and warmly greeted. They never had an issue with his mixed parentage. He quickly spotted his brother, Wolf. He also didn't miss the looks of several of the unmarried women, all who would welcome him warmly to their beds — unlike his little wife. Giving a quick smile to the group, he made his way to his brother before dismounting.

"Wolf."

"My brother has been too long gone from his home."

"Yes . . . too long. It is good to be here."

"You will stay with me."

"Thank you. I much need good company and a welcoming home."

After the evening meal the two men walked to the river.

"While I would like to think my brother comes because he misses his family, I believe there is something more."

"You're right, Wolf . . . I'm married."

"Married! And you did not send word to me?" He put up his stand to stop Brett from explaining, "I will hear of that later. Now though, you tell me you are married and so soon leave your bride? Why didn't you bring her with you?"

Brett let out a long sigh as he looked out over the water, the bleakness he felt clearly evident even in the growing darkness.

Before Brett could speak, Wolf asked, "Is it our family?"

"No . . . I'm not sure she even knows, it's . . ."

"You married a woman who knows nothing of your family?"

"Well I don't know much about hers either, but . . ."

"Brett . . ."

"Let me explain. Or try to. A few months ago one of the men, Henry Bascom, organized a deal to bring some mail order brides to town."

"A mail order bride? This is how White men now choose wives?"

"No, you know how it is in Alder Creek. You know there aren't that many women and, well, Henry put an ad in a paper and some women answered who wanted to marry and Jenna, my wife, was among them. From the outset she said she didn't want to get married, she was clear about that."

"Then why would she answer your paper? Why come with women who wish to marry?"

"I don't know. It's gotta be what's ever in her past. I met her and told her we'd marry, and she told me she didn't want to marry. Not anyone. I didn't listen . . . I wanted her and insisted she marry me . . . and she did. Things seem good and then just when I think we will make the marriage a real one, she pulls back. Each time it seems we are becoming closer, she moves away from me. Something frightened her before she came here, but she won't tell me. The other night it seemed as if she was ready to come to me, and suddenly, she ran and when I caught her she accused me of trying to rape her."

"I think you need to start from the first."

Brett picked up a stone and skiffed it over the water, releasing a long, tired sigh as he did. "Like I said, some of the men in town decided that they wanted wives and took out ads in some east coast papers, some women answered, the men wrote back and sent money for their trip out here. A number sent money hoping that more women would want to come west to marry and somehow Jenna ended up coming with them. Dusty Hendricks, you remember him?"

"Red hair?"

"Yeah, that's him. Well he had a funny feeling about Jenna and sent word ahead to Rick and I about it. I up and said she was my bride and gave her the excuse that my letter sending for her hadn't arrived yet. I knew as soon as I heard about her, I wanted her. Like momma said, I just knew. There was just something about her story that seemed to reach into my soul. I went with the others to meet up with the train and I knew who she was before I met her — I saw her and knew before any introductions were made who she was. I told her that I would protect her and care for her and that . . . well . . . I told her I wouldn't touch her until she was ready. That I would court her and would bed her only when she was ready."

Wolf's look showed his total surprise, just a moment before he burst into laughter. "You have a wife with a body made for making love and you haven't bedded her? Is this the White man's way?"

"It's not funny. Someone tried to rape her, I'm sure of it, but she won't talk about it."

"Do you know what?"

"No, and she won't talk. Things were going along pretty well. We'd hug, kiss — really kiss, hot kisses and then about a week ago we had some friends to dinner. One of the women she came west with and the man she married, Henry Bascom. They are so in love with each other, can't keep their hands off each other and when they left I . . . I, something went wrong. We were kissing, and I started to touch her. I wanted her to want me and I began to make love to her with my hands. At first, she didn't just accept it, she seemed to really want me. All of a suddenly she started to struggle, tried to get away and then she accused me . . ."

Wolf gave his brother the silence he needed to gather his thoughts before placing a hand on his arm.

"That's when she accused me of trying to rape her. I got angry, told her a husband can't rape his wife, that it was my right to take her. She ran off . . . it got ugly, yelling. I took off and stayed in town for a few days. Nothing changed when I got home, and I've been staying away. She wants an annulment."

"What do you want?"

"I want her. I want her as my wife . . . my true wife. But I don't see how it will happen. Like I said, she doesn't just not want *me*, she doesn't want a husband. She told me from the beginning she doesn't want a husband and I pushed her to marry me. All I want is her."

"Then you will have her."

"I can't, I won't force her."

"Then let her go, let her have this annulment . . . when she is ready, you will have your wife."

"You mean I'll appreciate another woman, maybe even an Indian woman?"

"Some man hurt her before." It was a statement, not a question and Brett nodded in acknowledgement of its truth.

"And you are sure you want this woman and the problems she brings to you?"

"Yeah, more than anything, I want her. I want this marriage."

"So? You are half-Indian—take her. Otherwise, let her go and find her heart. She will find her way to you."

"Wolf . . . I want her to want me."

Wolf sat quietly for some time, lost in his own thoughts. Finally he spoke.

"You have never reacted this way to a woman, never sought to spend your life with just one. This one, this Jen-na, has won your heart. I think maybe after having so many women desire you, that this one does not, makes you want her more. Let her go. She will find her way back to you. She must lose you so that she can find you."

"Are you saying if she wanted me I wouldn't want her?"

"No . . . that you are impatient for her because she does not have warm thoughts of you. Give her the time she says she wants . . . give her the freedom she says she wants. I think she will find it is not freedom she wants, but you."

Brett considered his brother's words as they sat in silence for some time. Could he let Jenna go? What if she didn't come back to him?

He spent the next two days visiting with his brother, trying not to dwell on his problems with Jenna. With a promise he would soon bring her to visit, he headed home, still undecided what to do.

Brett arrived after dark and tried not to disturb the rest of the house as he headed upstairs. Marta intercepted him and signaled him into the kitchen.

"Is Jenna alright?"

"She's fine . . . confused, but fine."

"What is she confused about? She got . . ." Brett clamped his mouth shut. He wasn't going to air his marital problems to everyone he knew even though it was clear Marta knew his marriage was a sham.

"She doesn't say much, but I see what you two do to each other. You want each other, but instead of nurturing your marriage you leave her for days."

"Marta, it's what she wants . . . she . . ." He shook his head. "I'm tired. As long as she's all right I'm going to sleep."

Brett made his way upstairs, stopping at Jenna's room to look in on her. Turning the handle, he slowly pushed open her door and quietly moved towards the bed. He stood for a few minutes drinking in her beauty. Her dark brown hair fanned out on the pillow, her breathing slow and steady, a small, yet sweet smile on her lips, calling out to him to kiss her. Lying on her side she had one arm tucked under her pillow while the other embraced the top of it. In the moon's glow he saw one of his shirts tangled with the pillow . . . as if she was holding on to him. At least in sleep whatever troubled her receded into the background.

He was up before Jenna in the morning, dressed quickly and gathered his gear to go back into town. He looked in on her before leaving and decided that he should at least leave her a note that he'd returned and that while he had to work today, he'd be home that night. To himself he hoped she would wait for him for dinner — perhaps they could enjoy a meal together and maybe talk.

Hearing the quiet click of her door, Jenna woke, her heart in her throat. The dreams had started again, but they were different. Now they would start with her and Brett together, walking hand in hand in a field. He would stop to embrace her, holding her close. She would look up into his eyes and see the love and commitment he promised her. In the dream Jenna, would reach up to entwine her fingers in his dark brown hair and pull his head down for a kiss that would start with a slight nibbling of her lips and quickly grow to the hotly passionate ones they had begun to share at her door at nights. As he did the night she accused him of trying to rape her, he brought his hand to her breast, at first gently palming it, teasing her nipple to exquisite hardness. Then the dream would change. It would no longer be Brett making love to her. He would change to Julian and he would be mauling her with brutal cruelty. She would struggle and he would only laugh as he would force himself on her.

Jenna didn't know if she screamed or called out. There was

no one to hear her if she did, not with Brett avoiding coming into his own home. She did know she would wake in a cold sweat, out of breath and terrified to move.

She knew he'd been in her room. Brett had come home, and it seemed he was leaving again if the sounds she heard outside the house were any indication. She wasn't proud of driving the man from his own home, not when she felt she should be the one leaving. Turning over, feeling a loneliness she hadn't known she could feel, she saw his note. As she reached for it, the familiar tearing rose in her heart. Jenna knew she was falling in love with him, hopelessly in love with Brett, but she couldn't love him. Not when he would one day arrest her. There was no way she could do that to a man like Brett.

So when he returned, she didn't venture downstairs. Instead Jenna sat in her room, looking out the window, wishing that somehow, some way she could go back in time and make it right. If only she had met Brett in another time and another place.

CHAPTER THIRTEEN

A few days later, when Jenna came downstairs to get a cup of tea, she saw Marta standing outside the kitchen door talking to a man that didn't look familiar to her. Approaching the door she saw that the man was as tall as Brett. His eyes were dark brown, so dark they seemed like obsidian, and he was wearing . . . *oh my God—he's an Indian! A real Indian!* As Jenna looked a bit closer, she realized he was an extremely handsome man—almost as handsome as Brett. Jenna stepped up to the door and boldly greeted the man. "Hello . . . Marta, is this a friend or family member of yours?"

Before Marta could answer, the man turned.

"I'm Wolf, Brett's brother."

"You're Brett's brother?"

"Yes, he is my brother."

"Then why are you standing out here? Marta, why didn't you invite, Wolf is it?" At his nod she continued, "Why didn't you invite him in? Please, come inside, have you eaten? Are you hungry? Thirsty?" Jenna reached past Marta, grabbed the man's arm, and pulled him inside. Wolf's came further into the kitchen and Jenna began to bustle around pulling out plates and asking him what he was in the mood to eat. She knew she was acting out of character, but the situation with Brett was unlike any she'd experienced before. Maybe, she thought, if she could get his brother to trust her, talk to her, she'd learn something about the man she married. Something that she could use to explain his behavior the past week or so and maybe find a way to convince him their marriage would never work.

Taking note of Wolf's appraisal of Jenna, Marta sought to quickly stop the growing admiration in his eyes. The couple had problems enough without adding another man to the mix, especially a member of Brett's family. "You knew your brother married, yes?"

Choosing to keep Brett's visit to his village a secret, until he learned if Brett had told her, Wolf only answered, "I'd heard something, but nothing specific. So I have come to see the woman my brother has chosen as his own."

"I married him, yes."

"This is good. This is very good. For too long now my brother has needed a woman of his own. He is fortunate to have one that is so lovely to look at."

"Well . . ." Jenna thought about an appropriate answer, one that would not offend Brett's brother, yet not create problems when Brett finally gave her the annulment she so desired. "He's a handsome and very kind man."

Marta's stunned look surprised Jenna, making her wonder just how much the other woman knew about their so-called marriage.

"Well, if you married my brother for only his looks, it is well he did not bring you to meet the rest of our family. He is, as you can see by looking at me, the ugliest of all in our family."

Jenna couldn't help but take an appraising look at Wolf. His broad chest was smooth and well developed. His belly was flat with rippling muscles, and his leggings left little to her fertile imagination . . . one she didn't know she had until she'd heard Belle and Bea talking about men and bedding and then, meeting Brett and feeling how hard he would become when they kissed.

"Well, sit down, Mr. Wolf, please sit down." Jenna gestured to the table and placed the plates down on it. "Marta, can you take out some bread and meat while I get Mr. Wolf a . . ."

"Please Jen-na, call me Wolf, as does your husband and the rest of our family and tribe."

She liked how he said her name, the hint of an accent and the way he broke her name into two parts. "Alright . . . Wolf . . . what would you like to drink?"

"Didn't you know all Indians like the firewater . . . liquor?"

Jenna blanched. "Oh, no, I didn't. I, weell, we, well, ahhhh, yes. Yes, we have some. I'm sure I saw Brett had some in the den. You wait right here, and I'll fetch you some." She rushed from the room quickly.

Jenna missed the look of disgust Marta shot him.

"When Mr. Brett hears what you just told her, he won't be too happy."

"Your Mr. Brett learns I'm here he's not gonna be too happy, either."

"He didn't ask you?"

"No . . . and in truth he told me much of his marriage but I wanted to see her ways, her manner for myself but he seemed concerned about some things and I thought it best to come see for myself. I also thought it best to come when he would not be here so I could see her as she truly is and ask you your thoughts. I wish happiness for my brother, yet I am unsure if she will bring him the happiness he deserves. She is a pretty woman. I can see why he chose her. And she is friendly, if not nervous.

"I can tell you I do not think Jenna has a prejudiced bone in her body. If she did, I think it would have shown long ago when she met Franco and me."

"Do you think she does not want the marriage because he is only half-White?"

"No, Jenna isn't like that. She seems to want a family or to have a big family but then turns to hide from it. She's not a mean woman, just something from her past keeps her from being too close to anyone."

As Jenna entered the den and headed towards the tray of liquor bottles, it crossed her mind that aside from the toasts at the weddings and some wine at their dinner with the Bascoms, she'd never seen Brett drink. He didn't seem to object to alcohol, just he himself didn't seem to indulge much. Maybe it was only full Indians who liked it so much. She'd only heard stories, but Wolf was the first full-blooded Indian she'd met. Marta was certainly friendly with him and he seemed very nice, so clearly the stories were wrong.

It hit her then . . . what had been nagging at the back of her mind. Brett was half-Indian. She hadn't really considered it before, but her husband was of mixed race. Was that why he was so possessive of her? Why he wouldn't listen to her? Was he afraid she had some sort of problem with his heritage? *Well, I need to put a stop to that nonsense and right quickly. Oh dear, the poor man probably thinks that's why I don't want to be married to him, not that I don't want to be married at all.* Putting her thoughts aside, she reached for the scotch and whiskey and headed back to the kitchen. As she placed the bottles on the table, she told Wolf, "I didn't know which you preferred so I brought both."

"Jen-na, I must apologize . . . Marta has taken me to task for my poor joke. I meant to tease you, not send you running around for something I only thought of as a joke."

"You mean you didn't want the liquor?"

"No, not with an afternoon meal. I thought you knew more of the . . . the things some people think and believe."

Jenna flushed, "No, I don't know much at all. Brett never even . . . well we haven't talked much about our families and their preferences."

Jenna and Marta ate a little to keep Wolf company while he told Jenna stories about Brett when they were children, how he grew into manhood living half the time in the village of their mother and half the time with his White father.

"So that's where he got those good looks from. I'd wondered."

Wolf was pleased to hear Jenna thought his brother handsome. At least they had that in their favor.

After the meal, Jenna and Wolf walked outside, around the corral and yard area, deeply engrossed in their conversation.

Brett rode up to the house. The scowl on his face grew when he saw his wife chatting with his brother like they were life-long friends. The jealousy rising up in him was not like any other feeling he'd ever experienced.

"Jenna, Wolf." Even as Jenna smiled up at him, reaching to place a kiss on his cheek he wondered with barely suppressed anger, *What is her game now?*

"Brett, you didn't tell me your brother was coming to visit."

"I didn't know myself." Feeling the tension emanating off him like a raging river overflowing its banks during a winter thaw, Jenna stepped back as if slapped, turned, and walked towards the house.

Wolf's eyes seemed to glow with angry tension while his face remained impassive. "I would not expect you, of all men, to treat his wife in such a manner."

"I would not expect you, my brother, to be so intimate with my wife."

"Intimate? Brett, you call walking in the air, sharing conversation with your woman intimate?"

"What would you call it?"

"Time spent with my brother's wife, learning to know her, hearing of my brother's health. We were out in the open the entire time. What angers you so?"

Brett pushed his fingers through his hair. His exasperated sigh was tinged with a sadness his brother had never seen. "I told you, she doesn't want me."

"So? Many wives to not want their husbands, at first. Wait till you give her a child, she will not let you out of her sight then."

"Give her a child? She won't let me touch her."

"She freely gave you a kiss in front of me."

"Yeah, probably for show."

"I am surprised. Jen-na I spent this afternoon with has been warm, friendly, caring, eager to hear the stories of her husband's youth."

"She's a great little actress."

"I think not. Why don't you tell me what has gone on since your visit?"

The brothers walked deeper into the yard, out towards the range as Brett told him about the past week. "I haven't been home much. I don't know what to say to her, what to do."

"It was my hope that if I could see her, I could find you an answer. It was a complete surprise when she came to the kitchen while I spoke with Marta. I promise you, my brother, I was outside the house with no intention of entering when your Jen-na came to the kitchen. She immediately invited me in, fed me and spoke to me as a member of your family. It is not your Indian blood that gives her concern in your marriage. She cares not from where your blood flows.

When the men returned, Jenna and Marta had put dinner on the table. She cast a wary look at her husband to see if he was still angry at her walking and talking with Wolf. Never having had a man jealous over her, or at least not knowing about it, she was caught off guard. Over dinner Brett seemed to relax and enjoy being with his brother.

Towards the end of the meal she told Wolf, "I prepared one of the guest rooms for you. I hope you'll find it comfortable."

"Why's that, darling?"

"Well it's late, I thought . . . that is, oh . . ."

"Oh what, Jen-na?"

"Is there a problem? Do you not like sleeping in a house?"

"I like it fine Jen-na, it is most gracious of you. I think what my brother meant was that I generally return to my home."

"Oh."

Seeing how downcast that statement made her, Brett asked his brother, "Do you think you would like to stay over this once? I can see Jenna has more questions to ask you."

Jenna brightened at her husband's question.

"Then I will stay. For my new sister, I will stay."

When he left the next morning it was with a promise to

return soon. Brett watched his brother leave, remembering his promise to protect and care for her, he knew in his heart he had to make a decision about Jenna soon because he couldn't live like they had been much longer.

"Wolf, I wouldn't hurt her . . . I cherish her," Brett had told the other man the night before. He hadn't been doing a very good job of either the past couple of weeks. Somehow that had to change.

CHAPTER FOURTEEN

Things continued much in the same way for the next two weeks. Brett spent two to three days at a time in town, coming home for a night, giving her only a cursory greeting, and returning to town the next day. Jenna finally decided she'd had enough and accompanied Marta into town for a weekly shopping trip. Her plan at first was to see if she could find a way to reach Brett, to at least return to a semblance of friendship. Then the fear of rejection crept in. She asked herself, if he rejected her, wouldn't he then grant her the annulment? So why did his reaction bother her so much? Maybe she really had fallen in love with him—imagine that—falling in love with your husband, the one you didn't want to be married to in the first place.

Before her fear took total control of the situation, she excused herself from Marta and marched down to the jail. She carefully planned her words and took a deep breath as she entered. At her entrance Rick stood to greet her and went to leave.

"No need to leave, Sheriff, I was just coming to see if you could spare my husband so he can take me to lunch." Phrased like that Brett was hard pressed to refuse and secretly he was glad, so very glad to see her.

"Well now, that sounds like a plan to me . . . get his ugly face out of mine for a bit."

At that Brett did scowl but got up to join is wife.

Once they were seated in Mary's Café he waited until they placed their orders before asking if there was something she wanted.

"I feel bad that I've driven you from your home. There isn't any reason for you to stay away."

"You haven't driven me away, Jenna, but there is a big reason for staying away."

"What reason?"

"Jenna, I'm trying to honor my promise to you. The only way I can do that is to stay away from you."

"Brett . . . that's not right. Look, why don't I come stay in town and . . ."

"No."

"But I haven't finished . . ."

"No."

"Would you let me say my piece?"

"No. You will not stay in town, at least not without me."

"Then what if I stayed with Belle and . . ."

"No. Jenna, you are my wife and my wife will stay in my house, our house. End of discussion."

She stood, putting her hands on the table and leaned over towards him. "You arrogant, domineering jackass. Are you so afraid that I might be right or have a good idea that you think you have to shut me down before I even say half of what I want?"

"Tell me what you are so afraid of and we can talk about whether or not you'd be safe here in town."

"I'm not afraid of anything."

"No?"

"No."

"You know, sometimes you call out in your sleep."

His revelation stunned her. Jenna bowed her head a

moment before raising it, she was sure that since there were no more dreams, at least none she remembered, that she did not call out either. Tears starting in her eyes, she denied his statement, "I don't, not anymore."

"Yes, you still do. Not so loud or often, but you still cry out."

Not wanting to talk about the dreams, Jenna looked to change the subject. "Please, Brett, I'm not a bad person, I just . . . marriage just wasn't something that I wanted. It has nothing to do with you or your family. It's about me and what I don't want for myself."

"Never said you were a bad person, didn't think it either. And I know you say you didn't want to be married . . . not ever . . . but you are, Jenna. You are married to me and will stay married to me. We have an agreement. And you can tell me till you're blue in the face that you aren't, but you *are* afraid of something."

She let go a frustrated sigh before asking, "Will you come home tonight, please?"

She'd reached out to make peace with him. It was time he accepted the olive branch, "I will if you will sit down and finish your meal."

Retaking her seat, Jenna and Brett finished their meals in companionable silence. Seeing Marta at the wagon, Brett stood and leaned over to give her a kiss. His intent was to merely give her a light brush across the lips, but when she unexpectedly parted her lips to welcome him into her, he gave her a tentative, yet still so very sensuous kiss. "I'll see you for dinner tonight," he told her as he lifted her into the wagon's seat.

Brett stood watching Marta guide the wagon out of town, letting Wolf's words return to him. His brother tried to tell him something, but it wasn't something that could be plainly said.

The sky was overcast by the time Brett returned home and he quickly stabled his horse. Coming in the house, he called out to Jenna and Marta that it looked like a storm was coming in. Over dinner he talked about Oscar Hooper, the town drunk, and some of his antics the past few days. "It's not that he drinks so much, or that he's sloppy, but the things he gets into. Sometimes I just don't know about him." He enjoyed hearing Jenna laugh and resolved to make more of an effort to bring funny stories home. Maybe he could win her over with laughter. When they retired, however, Jenna turned her head so that Brett could only kiss her cheek. Her moods seemed to change with the weather.

About an hour after they retired, the first clap of thunder sounded followed by what he thought was a blood curdling scream from Jenna's room. At first Brett wasn't too sure he'd heard the scream until another thunderclap sounded and was followed by another piercing scream.

"Jenna!" He rushed into her room as another thunderclap resounded. He heard her cry through the scream. She wasn't in the bed, or anywhere easily seen. "Jenna? Honey, were are you?"

"B-b-brett."

Her sob broke his heart. In the glare of the lightning he saw her huddled in the corner farthest from the window. In two long strides he was beside her and she flew into his arms. "Brett, I'm so scared, make it stop, make it stop."

"It's thunder, honey, I can't stop the weather, but I'm here now. I've got you." Not content just to have his arms around her, she grabbed on to him and clung as if trying to bury herself in his big, brawny body. She shook so hard he didn't think it would ever stop.

"Hold me, don't let . . . ahhhh!" Another scream tore from her lips as the thunder roared. The lightning flashes increased and the rain pounded the roof. With each crash Jenna grabbed tighter and tighter to Brett. It felt to him as if she was trying to bury herself inside him. He stroked her back and murmured endearments to her, reassuring her she'd be fine and he'd protect her. Slowly but surely the shaking was reduced to trembles and a flash of lightning showed her eyes to be pools of liquid warmth. Without encouragement or provocation, she raised her lips to his and kissed him. Sweet and slow at first and then deepening to the most primal taking Brett had ever felt. The way she claimed him rocked him to his soul. They had shared hot kisses before, but this kiss went beyond that. She continued her journey into his mouth, stroking his tongue with her own, tasting every corner of his mouth, nibbling on his lower lip, sighing in response to her own demands on his body. Without a thought her hands moved over his chest, feeling its strength and coming back to wrap her arms around his neck. Unable to control herself she clung to him and ever so slowly she began to rub against him.

The softly sensuous movement made him hard with need for her. To be one with her. To join as a man and a woman join. Without intending to, he brought his hands around her shoulders and back, pulling her into a close embrace. While her hips slid from side to side, he pulsed his back and forth, showing her the movement he would make when he took her, when he made her his wife in fact. They sat there, kissing, touching each other for an endless time.

Jenna yearned for him to touch her from head to toe. She wanted to feel his hand on her breast and more . . . innocent as she was, there was a part of her that knew she wanted not only his hands, but his mouth on her body . . . her whole body. But Brett only sat there, holding her, kissing her, building a hot need inside of her. But how to tell him? How to ask him to give her something that she could not turn back from.

As the storm pushed onward in its journey, the comfort of Brett's arms making her feel more secure than aroused, Jenna grew drowsy and while still cuddling with her husband, fell into a deep sleep. Brett rose and carried her to the bed. As he laid her down, she woke just enough to know he was leaving her. "Brett, stay with me, please, hold me, hold me in case it starts again."

He couldn't refuse her. Not this. Not anything. He climbed into her bed and pulled her close, and for the first time, she truly didn't resist. She laid her head on his shoulder, her arm around his chest while her leg crept over his hips. It felt so right. She was so much smaller than him, but they fit together like a hand in a glove. In that moment Brett knew without a doubt that he was hopelessly and desperately in love with her, and he knew that he had to let her go. Wolf's words came back to him and in his heart, he knew that he had to let her go. He'd never have peace with her so close and not having her, if she would not accept her marriage to him. He'd hold her tonight, savor what she felt like in his arms, and tomorrow morning he would tell her she was free to go, and he would hope Wolf was right, that once he let her go, she would want him. Brett had long believed a man's heart could not be broken. In that instant he knew he was wrong—his heart had well and truly broken. "Please," he asked the now silent night, "let my brother be right and have her return to me."

CHAPTER FIFTEEN

Brett woke shortly before Jenna and took those few minutes to enjoy the feel of her arms around him one last time and to revel in her unique scent. When she opened her eyes, he'd hold on to their warm brown depths in his heart and mind for the rest of his life.

When Jenna woke, she was momentarily confused at finding Brett in her bed, but it felt so right to have him there. Months had gone by since her head-long flight from Virginia and she could no longer deny her attraction to her husband. It felt so right to be with him, not just because of the storm the night before. She'd missed him when he stayed away so many days. She knew in her heart she wanted him. No one had come looking for her. She could be with Brett, she could make a life with him.

When he knew she was fully awake, Brett slid from the bed. As much as he wanted one last kiss, he knew if he did that, he'd never be able to let her go . . . and he had to let her go. It had to end. Today. Now.

"Jenna," he cleared his throat. He looked around the room as if trying to find the words. "Jenna, I can't do this anymore. I spent a long time yesterday thinking about us, our situation, how we got here, and you were right. We were a mistake. I realized when you and Marta left to come home that I had kept you from talking because I knew if I let you talk . . . we'll I'd get to where I did get last night, after the storm."

All she could do was just sit and stare, her eyes wide, it seemed a glimmer of fear entering them. But she didn't utter a word.

"So, when I go into town today, I'll have Edgar Samuels draw up the annulment papers. If he can't get them done tonight, I'll stay in town till their done."

"Brett . . ."

"Don't say anything, Jenna. I think we've said enough. I'd suggest you start packing today and think about where you'd like to go. I'll pay your way and give you some money so you can settle yourself. Dusty said it seemed you wanted to stay in St. Louis. Maybe that still appeals to you. I'll figure out some way to get you an escort or transportation by the end of the week."

"No. Brett, listen to me . . ."

"No, Jenna, enough."

When he turned and left the room, Jenna felt like she'd been kicked in the stomach. And he'd done it again . . . said his peace without taking a moment to listen to hers. It felt worse than the day her mother died, worse than the day she'd found her father. "Oh, Brett, no, no . . . I love you." But he never heard her whispered plea.

Marta didn't think too much of Jenna not coming down for breakfast. She'd heard the younger woman cry out in the night and had started upstairs herself and then stopped when she heard Brett rush into her room. But when lunch came and there was still no sign of Jenna, she got worried. Going upstairs and knocking on the door, she became even more concerned when there was no answer from within. Marta pushed the door open ever so slightly and saw Jenna curled in a ball on the bed crying. Her red rimmed eyes looked sadder than she had ever seen anyone else look.

"Ah, Jenna, what is it? Are you sick? Did Mr. Brett say something really hurtful?"

"Oh, Marta." The tears started afresh, and she flew into Marta's arms. "He's sending me away. He's giving me an annulment."

"Annulment? You are married, you can't annul . . ."

"We never . . . oh, Marta, I can't lose him, I can't."

"What do you mean you never? You mean you never shared his bed?"

"No. Marta, I was so afraid. I . . . things happened before I came here, and at first, he promised he wouldn't force me, and those things that scared me they didn't go away and . . . oh, Marta, I love him."

"I know you do, Mrs. Brett. But does Mr. Brett know?"

"No. Marta, I've pushed him away, over and over. I've pushed him away and I thought, I really thought he'd be there. That someday I'd feel like it was ok, but I love him and this morning he said he's giving me an annulment."

"You wanted this?"

"At first yes, but Marta, I love him, and I want to be his wife, really and truly his wife. What am I going to do?"

Marta thought for a minute and finally told her, "You need to tell him you love him. But first, you need to freshen up, put on your prettiest dress and for dinner tonight, we will make it very romantic. Then you will tell him you love him."

"Do you think it will work? Do you?"

"I know he cares for you, Jenna. I think you will open his heart."

Feeling a little better Jenna got up, took a long, hot bath, washed her hair and then brushed it to a luxurious shine. Then she looked over her dresses and at first was going to put on her wedding gown . . . but then she decided that a deep blue dress that he'd bought her as a surprise would be better. Marta had sent Franco to town to be sure Brett came home that night — that whatever papers he needed could wait, that he was needed at the ranch. Jenna finished the last touches on the table just before the men returned.

"Marta, what's wrong?" Despite Franco's assurances that nothing was wrong, Brett still worried about Jenna.

"Nothing Mr. Brett. You go on into the dining room and see the nice dinner *Mrs.* Brett made."

Her emphasis on *Mrs.* did not elude Brett's attention. Stepping into the dining room he saw Jenna lighting the last of the candles on the table. She was like a vision, stepping out of his dreams.

"What's going on, Jenna?"

"Nothing. I just wanted to have a nice dinner with just the two of us."

"You send an emergency message to me in town, bringing me home, just for dinner?" His anger at what he perceived to be her deception was evident.

"I didn't . . . Franco told you it was an emergency?"

"He said you needed me at home but couldn't say why. What was I supposed to think?"

"Just that . . . that I wanted, needed to see you. Just that I wanted to have dinner with you — to talk."

"I think we talked enough, don't you, Jenna?"

"No. No, I don't. You talk and demand I listen. *You* don't listen. You demand, you order, you dictate, but you never listen to me. Talking is a two-way street. That's why you talk and then I talk and then you talk, and I talk again. And when I'm talking, you listen to what I have to say, and you acknowledge that what I say has value."

"It's a little late for that, Jenna. You wanted an annulment. I told you, you could have it. There is no reason for us to talk."

"If it's over between us, why did you rush home to me?"

"I didn't want a scene or a mess to clean up."

Tears sprang into her eyes, making their deep brown color glisten so they looked like molten chocolate. She angrily wiped at her eyes, cursing the tears that threatened to spill. She wanted to win him back with conversation, not with emotional blackmail. Anger at the tears gave her a strength she didn't know she had, and she pushed Brett down in the chair behind him. Before she even knew what, she was doing she leaned into him and then climbed up on his lap, pinning him with her own legs. Reaching to the table, she grabbed a napkin and held it close to his face.

"You are going to listen to me, and if you won't sit and listen to what I have to say I'm going to stick this in your mouth so you can't speak. Do you understand, you stupid jackass?"

"Lovely language, Jenna."

"Do you understand?"

"I'm waiting." Not that he couldn't uproot her from his lap — she wasn't very heavy — but his curiosity about what she was up to intrigued him so he sat beneath her, not moving a muscle, except for one part that he couldn't seem to control around her.

"Brett, I don't want the annulment. I don't want to leave you. I want this marriage."

"It's too late, Jenna, I tol . . ." Before he could utter another sound, the napkin was shoved in his mouth. His eyes popped open in surprise and he found it was all he could do not to laugh at her actions. Not that his marriage was a laughing matter. She'd hurt him over and over with her rejections and now that he'd finally given her what she wanted, she was saying she wanted to stay with him.

"Are you going to listen to me?" When he nodded in the affirmative, she continued. "You were right. I was . . . leaving a bad situation, one that frightened me, one that would have hurt me. I had to get away, so I came west, but was only going to go to St. Louis except I ended up with the bridal train and didn't have a choice but to keep coming here. I tried to leave in St. Louis—and Dusty stopped me. He told me . . . he said . . ."

The tears springing to her eyes showed her hurt and they clawed at Brett's heart. Not unlike how he ached for her during the storm last night when she cried out her fear.

Drawing in a shaky breath, she continued, "I didn't want to get married. I didn't want an arranged marriage. I wanted a marriage based on love and mutual respect. When you came thundering in, you were so big, your presence so powerful. And you seemed like such a decent man. When you said you would protect me but wouldn't force yourself on me, I felt it was unfair, that *I* was unfair. You deserved better than me. You weren't getting anything out of the bargain. I had nothing to give you back—nothing of value, nothing in exchange for your protection. You didn't know me, you didn't know anything about me. And over the past few months I started to care for you—really care for you. Brett, it scared me to think I was falling in love with you, but I was and I denied it to myself."

She saw his look of incredulity. But he still sat there

listening to her so she went on. "Then last night, the storm . . . Brett, my whole life they have scared me. Thunder and lightning has frightened me more than anything. My momma wasn't strong, and I had to act so brave all the time, but I was scared, so scared. There was nothing worse in the world for me than thunder and lightning, but not once in my whole life was someone there, not once did anyone care or hold me or care for me in any way during one. But you did, you were there, and I knew that this morning, accepted what I have known for a long time — I am in love with you and that I really do want a marriage with you. A real one."

He sat looking at her, waiting. She finally removed the napkin and said, "I don't want the annulment, Brett, I want you."

He waited a moment, his own thoughts rolling. She was offering him what he wanted, wasn't she? A marriage, a real marriage. Or would it be? Could he trust that she really did love him? Or did she only think that because of the storm? He wanted . . . needed her love. But he wanted it to be real, true, not a fleeting emotion. As much as he wanted Jenna in his life, he could not put his heart in his hand again. He finally asked, "Are you done?"

She nodded, and drawing in a breath he told her, "As you said, Jenna, marriage is a two-way street . . . and for too long I was the only one participating in the marriage, or trying to. Simply feeling safe during a storm does not constitute love. You are confusing love with feeling safe. I do want the annulment and I don't want you."

Had he slapped her across the face, it would not have hurt as bad as the words he had just spoken. In horror and humiliation, Jenna rose off him and ran towards the kitchen and out the back door. Tears blurred her vision and in her head-long flight, she ran out towards the fields. Her footsteps pounded in her own ears making her think of the sound of Julian coming after her. She ran until she hit the tree line, the tears falling faster and faster, her sobs causing her to gasp each breath — crying so hard, running like she'd never run before, not even the night she killed Julian, she didn't see the hole in the ground ahead of her. Tripping into it, she stumbled and fell, hitting her head on a nearby rock. The last thing Jenna saw was a flash of lightning in the distance. Her last thought was that she would die in the oncoming storm, but not of the blow to her head or the thunder or rain, but from a broken heart.

When Jenna bolted up and left Brett's first thought was that his torn emotions would finally heal. The decision to let her go hadn't been easy, it tore him apart. He was totally and irrevocably in love with her, but he couldn't go on wanting his wife and having her continue to refuse him. He couldn't believe she suddenly fell in love with him. Whatever it was that had frightened her, and he knew it was more than the attempted rape, that drove her to him was going to continue to eat away at her and smother their relationship. He knew, he just knew, that when the fear of the storm passed, she would regret her words and decision and would try to leave him again. His heart could not take her breaking it again.

After a few minutes, he got up and wandered into the library, then upstairs to his room, stopping to look in her room to what? Tell her he loved her? To tell her he didn't want her to leave? His emotions so tumbled, his heart breaking all his mind registered was that the bed was unmade, the rumpled sheets holding her scent, the room looked like a storm had blown through it. *What is her game now?* Brett's own emotions raw, he wandered towards his room when the first clap of thunder sounded overhead.

Jenna! She'd be frightened, if her reactions last night had been true, she'd be terrified. *She's not my problem, not anymore.* And then he moved, his heart contracting—room to room calling her name.

"Mr. Brett?"

"Marta, where is she? She's terrified of storms. Do you know where she went?"

"Out."

"Out? What do you mean out?"

"She ran out the door, towards the woods."

"When?"

"Right after you told her you didn't want her." Marta was clearly unhappy with him, but he couldn't worry about that now. He needed to get to Jenna.

"You're sure, Marta? She ran towards the woods?"

"Of course I am. You want me to show you?"

"No, I'll find her."

Marta called to Franco telling him to help Brett search for Jenna.

Brett tore out of the house and ran towards the woods, calling Jenna's name. Brett called for her over and over, but his calls were lost in the winds that came with the pounding rain and thunder booms. Together they searched the area, trying desperately to hear her respond.

Jenna lay on the ground in the woods, the rain pelting her and bringing her back to consciousness. Just as she became aware, another thunderclap sounded, louder than she could ever remember one sounding before. Looking down at her dress and the dirt beneath where her head had been were soaked in blood. Raising her arm to feel her head where it hurt so bad, she felt a sticky wetness. Bringing her hand before her eyes, she saw more blood. She wasn't sure if she was dizzy from hitting her head or from seeing all that blood. Shaking from both the cold rain as well as her terror from the storm, Jenna could only curl into a ball, tears of fear and grief flowing down her cheeks.

"Jenna! Jenna, answer me! Where are you? Jenna!"

"Brett," her voice barely a whisper. "Oh, Brett, I'm sorry, I'm so sorry, I do love you, I really do."

"Jenna."

It was him. It really was him calling to her. Just as she opened her mouth to call his name, another clap sounded, and a scream of pure terror poured from her mouth.

"There — Franco — there." Brett raced toward the sound of her scream and found her still curled in a ball on the ground, her tears mixed with the blood and dirt from the ground and the rain. He was beside her in an instant, cradling her in his arms. Not knowing if she shook from the cold or fear, he began to carry her towards the house. "It's okay, Jenna, I've got you. It's okay, sweetheart."

He wasn't sure if she heard him or even knew he was there, she just kept softly responding, "Brett, oh Brett, I love you. I love you, please don't leave me."

Franco ran on ahead to tell Marta what had happened and to get a warm bath prepared for Jenna. She'd been out there long enough to take a chill and he saw the bleeding gash on her head. Franco began to heat the water while Marta went upstairs to get her bed ready for her. Brett entered a few minutes later and nodded to his friend when he saw him preparing the bath water. He carried Jenna upstairs, her constant litany of, "Brett, I love you, please don't leave me," not letting up for even a moment. Seeing Marta in Jenna's room, he carried her in. Marta immediately directed him, "Get those wet clothes off of her before she catches a serious chill."

Brett's hands moved to the ruined dress, unbuttoning it to pull it off her followed by her petticoats and finally her undergarments. He'd never seen his wife naked before and the site of her lush body curling into him was like a kick in his gut. Despite his fear that she was hurt his groin tightened, his cock demanding he take her . . .that he make love to her.

Franco had already started to bring up the hot water while Marta pulled out a warm night shift and extra blankets. Hearing the couple ending the room Brett drew a blanket up to cover his wife. So lost was she in her litany of loving words to Brett, Jenna no longer seemed to hear the storm howling above them. She didn't even react to the thunderclap or the cut of the lightening. As he pulled off the last of her undergarments his mind barely registered that for so long he'd wanted to peel the clothes from her, but not like this. Her shivers were so strong they seemed to shake him as well. After what seemed an eternity, he lowered her into the tub, pushing her down into the water to cover even her shoulders. He began to rub her briskly with a washcloth, trying to stimulate some warmth in her. Finally, her shivers began to subside. But with the water cooling he didn't want her to chill again so he lifted her from the tub and rubbed her briskly with a towel. After carrying her to the bed, he began to tuck her in, pulling the blankets up to warm her . . . and her litany changed, "Brett, please, hold me, please just for awhile, just hold me."

Her pitiful plea cut into his heart — Brett Parker was in love with his wife, his wife who told him over and over for months she didn't want him . . . and now, tonight, she'd told him she loved him and he rejected her . . . sending her out in to the storm, a storm that terrified her to the point she seemed to only be able to babble. He didn't want to lose her. Not now, not ever.

Quickly shedding his own clothes, Brett climbed in the bed beside his wife and used his body to warm her. At long last the shivering stopped, and Jenna slept. His cock hard with desire, his heart hurting, his mind confused . . . and concern what she would do when she regained full consciousness and found him naked beside her.

CHAPTER SIXTEEN

Somehow, while the storm raged, the couple fell asleep. It was Jenna who woke first the next morning, feeling a hard, but warm body beside her. Seeing the rise and fall of Brett's smooth chest the events of the night before came back to her. Brett had told her he didn't love her, didn't want her and it was over. *So why is he in bed with me — naked in bed with me? Did we make love?*

Brett slowly came awake and felt her silky hair caressing his shoulder while her soft breathing fanned across his chest, the desirable body of a woman beside him . . . Jenna. Their fight the night before came back to him . . . along with her flight from the house and how he found her. Glancing down, he saw her big brown eyes on him. The question was clear in her eyes.

"We didn't make love, Jenna. I didn't touch you, not that way."

Her eyelids lowered, and the slight blush on her cheeks was becoming. Slowly, she opened her eyes as she raised herself up, sliding further on top of him. Her lips hovered above his just for the briefest of moments before she lowered them to his, the tender brush of her lips just before she whispered, "Then we should do so now."

Before Brett could respond, her lips captured his in the same manner he had begun his passion-filled kisses to her in the past. At first startled by her boldness, he started to pull away. In the beginning he'd thought it was because of his mother's side, that she had somehow found out about her side of the family, that he was half-Indian she rejected him. But the warm welcome she gave his brother, Christ, she *hugged* Wolf and wouldn't give him, her own husband, the time of day.

No, there was something more and he couldn't do it anymore. It was too long and too much hurt. He didn't want this, did he? Her kisses grew more insistent and try as he might, Brett's body refused to listen to his mind. Finally he pulled away from her. Taking her wrists in one hand while he held her in place with the other, shifting so her hips couldn't continue their tentative grinding against his, he drew in a long steadying breath.

"Are you sure, Jenna?"

"Yes."

"No doubts, no reservations? No recriminations, because once I make love to you the marriage is firm, there will be no divorce. You will share my bed, every night, you will sleep by my side. You will be my wife, completely and fully. Is that what you want?"

"Yes, Brett, yes I do. I didn't come here wanting this, but Brett, I want you. I want to be your wife."

Try as he might, he couldn't keep the hurt and fear from his voice, "Why? Because you're afraid of thunder? That's not a reason to marry someone."

"No, oh, Brett. I told you last night, I knew I was falling in love with you long before the first storm. I just kept fighting it, but when I felt how you held me, how you cared for me, really cared for me I knew it was what I wanted."

Brett slid the hand that he'd used to hold Jenna away from him to her back, drawing her closer to him, while the one he'd used to hold her wrists moved behind her head, just before his lips met her he whispered, "I want you, Jenna. I want you more than I've ever wanted anyone or anything in my life."

With that, their lips met, at first softly teasing, testing, tasting until Brett slid his tongue into her mouth, lingering just inside, savoring the taste and texture of her mouth. Even though he'd kissed her a hundred times in the past few months, this kiss was special. It had to be special because it was going to set the pace, the tone for the rest of their lives. He had to make it good for her, so good.

She eagerly took him to her, her response a demand for more, and Brett gladly gave it. Holding himself back, denying himself the feel of her body for just a bit longer, giving her the chance to adjust and wanting to experience her every move, Brett groaned. His cock hardened, responding to her little whimpers of pleasure. He felt her tentatively touch him, her hand sliding slowly up his arm, coming to rest on his upper arm. She stroked and gave a slight squeeze to his bicep before continuing her journey up to his shoulder. As her hand traveled upward, she slid her hips closer to his, the brush of her satiny skin against his groin making him even harder.

After the slightest pause, her hand moved downward, towards his chest, stopping as her thumb passed over his nipple. She stopped there and in the soft morning light, he opened his eyes to see her staring at his chest. At first he was alarmed when he saw her staring at her thumb resting on his nipple. Then he realized she was, for some reason, enthralled by what she saw or felt. Her thumb moved again, slowly, sensuously over his nipple. He almost missed the look of wonder in her eyes. Brett let her play for a short time before sliding his hands along her ribcage to her breasts, his thumbs moving to stroke across her nipples, teasing them to share the hardness of his own. Holding the warm globes in his hands, he pulled ever so slightly on her nipples, bringing a gasp of pleasure to her lips just before he dipped his head to lick at them. He was quickly rewarded with their hardening in pleasure. She leaned into him, encouraging him to continue his erotically sensual assault.

He was quickly rewarded with her passionately whispered, "Oh, Brett, Brett, that feels so good. Don't stop, don't ever stop, it feels sooooooo ahhhh oh, oh, Brett."

"Do you like that, Jenna? Does it feel good?"

"Better than good. Oh, Brett, if I'd known . . ."

"Now you do, and, Jenna, it gets better. I promise you, it gets better." Her indignant "oh" when he lifted his mouth from her one breast was quickly replaced with a sigh of pure pleasure as he moved to the other while at the same time his hands began their own dance of pleasure, caressing her, kneading her breast, stroking her hip. With his hands and mouth, he showed her how he would make love to her not only this morning, but for the rest of their lives. He only roared almost as if in pain when her hands came up to his shoulders and pushed at him every so slightly. His fears again coming to the surface, fears that she would reject him, Brett fought the anger that sought to boil to the surface—was she playing him for a fool again? In the dim light he saw her dilated pupils and fought for control when her tongue darted out to lick her lower lip before she leaned down to his chest and ran her tongue over one of his own nipples. The warm moisture of her mouth as she drew his nipple within, her tongue licking, stroking, before she sucked on it, excited him more than words could express. When he groaned, she sucked just a bit harder before again lathing it with her tongue. Anger fleeing as he realized she mimicked his love making while trying to know him.

Unable to help himself, Brett rolled ever so slightly so she could pay the same attention to the other nipple. Relief mixed with desire when he realized she only wanted to excite him as much as he was exciting her. As her mouth moved to the other nipple, her hand came back up to reclaim the one her tongue had just left. Her long hair tickled his belly while her hips pulsed against his groin, her hand and mouth making him more aroused than he thought possible. When she paused, looking up at him in wonder, he waited only a heartbeat before taking her lips in another hot kiss. Their tongues danced with passion, their breath in short pants. She pulled away, ever so slightly and this time he waited to see what she was about.

"Oh, Brett, you are so beautiful. I've wanted to touch you for so long, so very long."

"Why didn't you, Jenna?"

"Because it wouldn't have been right."

"I'm your husband, Jenna. It's your right to touch me, to kiss me, to be with me."

"Am I doing it right, Brett? Am I making you feel as good as you're making me feel?"

"Oh yeah, sweetheart, oh yeah. You make me feel so good, Jenna. I want you so much sweetheart, so much."

"Make love to me, Brett, please, make love to me."

"We are sweetheart, this is part of it, I promise. I gotta ask you one thing though, ok?"

Without stopping her hands searching strokes on his body, she nodded.

"Don't be offended, Jenna, I just need to know, just so I don't hurt you, okay?"

"Know what, Brett?"

"Have you been with, has there . . ."

"No one, Brett, only you."

"I'll be careful, sweetheart, it's gonna hurt. I'll do what I can to keep it from hurting bad, but it'll hurt. I don't want to but . . ."

"It's okay, really. Belle told me . . ."

"Belle told you what?"

"That it hurts the first time, but after that it's so good, so very good."

"Wh-when did Belle tell you that?"

"On the trail—her sister's married and her sister told her. You know, since she didn't have a mom here to tell her things, her sister told her—she told Bea and I about it."

Relief coursed through him, in small part that no one knew she'd denied him until now, but mostly because she was prepared for what was to come, at least as prepared as she could be. The hand he'd had on her hip slid down her outer thigh and moved between her legs, then stroked upward along her inner thighs.

"Ahh, Jenna, your skin's like silk, like softest silk. You feel so good, darlin', so good." His hand reached her mound and one of his long fingers sought her nether lips, moving just inside. She gasped just before he brought his mouth to hers, brushing her lips with his. "I'm going to show you a bit of what you'll feel, I'm gonna get you wet, sweetheart, I'm going to get you nice and wet for me, ok?"

She nodded as his finger slid further inside only to withdraw and slide back in again. "How does this feel, Jenna? Does it feel good?"

"Oh, Brett, oh yes. Don't stop, please don't stop."

He joined another finger with the first, spreading her nether lips just a bit further, quickening the pace of his strokes. "How about that, Jenna? Does that feel good, sweetheart?"

"Oh oh, ah, oh, Brett, Ohhhhhhhhhhh." He felt her contract around his fingers, her climax making her more ready for him, wetter for him. He reached for her hand and brought it to his cock.

"I want you to feel me, babe, just a little, just a little touch." She shifted so she could not only touch the tip of his cock, but to take him in her hand. He was so big, so hard, she couldn't quite wrap her entire hand around him, but she had no problem stroking downward to the base and back up to the tip.

"Are you going to fit in me, Brett?"

"Yeah babe, I will."

"Are you sure?"

"Oh yeah, I knew the minute I laid eyes on you, we were made for each other. It may be tight as first, but I promise, I'll fit." Brett moved to kneel between her legs, pushing them further apart before leaning forward, bringing the tip of his cock to the entrance of her channel. "Relax, Jenna, let me in. Let me be with you." Slowly, bit by bit he moved into her, a slight way in and he withdrew ever so slightly, moving in a little further, pulling back a bit. Slowly, building up a needing pressure in her sex channel until he met with her maidenhead. He moved outward just a bit before plunging in to the hilt, his balls meeting with her slit. Then he stilled, giving her a chance to take him, to feel his size. She'd gasped at the pain, bit at her lower lip to keep from crying out. She was so small, so tight, it took every ounce of his strength not to take her hard and fast. Months of wanting her, trying to sleep while his cock throbbed with desire for her finally ended. She was his, now and forever. Jenna was now his wife in every way. She wiggled beneath him and at first Brett thought she was afraid, that he'd hurt her so bad that she was now struggling to get away from him. To his surprise her hands slid down to grab his butt while her legs wrapped around him.

"I need more, Brett. I want more of what you did with your hand. I don't care if it's wrong, I want that Brett, I want it from you."

He groaned, a sound of pure desire before he began to rock his hips back and forth inside of her. His lips claimed hers while his hips pumped; his tongue sought hers while his hips pumped faster. The sounds of pleasure coming from her throat, soft little purrs that sent shards of pleasure into him demanding he pump harder into her. Just when he thought he couldn't hold his own need back a moment longer, her channel contracted around his cock, squeezing him and beginning to milk his nectar into her. "Jenna!" he roared as he came, pumping until every last drop was drained into his wife. He collapsed on top of her and lay there, spent. Her hands had moved from his butt to his shoulders and she hugged him to her. When he moved to raise himself up, her legs quickly came up to restrain him.

"I don't want to crush you, babe."

"Don't leave me."

"I'll be right here. Right by your side." She released him and as soon as he moved to her side, she rolled to him, her arms moving to go around him. They lay there, cuddling for some time before Jenna tipped her head back, a small frown of worry on her lips.

"Brett . . . was it good for you? Did you enjoy it with me? Did I do it right?"

"Better than good, sweetheart. It's never been that good before."

"Will it always be that good?"

"I hope so, and I think, based on how good I feel now, it's going to get better and better for us."

She ran her fingers into his hair, enjoying its texture, her finger tracing his ear as she drew in a breath. "I like touching you."

"I like you touching me."

"Yeah?"

"Yeah . . . do you like me touching you?"

She moved closer to him, her nipples burrowing into his chest. "Very much, I'm sorry I made you wait . . . I feel kind of peeved at myself because, well, we could have been . . . you know."

"It's okay, Jenna. We're together now and I won't let anything pull us apart, not now, not ever."

"Are you sure?"

"Absolutely."

"Prove it to me."

A slight feeling of panic constricted in his chest "How? How do you want me to prove it?"

"Make love to me again."

Relief replaced the panic when he assured her, "I will, trust me. I will make love to you every chance I get."

"Now, Brett, I want you now."

"I don't want to hurt you, Jenna, you may be tender, too tender to . . ."

"Now, Brett . . ."

CHAPTER SEVENTEEN

It was mid-afternoon before the couple emerged from the bedroom. Jenna blushed as Marta gave them an appraising look when they entered the kitchen. If Brett noticed, he certainly didn't let on when he asked Marta for some coffee and whatever food was easy to put together. As Marta served them, she asked Jenna how she felt. At the younger woman's deep blush Marta explained, "That was quite a bump you took on your head last night, so much blood when Mr. Brett brought you in."

"I was bleeding, wasn't I?" Both Brett and Marta nodded in the affirmative. "A lot?"

"Yeah, head wounds do that, they bleed a lot and look worse than they are." Brett assured her.

"All of them?"

"Yes, don't worry sweetheart. We checked you carefully for a concussion—and the blood, it looks really bad, but it stops pretty quickly, and it looks scarier than it is."

Jenna considered that while she ate. Head wounds bleed—a lot. She'd hit her head on a rock, it bled—she was fine. What if . . . she'd struck Uncle Julian in the head, along the temple. He'd fallen unconscious and she saw him bleeding. It was the blood that made her think she'd killed him. But if head wounds bleed . . . then maybe he wasn't dead! It would mean she wasn't a murderer! No wonder no one had come looking for her . . . if she hadn't killed him, he would be too embarrassed by the fact he'd tried to rape his own niece. She was free. Jenna was free and that meant she could stay with Brett

without worrying that her husband would be tasked with arresting her if she was found out.

The next few weeks were perhaps the happiest of Jenna's life.
Even more so than growing up safe in the care of her parents.
On the nights Brett did not have to work, they would ride in
the early evening. Jenna became quite skilled riding astride
her horse. If lack of knowledge about her past bothered him,
Brett he didn't let on, and seemed content to enjoy her for who
and what she was right then. Often, at his urging, they would
retire early, walking hand in hand up to his room. Some
nights he would tear at her clothes, impatient to have her naked beneath him, on others he was content for them to undress as a part of their foreplay. Jenna was an equal partner in
their lovemaking, often initiating their love play herself. If
Brett had been in love with her before, he was even more so
with the adventurous yet loving and caring woman in his bed.
He loved how her eyes would darken and her breath become
passionate little pants as she would run her hands over his
body.

Mornings were no different except their lovemaking was
slower, more languorous. When Jenna discovered *love bites*
she immediately took to leaving Brett with at least one each
morning — to be sure any other woman having a look at him
would know he was taken. That small bit of possessiveness
on her part brought reassurance to Brett.

When he'd return at night, she'd come out to the barn and
slide her arms around him, beginning with kneading his flat
belly and moving her hands up to his chest. The first time she
rubbed her own groin against his butt she suddenly froze; embarrassment evident on her face until she realized how it excited him. After that, when in private, she took every oppor-
tunity to rub against him . . . and when others were around,
she always seemed to find a way to touch him in that

sensuously seductive way she seemed to find around him. His wife learned quickly and enjoyed learning him as much as he enjoyed her doing so.

It was on a Tuesday morning as Jenna waved to Brett as he rode off that she had an odd prickle trickle down the back of her neck. She ran after Brett, calling to him until he stopped and dismounted to see what had disturbed her. "What is it, Jenna? What's wrong?"

"Nothing, Brett I . . . I just, oh I'm being silly. I just felt like I needed to tell you I love you, that I love you more than life itself and I couldn't bear it if you left me."

Pulling her into his arms he held her a moment before telling her, "Jenna, darling, I love you more than I ever thought a man could love a woman. Trust me, I'll always come home to you."

"I know, I know, I just wanted . . . needed to . . . make sure you know I love you. I really do, Brett. I love you so much." She pulled his head down and kissed him like a thirsty man taking a long-awaited drink of water.

"You okay now?"

"Yes, I guess maybe I just like telling you I love you."

"And I like to hear it. I'll try to get back early tonight, maybe we can take a ride before it gets too dark, huh?"

"That sounds good, I'll see you tonight." Jenna skipped towards the house. Feeling much more at peace, she busied herself straightening their room. How good it felt to think of it as *their* room. Moving to make up the bed, she picked up Brett's pillow and inhaled deeply, his scent causing the now familiar moisture to pool between her legs. Smiling to herself she knew that any riding to be done tonight was going to happen right here in this bed.

Rick looked up at the sound of his office door opening and

closing with a firm click. Something about his visitor disturbed him. There was nothing out of the ordinary about the tall, slimly built, dark-haired man. As he approached, Rick saw that the dark hair was laced with gray and while slimly built, there was power in the man's body. Not strength from an honest day's work. When the stranger arrived in front of Rick's desk, he looked up into the coldest eyes he'd ever seen. They were an odd shade of blue, almost like they had been submerged in water, taken out and put in the man's eye sockets.

Rick stood to greet the man. "Help you, sir?"

"I'm here to collect my property."

"Your property? If someone has left something for you, I don't have . . ."

The man pulled a sheaf of papers out of his jacket and held them up to the Sheriff. "I'm here to collect a runaway slave."

Rick half fell, half sat in his chair, stunned. *A runaway slave? Here in Adler Creek? There weren't any darkies here. What did the man mean?* "Mr . . ."

"Carlman, Julian Carlman."

"Mr. Carlman, we don't have any runaways here. In fact, I can't say as we've ever had a Negro come through town at all."

"Oh, she's not a Negro, Sheriff. And from what I understand, she's here. I'm looking for Jennifer Matthews."

"Wish I could help you, but there's no Jennifer Matthews living here."

"Perhaps you would know her by her married name?"

Something about the man in front of him turned Rick's stomach. There was just something . . . dirty . . . yes, dirty about the man. "Mr. Carlman, we aren't a very big town. I can tell you, we don't have a Jennifer here."

"I'm sure you do. I have . . ." he pulled out what appeared to be a newspaper, " . . . a picture appeared in our local paper about some mail order brides that came here . . . I'm sure

Jennifer is somewhere in your town."

"I wish I could help you . . ." *Like hell I do*, "but I met all the brides when they arrived and there was no Jennifer among them."

"Then she's changed her name. Sheriff, a runaway slave is by his or her very nature deceitful. My sources tell me she is here." Carlman held up the newspaper for the Sheriff. "Please, take a close look at the woman here towards the edge of the photograph, Sheriff. That is my Jennifer. Are you sure you don't know her?"

Rick looked at the photo, his normally healthy complexion turning white.

"I see you do. Might I ask what name she is using?"

"Jenna, that's Jenna Parker."

"Would Parker be the name she is using or did some poor soul end up married to her?" Normally calm and in control, Julian felt his gut clench. If Jennifer had married then some other man had taken her maidenhead, some other man had bedded her. Jennifer, the woman he had intended to possess since she was a little girl would have given her sweet body to another man. He vowed to kill any man that touched what was meant to be his, what he worked so hard to claim as his own.

"Parker would be her married name — she's married to my deputy, Brett Parker. *If* in fact Jenna is the same person you are looking for."

"I'm sure she is and as soon as she can be sent for, I will take custody of her and return her home where she belongs."

"Whether she is or isn't, Mr. Carlman, the Wyoming territory does not recognize slavery and, she *is* a married woman."

"Sheriff, these papers are her indenture papers, signed willingly by her in payment of the debt she owes me. She belongs to me and I will bring her home."

Before Rick could reply, Brett walked into the office. For Rick a day that had started bad had just gotten worse.

"Rick."

"Ah Brett. This here is Mr. Carlman, Mr. Julian Carlman. It seems . . ."

"I want my Jennifer back."

"Excuse me?" Brett had begun to extend his hand to the older man but withdrew it at his statement.

"She now calls herself Jenna, but she is my property and I am here to bring her home."

"Mr. Carlman," Rick interrupted him. "The papers say she is indentured . . ." He stumbled trying to make sense of the documents Carlman had just given him.

"I paid her debts, she signed the papers giving herself to me. I intend to bring her home."

Carlman kept his anger in check, but just barely. Appraising the tall, good looking deputy, Carlman thought, *So the little bitch gave her body to this man and he had the pleasure of busting her sweet cherry. It should have been mine. Mine. And she will pay for that along with making me chase all over the country in search of her.*

"Look, Mr. Carlman, Deputy Parker just arrived. He has no idea of what we've been discussing, and I can assure you, his wife won't be going off anywhere while we sit down and talk about this."

"If it's money for a debt," Brett started, "I'm happy to pay you whatever is owed."

"That is considerate of you, Deputy, and what you say may

be true, Sheriff, but I believe it best you know I have, in addition to her indenture papers a warrant for attempted murder
from Maryland and I have brought a legal escort with me to
ensure she gives me no further trouble. Deputy, if you would
either send for Jennifer or give me directions to where she is,
I will retrieve her and take her off your hands."

"You will do no such thing." Fortunately for Brett, Rick saw
him ball up his fist in preparation for striking Carlman and he
moved across the room before the fist flew.

"Brett, you pull up a chair and park yourself on my side of
the desk. Mr. Carlman, I don't care if you brought the entire
militia for the State of Maryland with you, this is *my* town and
I am the law here. No one is going anywhere or *fetching* anyone until we sit down and I have a chance to look at these
papers of yours. And then if, and that's a might be if, they are
true, we will wait for the magistrate to come through to make
a decision. Wyoming does not answer to the laws of the State
of Maryland. We do not recognize slavery or indenture. And
knowing Jenna like I do, she would not have left her home
without good reason."

"I understand your concern, Sheriff, and I will concede that
there is little chance she will run off while her husband is
here . . . although I can attest she does have a penchant for
running."

Brett digested Carlman's last statement. He would have to
agree about Jenna's need to run, from what Zeke and Dusty
had told him, Jenna had tried to leave the bride train in St.
Louis and had held him at bay for months. But if she was running from Carlman, just from his first meeting of the man, she
may have had good cause.

"Jenna's home, safe and sound. She doesn't leave unless it's to come here to town."

"Fine. I hope we will find her there when you see the right of my claim."

"Alright, Mr. Carlman, why don't you tell us your story."

"Thank you. I'll try to be brief. You see, I met Jennifer's father some years ago and lent him some money. Along the way my dearly departed sister, Dorothy, met and married him despite my warning that he was, well, in a word unsavory. The man was not the best when it came to money matters and despite my attempts to assist him, he got further and further into debt. In March of this year it seems he was no longer able to pay any of his bills. He had contacted me and asked me to come speak with him and asked me if I would provide for Jennifer. I agreed that I would marry her and we were ready to set a date when her father killed himself. A tragedy to be sure. For some reason Jennifer took it in her head that she wanted to pay her father's debts and told me that if she married me she would be even further in debt and she, herself, offered to indenture herself to me. Believe me, I argued with her, but she was adamant, she wanted to pay me back."

Brett considered what Carlman had said—and Jenna was like that. She'd wanted to pay him back for her trip west. At least she was ethical about paying her bills. And he didn't blame her for not wanting to marry the man in front of him.

Carlman continued, "So I had my lawyer draw up the papers, had Jennifer seek her own counsel to be sure they were fair and I assure you, I told both of them that what I wanted was to marry the girl, make her my wife and spoil her to pieces. She finally conceded to leave a clause in the document that states that if she chooses, at any time she can marry me and the debt would be paid.

"After her father's funeral we went to my home in Maryland and I don't know if it was grief or her own madness, but she came after me with a lamp and struck me in the head. I'd heard her call out for help, went in to help her and she came up behind me and struck me in the head. To tell you the truth I'd wondered if perhaps she had something more to do with her father's death."

"Excuse me, Carlman."

"Deputy?"

"Are you trying to tell me this Jennifer of yours killed her father?"

"I assure you, Deputy, I have no doubt that the woman who calls herself Jenna is *my* Jennifer. I didn't mean to infer she held a gun to his head or did anything else so overt, but rather somehow persuaded her father to do so. I'm sure you've seen how manipulative she can be."

Brett had to consider that. Jenna had persuaded him to . . . no, that wasn't true . . . was it? Did she manipulate him into offering her protection without sharing his bed? No, no, even before she knew him and that he meant to marry her, he'd offered her protection and his name and it was he who promised that he wouldn't touch her until she was ready. He knew she was hiding something—but this was much more than he expected; if, it was true.

"Anyway, when I came to, I found that not only had my dear Jennifer left, run off, but quite a bit of money was taken as well. I couldn't imagine what had happened to her until this article appeared in our paper." Julian pushed the newspaper towards Rick and Brett, pointing out the picture of the woman he called Jennifer.

As much as Brett wanted to deny it, the woman Carlman called Jennifer was Jenna, his wife.

"Well, Mr. Carlman, you tell a compelling story, but I'd like to hear what Jenna has to say, this may well be a woman who only looks like Brett's wife, you know?"

"I can assure you, Sheriff, this woman is my Jennifer and I

will thank you to have her brought to me as soon as possible."

"Well that would be well and good, Mr. Carlman, but I believe we need to hear Jenna's side of the story and then leave it for the traveling magistrate to decide. You *do* agree that would only be just, don't you, Mr. Carlman?"

"I do, to a point, but I believe you will agree that Jennifer should be brought to me and turned over to my custody while we await these proceedings."

"No." Brett's voice was deceptively quiet. Rick could clearly see the rage boiling in his eyes. The question was, was he angry at Carlman, Jenna or both?

"No? Deputy, she belongs to me."

"She's my wife, Carlman. She stays at home with me."

"And to what end? So you can impregnate her and make her useless to me? You already pierced her maidenhead, that is bad enough."

Brett paused a beat at the last statement Carlman made, wondering why an uncle would care about his niece's virginity. The way he said it sent a chill up Brett's spine. "Carlman, what happens between my wife and I is no one's business but ours. She stays . . ."

"Excuse me." Rick cut both men off. "I suggest we first ascertain if our Jenna is the same person as this Jennifer you're talking about. If she is, well then it seems to me it only be right she have her say. If — and that's a big if — she has done something illegal, then we need to hold her in custody — here at the jail — until she can have a proper hearing. Understood?"

"Of course, Sheriff. How soon can I see my girl?"

Before Brett could react, Rick cut him off. "I suggest we ride on out to the Parker ranch and we'll see if Jenna knows you.

We'll take it from there."

"Agreed. Shall we leave now?"

"Brett?"

"Sure. Let's go." His voice tight and like iron.

As they left the jail, Carlman signaled to the bounty hunter, a disreputable looking man, even for someone who's been on the trail for as long as it took to get to Adler Creek, he'd brought with him and the four men rode out to the ranch. Brett looked the bounty hunter over and decided the man was not of the highest intelligence and it stood to reason he would be slow on the draw if it came to that . . . if he couldn't think himself out of a room with two doors he wouldn't know when to draw.

When they arrived at the ranch, Brett led them inside while at the same time calling for Jenna.

Surprised her husband was home so early she skipped down the stairs and hurried over to him . . .

She smiled as she approached him. "Couldn't wait to pick up where we left off this morning, could you?"

She'd just reached Brett's side, turned to greet Rick, and stopped dead in her tracks. Her face lost all color just before she collapsed. Brett reached to catch her just before she hit the ground.

"I believe, gentlemen, you have your answer, it is my Jennifer."

CHAPTER EIGHTEEN

Brett carried Jenna into the living room and gently laid her on the couch while Rick went to pour a brandy. Ignoring Carlman while Brett tried to rouse her, worry coursing through his veins.

As she slowly came to, she whispered, "Brett," but it was Carlman who came into her line of vision.

"Hello, Jennifer dear. I've come to bring you home."

"No, no, it can't be. You're dead." No, not dead. He had a head wound, he bled, no, he wasn't dead. He was alive and here in Brett, their, home.

"Ah, so there you are, Sheriff. She is my Jennifer and you have your confession of attempted murder. There should be no further delay in returning her to my custody."

"That's not the way it's going to happen, Carlman. I told you in town, if Jenna is the person you knew, we would take her into custody and await the magistrate and that is what we will do."

"Brett, no, you can't let him near me, please, don't let him near me." Her fear of the older man clear in her voice.

Trying to allay her panic, he handed her the brandy Rick had poured for her while telling her, "I don't plan to, darling, I don't plan to."

"You don't have any choice in the matter, Deputy."

"Jenna, do you know this man?"

"Yes . . . Brett, he . . . he . . . he tried to . . ." She grabbed on to him as if her life depended on the contact with him, her fingers tangled in his shirt, and sobbed uncontrollably. Brett held on to her, cradling her in his arms until she had cried herself out.

"Jenna, did you try to kill this man?"

"No! Oh, Brett, no. He tried to rape me. This is the man who tried to rape me. He's my uncle and he tried to rape me."

"Now, Jennifer, Jennifer, no more lies. Enough of your playing. I've already told these gentleman how your father owed me such a large sum of money and when he couldn't pay it back, he committed suicide.

"I told them how I offered to marry you but instead you wanted to pay your father's debt and offered yourself to me as an indentured servant. I brought the papers with me to show the authorities that you did agree to indenture yourself to me. Now, dear, I can understand your upset and depression at your father's death, but when you attacked me for no reason, well, my dear, you shocked me. I was quite dismayed when I came to, found you and all that money gone."

He paused as if for effect before continuing, "I've searched for you for months and it was only by chance I came across the photographer's picture of you in the paper. Now, if you will come home quietly, without any fuss, I'm willing to let bygones be bygones—you will need to reimburse me for the expenses in trying to find you—but don't worry, we can attach it to your service years. And, of course, you will have to make up the time you have spent away from me. Unless, you want to marry me, immediately."

"She is married, Carlman, to me."

"Ah, Deputy, I'm afraid that may not be so. What is the name on the marriage certificate? Jennifer Matthews or Jenna something-or-other."

Brett paled, but he couldn't speak . . . he'd married someone who didn't exist. Jenna Martin wasn't a real person. Jennifer Matthews was.

"I wouldn't marry you if you were the last man on Earth," she stormed at Julian. "You disgusted me as a child, you disgust me now. I love Brett and I will fight to stay with him."

"How much do you want, Carlman?"

"Excuse me?"

"How much? How much is her contract for?"

"Quite a large sum, Deputy, but she's not for sale. I have wanted to marry Jennifer since she was a child. I waited a long time for her — I *will* have her."

"No. No. I will *not* marry you. Nothing could persuade me to commit such a vile act. Rick, he's lying. I never signed any kind of indenture papers."

"Jenna, why don't you tell me your side of this, alright?"

"Yes, thank you, Rick, thank you." She paused and drew in a slow breath in an effort to calm herself. "My father was a wealthy man, we lived in a large house, a mansion by some standards, in New York City and my parents loved each other. This man here," she gestured to Carlman "is my mother's brother and, Rick, for as long as I can remember, as a child, he was always touching me. And not in an appropriate way. He'd touch my chest, my bum, he'd tell me that he would, that he'd . . . that he would bed me. My mother died when I was eighteen. She was in a horrible carriage accident and it killed her. My father blamed himself and then killed himself out of grief from my mother's death a few years before. The note he left said it was because he couldn't live without my mother. But he was a wealthy man. Uncle Julian coincidently was in town on business when my father died and at the time he said it was fortuitous he was there because he was the guardian my parents had chosen for me. He showed me my father's Will making him the trustee of my inheritance.

Immediately after my father's funeral, Uncle Julian insisted we return to his home in Maryland — that his business had been delayed too long. We arrived two or three days later and the first night there he snuck into my room and attacked me. He tried to rape me."

"Jenna, that doesn't explain the indenture papers."

"I don't know about them. I don't. But I can tell you after the funeral Uncle Julian made me sign a bunch of papers."

"Jennifer, I never forced you to sign anything."

"No? You kept pushing papers in front of me and when I would try to read them you told me I didn't need to bother, I didn't need to worry about them. It seems I did. But I never, not ever, said to you I would indenture myself to you to pay my father's bills. He was a wealthy man."

"I'd like a minute with my wife."

"I think not."

"Carlman, my Deputy just found out his wife may not quite be who he thought she was — they aren't going to leave the house — let him talk to her."

"Ah, but, Sheriff, they can't be married, as I said, the name on the wedding cer . . ."

"Carlman, you are trying my patience, step out into the foyer with me . . . *now.*"

Seeing that he stood a better chance of gaining the advantage by stepping out of the room, Julian conceded. It crossed his mind that he could use this with the Magistrate by pointing out how generous he was but that the Deputy conspired with Jennifer against him — and perhaps he could even discredit the Deputy by making it seem he'd conspired with Jennifer. The man had bedded Jennifer, *his* Jennifer. He'd taken her sweet cherry — something he'd bided his time to have for himself for years. And the tall, heavily muscled, man stole that

187

from him. For years Julian had fantasized just how it would be when he took Jennifer the first time; in fact he'd practiced on many of the female servants he had in his . . . care. He wanted it to be perfect when he took Jennifer so he'd rehearsed, enjoying each sexual encounter, but that brute and taken her maidenhead . . . worse, she'd probably willingly given it to him. Oh yes, he'd find a way to discredit the good looking Deputy and hurt Jennifer in the process of doing it. He'd have to carefully plan her punishment so he could enjoy it to the fullest.

"Of course, Sheriff, you're right, they should have a few minutes to say goodbye."

"It's not goodbye, Carlman."

Julian and Rick left the room. Jenna watched Brett pace a few minutes, not knowing what to say. Finally he came and stood before her.

"I always knew you had a secret. I never thought it would be something like this."

"Brett, I . . ."

"Damnit, Jenna! You tried to kill the man!" Despite his whispered words they thundered in Jenna's ears.

"No, Brett, no I didn't. He attacked me and rather than be raped, I fought, and I grabbed whatever I could to stop him. He was proud of the fact that no one would come to my aid. And, Brett, he had a rope with him . . . he meant to tie me up or do something with that rope."

Brett sighed deeply, looking around the room as if an answer lay somewhere in there. His mind wandered back to how early on, at night, she would cry out and when he'd go to check on her would see her struggling against an unknown attacker in her sleep. And the night he'd tried to seduce her, the night before he decided to give her the annulment she wanted, she'd panicked—she said someone tried to rape her.

"What happened after you hit him?"

She exhaled slowly before continuing. "He was bleeding, from the head, bleeding so much and he didn't answer so I grabbed a few of my things . . . *my things*. I didn't take any of his money."

Brett thought he could vouch for that—she had nothing when she arrived and wanted to work to pay him back. If she had money, she would have just tried to hand it to him. "And?"

"And I snuck out of the house, made my way to the train yard and climbed into a box car and waited inside until it left. We traveled for I guess a day—I couldn't tell from inside. But when we stopped we were in Virginia and I found the tavern where the brides were leaving from and thought I could hide with them. That no one would notice another woman. I had thought only to get away . . . St. Louis seemed safe and . . . and I was going to stay there. Change my name, get a job, stay there."

He saw Jenna became more and more upset as her story came to when she met him.

"But Dusty found me and told me that I'd essentially been, that I'd been . . . bought. He said that some man had paid good money to have me as a bride and he was going to deliver me to that man. Do you have any idea how that sounded to me? Do you understand how it felt to know that I may have escaped one nightmare for another, worse one?"

"Am I a worse nightmare, Jenna? Am I? My God who have I been living with the past few months?"

At the last Brett raised his voice loud enough for the two

189

men in the foyer to hear him. To Julian's mind it fit well with his plans—he could use the Deputy's anger at little Jennifer to build his case. Yes, he could keep feeding him information about Jennifer to turn him against her—and send her packing back to him and his bed. And he'd make her pay, oh how he'd make her pay—night after night and even sometimes in the day time he'd leave work early to make her pay.

"You were the one who picked me, who came after me. You were the one who insisted I marry you."

"And at every step you tried to avoid it, avoid me. You know, Jenna, I thought it was because of my mother, because I'm half-Indian. But that wasn't it at all, was it, Jenna? Or is it Jennifer?"

Realizing he was turning on her, had perhaps already done so, tears flowed more freely. "No, Brett, no. Brett, I love you."

"Which one of you? Jenna or Jennifer? And if it's Jenna, what if Jennifer doesn't feel the same." He turned to walk to the door.

"Brett. No! Please, listen to me."

But he didn't. He opened the door and told Rick he could take the prisoner into custody.

Despite Julian's well told story and imposing documentation, Rick had reservations, strong reservations, about the truth of it all. There was something wrong about the way Carlman spoke to and about Jenna. When he looked at her, it was lewd and lascivious, the way a rough man looked at a lady of the night, not his niece. What he'd heard of Jenna's story rang true, and she certainly was upset right before Brett brought her out of the room. Something wasn't right . . . but he knew that from the first he'd heard about her from Zeke, something

190

was odd. And then her reaction to Brett—and how Brett acted about her, wanting to get out on the range to meet them, getting her aside before anyone else could talk to her. He looked over at her—the way she was slumped over on her horse she looked like it was the end of the world. Well, he supposed it probably was the end of her world. A few months ago, no, she probably would have been glad to have been taken from Brett's place—at least based on what Brett had told him. And then all of a sudden, right after that storm where she fell and got hurt, things changed. It was like that hit on the head knocked some sense into her about what a good man Brett was. And ever since then, she'd been one of the most loving wives he'd ever seen. Maybe she was telling the truth . . .

All he knew for certain was Brett could not weather another betrayal, especially not one from Jenna.

When they arrived in town Rick rushed over to help Jenna down. She may have treated Brett bad when she first came with her not wanting to marry him and holding back from being a true wife. A husband and wife should share things, that's what a marriage was supposed to be. Like what Brett's parents had, not what he'd seen in his own home.

But Jenna also made him happy, happier than Rick had ever seen him. And with how skittish she was around Carlman, he'd do his best to keep the man from her. As he lowered her to the ground, speaking so softly he almost missed it, she implored him, "Please Rick, don't let him take me. Not just because he's a liar, but because I love Brett, I really do love him."

Carlman approached but Rick shouldered him out of the way and escorted Jenna into the jail. It was going to be hell to pay when the other ladies found out she was incarcerated. He decided to have Tom go ask Belle to come on in to the jail. If anything maybe he'd be able to convince her to have the other women also come by and do what they could to make sure

191

Jenna was never in there alone. He knew in his gut that if he left her alone for more than a few minutes Carlman would make a move on her and it wouldn't be pretty. As he locked her in the cell, he told her that he'd asked for Belle to come by.

"Oh, Rick no, please, I can't handle anyone else hearing those horrible lies he's made."

"Jenna, they're gonna hear anyway. When the magistrate comes, they'll hear. And to be honest, I think you stand a better chance of a fair trial here than you would anywhere else."

"I know, Rick, I know . . . it makes me sick to think of that man touching me again. Rick, you have to believe me, I never signed those papers and the only reason I hit him was because he was going to rape me."

Rick sighed before answering her, trying to collect his thoughts. "Jenna, I believe you. You had problems here with us for a bit, but the past few weeks things have been good. I've never seen Brett happier. I know you're embarrassed, but Belle's a good woman, she'll understand and help. I know she will."

When Belle arrived, despite Carlman's bellowing that he wanted to see his *girl*, Rick took her right into the holding area. Before Belle could see that Jenna was in a cell Rick stopped and turned to her. "Belle, I know you aren't going to be happy with what I'm going to tell you and what you're gonna see, but you gotta believe me that it's for the best."

"What's going on, Rick?"

"Jenna's here, it's mostly for her safety, but she's here."

"Here in a cell?" Belle peered around him and saw Jenna standing there, tears again flowing.

"Jenna? What's going on?"

"Oh, Belle. I . . . I'm . . . oh, Belle, please don't hate me."

Belle approached the cell and glared at Rick. "You gonna tell me what's going on here, Sheriff?"

She called him Sheriff . . . she was mighty angry, no doubt

about that. Well, that might help Jenna.

"Now, Belle, I want you to hear me out before you make any judgments, ok? Will you listen to the whole story?"

He watched as she appeared to think about it a moment before replying that she would.

"This afternoon a Mr. Carlman arrived here in town. A Julian Carlman. He brought some papers saying that Jenna's name is Jennifer and that she's an indentured servant of his. He says she tried to kill him for no reason and then she ran away. Apparently that photographer that was taking pictures at all of the weddings put one of her in a paper that this Carlman saw and he came here looking for her."

"Jenna . . . is that true?"

"No, Belle, no it's not. Well, yes, part is true. Yes, it's true my name was Jennifer, but he's my Uncle and when my papa died a year ago, he told me he'd been appointed my guardian and he had a bunch of papers for me to sign. Before I could even pack my things, he moved me to Maryland to his house and the night we arrived he came into my room and tried to rape me. I fought him, Belle, I fought him and when he wouldn't let me be I grabbed whatever I could find and hit him in the head. When I saw all the blood and he didn't get up, I ran and it was the next day I met you ladies."

"So was that why you wanted to stay in St. Louis? To hide from him? That was why you never wanted your picture taken?"

"Yes, Belle I didn't want to trouble anyone else. I didn't want anyone else to be hurt by him. But Dusty told me I didn't have a choice, that I had to come here. And then when Brett said that I was his bride, he didn't give me much of a choice. Not that he was bad or cruel. He told me he'd protect me and I thought that in time, he'd see we didn't suit and he'd give me an annulment. Only he kept trying. He really did court me and I fell in love with him. Belle, I can't imagine a life without him. He's the very air I breathe and he won't listen to me. Oh, Belle, he believes Uncle Julian, not me! What am I going to do Belle, what am I going to do?"

"Well we're gonna fight for you, that's what we're going to do, isn't that so, Rick?"

"That's why I asked you to come, Belle. I don't get a good feeling about this Carlman and . . ."

"So why do you have Jenna here? She can stay with us at our place. We have plenty of room. If Brett won't do the decent thing, she can stay with us."

"It's not just a matter of Brett not doing right by Jenna. This is going to have to go before the Magistrate. Carlman has accused her of being a runaway indentured servant and that she attempted to murder him. Both are pretty serious accusations."

"So we'll post a bail for her."

"If I thought Jenna'd be okay I wouldn't have any problem with that. It's Carlman I don't trust. And there's no way I'd say she should go home to Brett's because I really think that would make more problems for the two of them. I think she'll be safest here, especially, and this is where you come in — you and the other ladies. If you can take turns just sitting here with her at least during the daylight hours, she won't be alone. He won't be able to get to her."

"Of course. I'll contact the other women right now and we'll set up a schedule."

"Belle, no."

"Why not, Jenna? Or oh . . ." Her friend was clearly flustered and searching for the right thing to say. "Should we call you Jennifer now?"

"No, Belle, Jennifer Matthews died a long time ago. It's Jenna, Jenna *Parker*. Oh, Belle, Rick, I'll get him back, won't I? Brett will come back to me, won't he?"

"I'm gonna talk to him, Jenna, but, well the man's hurtin',

I can tell you he's hurt and feeling betrayed. I'll stay around till Belle gets back — and I know you don't want it to go further, but do you see why we need to?"

"Yes. It makes sense. I don't want to be alone with Uncle Julian, not even for a minute."

"Fine. I'll go call a meeting and I'll explain things and bring you back some dinner. Would that be okay, Rick?"

"Sounds good, Belle, and thank you."

After Belle returned with Millicent and a schedule of when the other women would arrive, Rick headed back to the Parker Ranch. He was determined to try to talk some sense into Brett. Even if Brett wouldn't accept Jenna as his wife, he needed him to stand by her to protect her from Julian Carlman. Carlman hadn't been any too pleased when Rick told him that there would be no male-female visiting hours without him or one of his deputies there. When Carlman tried to argue that Jenna was his niece, Rick reminded him that he had said he had intentions to marry her himself and she was a married woman and . . . it would be highly questionable to allow a crime victim alone in a room with a suspect. Rick was mighty pleased with himself for turning that table against Carlman.

By time he got to the ranch, Brett was in a fine state, if being skunk drunk was a state someone should be in in the middle of the day.

"What are you doing back here, Rick? Didn't you ruin my day, my life, already by bringing that Carlman out here earlier?"

"We need to talk, man. I need you to focus on what I'm saying and we need to talk."

"I'm not that drunk. I'm mostly just angry, angry at him, angry at her. The woman lied to me . . . shit, she didn't even give her own name. She made up a name. She tried to kill a man, she ran away . . . she probably lied when she said she loved me."

"No, she didn't lie about loving you. Believe me, she didn't lie about that."

"So what do you want from me?"

"I don't care what you do once Carlman leaves, but I need you to stand by her while he's here. I don't like the man, I don't get a good feeling about him."

"So what do we do?"

"Right now I have Belle and the other women staying with her during the day time. Tom and I will take turns sleeping in the jail at night. I don't trust Carlman near her. We keep her in protective custody till the magistrate arrives and my money is on that Carlman's lying and that he really did try to rape Jenna."

"Jennifer, didn't you hear, her name's Jennifer"

"Brett . . ." Rick warned him.

"Alright, alright. It seems to me it's her word against his, and we gotta hope we get a Magistrate that sees things right."

"So you gonna work it out?"

"I don't know, Rick, I don't know. I promised her I'd protect her and I'll do that, but after, I'm not making any promises."

"That's fine. I just wish we had someone else to ask about it."

"What about Kendrick?"

"Kendrick?"

"Yeah, your brother. He's a U.S. Marshal . . . and he's back east. Maybe he can do some checking and see what he can find. We'll ask him to take a look into this and see what he can find out."

For the first time all day Rick felt like things were going to go the right way for Jenna . . . and Brett. If they could prove that Carlman was lying, Rick would have to see his wife did what she had to just to survive.

Together they rode back into town, went to the Emporium, and sent a telegraph to Kendrick Parker asking him to look into the deaths of Dorothy and William Matthews. That was where it started with Jenna and Carlman and that was where they would start to find the answers. Kendrick responded a few hours later that he was starting on the case immediately.

CHAPTER NINETEEN

It was almost three weeks later the Magistrate arrived in town on a cold late-December morning. Through the whole time Belle and the other women had arrived at the jail early each morning and one of the women stayed with Jenna through each day. Rick or Tom slept in the jail each night. Each morning, Carlman showed up demanding to see his niece and each day Rick informed him that if he was going to persist in pressing charges for murder and as a runaway indenture he would not allow him, as the victim, to be with the suspect. Brett never came by, he never even asked after Jenna. Jenna seemed to get more and more depressed each day and Rick had no doubt it was because of Brett, not Carlman. Rick would have punched him over that except he knew that Brett went to the Emporium every day to see if Kendrick had found anything out that would help Jenna. When he'd asked Brett why he didn't even ask after Jenna Rick saw the hurt in his friend's eyes. Brett told him he couldn't he just couldn't because he knew when it was over he'd lose her. One way or the other, he said, he would lose her.

"I can't, Rick, she never trusted me to tell me what happened, what she was running from. And then me, fool that I am, I didn't stand by her when he showed up. There's just too much water under our bridge and I have no doubt when it's over she will leave me. It's better I just start to walk away now."

Things looked pretty bleak when the day of the trial arrived with not so much as a howdy-do from Brett's older brother.

The morning of the trial, as usual, Brett went to the Emporium to see if there was a message. After being told once again that no, nothing had arrived from his brother, he walked out into the blustery morning and against his mind's direction he looked towards the jail. He was greeted by the sight of Rick guiding Jenna out of the jail and towards the saloon which was being used as the courthouse. He wasn't going to go to the trial, he couldn't look at her after her betrayal, but of their own volition his feet began to move towards them. Just as he stepped off the walk, Adam Brewster burst out of the Emporium.

"Brett! It's coming, Sam said to get you and tell you your brother is writing."

Brett spun on his heel and pushed into the store, his long strides eating up the distance to the telegraph. Standing before Sam and his machine, his impatience was obvious.

"We'll have it in a minute, Brett, just relax." When the machine finally fell silent, Sam looked up at him and smiled.

Brett grabbed the piece of paper and quickly read its contents. While he'd hope it would say Carlman was lying and that Jenna was just Jenna, not this Jennifer person, it didn't do that. What it did say, though, was much, much more important.

CARLMAN VERY DANGEROUS — STOP

CARLMAN POSSIBLY MURDERED DOROTHY MATTHEWS — STOP

CARLMAN DID MURDER WILLIAM MATTHEWS — STOP

CARLMAN INVOLVED IN SHADY DEALS—MANY—STOP

DEALS INCLUDE FORGERY, HUMAN TRAFFICING, SMUGGLING—STOP

MAY HAVE KILLED OR SOLD NEICE JENNIFER MATTHEWS—STOP

IF STILL IN YOUR TOWN, ARREST, HOLD FOR FEDERAL OFFICER-STOP

HARD COPY REPORT FOLLOWS FASTEST ROUTE-STOP

U.S. MARSHAL KENDRICK PARKER, NEW YORK, NEW YORK-STOP

Jennifer was innocent! Everything Carlman had said was a lie! Jennifer had been in more danger than even she knew. But the fact remained, she didn't tell him, she didn't trust him and kept perhaps the most important information about herself from him. How could he have protected her if she didn't tell him? It hurt more than anything else had ever hurt him and it was the one thing he could never forgive. He knew from the beginning she had something to hide, but this . . . this was unforgivable. She should have told him. Not even how deeply he loved her would allow him to forgive her for this betrayal.

But he was a lawman and he could not let scum like Carlman loose. He'd killed Jenna's parents and who knew how many others. And how many had he sold into slavery? He was glad Jenna escaped . . . but she didn't tell him . . . she didn't tell him.

Brett ran to the saloon. He entered just as Jenna was called to the stand. Signaling to Rick he rose and headed towards him. Brett held out the paper. "Carlman's a kidnapper and a killer. Kendrick has proof."

Rick took the telegram and quickly read it, whistling through his teeth. "Damn."

"That's what I thought. We need to take him into custody and hold him till Kendrick and the Marshals arrive. I imagine they will want to return him to Maryland or New York to stand trial."

"I'll approach the magistrate when he takes a break, from past experience I can tell you no matter what the news he doesn't take too kindly to being interrupted."

"Yeah, but what if Jenna says something that makes it worse for her?"

"I don't think that's an issue . . . anything she says will just show how he manipulated her." They moved to sit as Jenna began to give her oath.

"State your name."

"Jenna Parker."

"Excuse me, your honor," Carlman interrupted. "Right there you have proof of what a little liar she is. Her name is Jennifer Matthews—Jenna Martin is a name she made up. It isn't her name, so when she married Mr. Parker it was a lie. She didn't walk down the aisle as Jennifer Matthews, but with a made up name."

Jenna looked to the judge who considered the matter a moment before speaking. "All right then Mrs., or Miss, state all your names for the record."

"In the past I was called Jennifer Matthews, I used Jenna Martin to travel and the name I choose to live with is Jenna Parker."

"Thank you, Mrs. Parker. Now, you have been accused of breach of contract, running away from an indenture, attempted murder and stealing. How do you plead?"

"Not guilty. I didn't do any of those things."

"Fine, so why don't you tell me your story?"

"All right." Jenna paused a moment to collect her thoughts, relief flooding her when she saw Brett. In her heart she knew he was there because he cared for her, not to see her reviled. "My pappa killed himself about a year ago. I came home and found him in his study after he'd apparently shot himself in the head. My uncle, Julian Carlman, the man sitting over there, happened to be in town that day on his own business and he stopped to call shortly after I found my father's body. He took charge of things and the next day he had several papers for me to sign. To be honest, I didn't look at any of them closely—Uncle Julian told me that he would take care of all the funeral arrangements for my father and I thought that was what it was all about. The day after my father was buried, Uncle Julian took me to his home in Maryland. I had just gotten ready for bed that night when he came to the door and he . . . he . . ." Jenna began to cry, the tears quietly flowing down her cheeks.

"Go on, Mrs. Parker."

She continued, her speech broken. "He ripped my night shift, pushed me on the bed and tried to force himself on me. He told me I owed him and he was going to . . . he wanted to . . . Your Honor, it was awful. I don't think I've ever been so frightened in my life. He wouldn't listen to me. I called for him to stop and he told me that no one in his house would interfere with him. And . . . and when he wouldn't stop, I grabbed for whatever I could find and I finally found a lamp and I hit him with it. I must have hit his head because when I got out from under him I saw all this blood from his head. I became even more frightened and grabbed my satchel, threw what I could in it—of my own things, I never touched his money—not once. I took my own things and left."

"So you didn't know if the man was dead or not?"

"No sir, I didn't. I was too scared."

"So you didn't know if he was alive and you could have helped him?"

"No, sir. I knew if he was alive, he'd come after me again and I felt for my virtue and my life I needed to get away from him."

"And why did you change your name?"

"I knew someone would look for me. I knew it, and I didn't . . . I knew that no one would understand he tried to rape me and not understand that I was only defending myself."

"So you came here and married Deputy Parker. Any kids yet?"

"Excuse me, Your Honor?"

"Yes, Mr. Carlman?"

"I would like to call for a mistrial—clearly your friendship with the deputy is clouding your judgment about this woman."

"Sit down, Mr. Carlman. You'll have your say and then I'll be asking Mrs. Parker a few more questions at some time. For now, Mrs. Parker, thank you and go have a seat. I see your husband arrived and he looks like he's got something on his mind."

Jenna looked up to see Brett had moved to the other side of the room. She'd always thought him not just a physically big man, in many ways he was larger than life the way he'd come along and just taken charge of things for her. As he approached, she saw his look was grim which meant he didn't really want her to come stand by him. Before she could decide, Rick approached and took her arm. He leaned over and whispered in her ear. "We found out more about Carlman than you can ever imagine. What you will hear in a few

minutes may upset you, but, Jenna, it will mean your freedom."

"What good is freedom without Brett in my life, Rick?"

"He'll come around, sooner or later. He'll come around."

Rick sat her down and turned to the magistrate. "Sir, if I
might approach, I have something I think you should see."

"That's fine, Sheriff."

Rick approached where the Magistrate sat and handed him
the telegram. The man's face first started to turn white and
then became quite red.

"You sure about this, Sheriff?"

"As much as I can be. You know Marshal Parker's a good
man, very thorough."

"Yes, I've heard of him. How long you think before his report arrives?"

"Hard riding, a few weeks."

"Fine. Sheriff, please take Mr. Carlman into custody."

A murmur moved through the courtroom, the townsfolk
clearly happy that the man who wanted to hurt their Jenna
was now in trouble, but also a bit disappointed that they
weren't going to get their show. Jenna sat, bewildered, all she
knew was there was something on that paper that disrupted
things. Was there something on it that Rick thought would
upset her more than she already was?

"Now see here, Your Honor." Carlman attempted to shrug
off Rick's hand. "What is the meaning of this? I demand an
explanation."

CHAPTER TWENTY

Jenna watched as Julian was led from the saloon-turned-courtroom, her bewilderment clear on her face. With Rick and Tom escorting him to the jail, she only had Brett to turn to to find out what was going on, if, he would even speak to her. It hurt that he thought she should have just lain there and let Julian do what he wanted with her. It hurt so bad. But then, wasn't sex all Brett had wanted from her? He'd never asked her what she wanted. Oh yes, when it came to clothes or something for the house, which she never accepted because she didn't want to take more of his money and it was, after all, his house. She wasn't about to reorganize things from how he had his life arranged. And what about Marta? She didn't want to make the woman uncomfortable in the home she'd lived in for how many years?

No, it was what she wanted from life — like children or to travel or what even what she thought of a book she'd read. He never even took her to meet his mother's family. Oh yes, his brother came for that visit, but Brett never took her to see his family. Was he so ashamed of her he didn't want his family to see her or get to know her?

And now, now it was too late. He wouldn't look at her, let alone talk to her. He was done with her and all because she wouldn't let Julian rape her. To her surprise, as Rick led Julian from the saloon, Brett walked towards her, his face grim.

"What's going on, Brett?"

Her soft voice jolting through him caused the all too familiar tightening in his groin. Oh he was always hard around her, and the weeks before Carlman arrived were the happiest of his life — not because they made love every day, on some days all day. No, because she was a part of him, part of his life. She asked him questions about himself. She listened. She made his life better without even really trying. And he was hoping her love for him was strong enough that she would one day give him children. But the bottom line was she didn't trust him . . . she said she loved him, but if she did, why didn't she confide the one thing that really affected their life together? And even with that betrayal, here he stood, probably harder than he'd ever been in his life and wanting to bury himself in his woman — no, no longer his woman, just this woman — so deep he'd never come out.

"Rick and I contacted my brother, Kendrick, the one who's a Marshal and I asked him to look into this situation with Carlman. Seems your uncle was engaged in more than just attacking you — if that's what he did."

Jenna had to bite her tongue to keep from cursing Julian with every foul word she could think of, but she wanted to know what Brett had learned. "What did he do?"

Brett opened his mouth to speak and then seemed to think better of it. He gave a quick look around the room, took in the people milling about looking at them. More likely than not she was going to be upset, devastated, by what he needed to tell her. "Not here, Jenna. Walk with me."

Hope soared in her heart — he wanted her! He wanted her

back and was going to tell her he loved her and that he was going to bring her home!

They started up the street and wandered into the park area with its pretty white gazebo that the women had gotten the men to build in the past few months and sat down under its romantic canopy. The snow on the ground made it look more like a storybook scene than ever. Even in the cold, Jenna felt warm just being next to Brett.

It broke his heart, almost, when she looked up at him with those big, trusting brown eyes. Brett took her small hands in his big ones and seemed to study their joining as he held them.

Drawing in a deep breath, he realized he was stalling for time and that wasn't going to make this any easier. "Jenna, were your mother and uncle close?"

"I suppose. She was the one who wanted him to be my god-father and guardian. He'd come to visit several times a year . . .but stayed at a hotel. Not with us and, and, well now that I think of it, it was odd. We had a big house, plenty of room. Why?"

"Jenna, Kendrick has proof that Carlman killed your father."

"No, Papa, Papa, Brett, my Papa . . ."

"Was killed by Carlman. Kendrick says he has proof that he did. I don't know what it is, yet, but he's sending the proof."

"I knew Papa wouldn't take his own life, I *knew* it . . . but why would Uncle Julian kill him? Brett, that doesn't make sense."

"It does if it's true that Carlman was in debt and getting further in. Again, the proof is coming, but it would seem that Carlman attributed all of his own bad judgment on your father. Somehow he manipulated things to look like your father killed himself."

Jenna fought the tears starting to form in her eyes . "What did that have to do with my mother?"

"Kendrick thinks Carlman had something to do with your mother's death, also."

"No, Brett, she was in an accident. That's what the police told us."

"Maybe a staged accident. I trust my brother's judgment, but we'll see on it. Carlman also has a history of human trafficking and there was a chance he would have ended up . . . well your life may have been in danger, Jenna."

"Yes, I know and now you know, too. Oh, Brett, do you understand why I ran away? Do you understand why I was so frightened?"

"I understand your fears and what you did, but . . ."

"Oh, Brett!" She launched herself into his arms. "I love you so much, I love you more than I ever thought . . ."

"No, Jenna." He pushed her back away from him. "I understand why you did what you did, but not why you kept it from me. If you really loved me, you would have told me. You would have been honest with me. In the beginning I could understand, but after we, after things got better for us . . . you still kept it from me. I just feel that too much has passed between us, more than either of us could ever overcome."

"I didn't know how you would take it and I'm sorry I didn't trust you. But, Brett, the one thing I have never doubted, the one that that has never changed, is that I love you. With all my heart I love you."

"You never even told me your real name, Jenna." He stood, raking his fingers through his hair, his pacing showing his agitation.

She stood to stand as near him as she could while he continued to move the length of the gazebo, "If I had and they sent out a notice about me being wanted for murder, what would you have done? How would it have felt to arrest your wife?"

"I'd like to think I would have listened to you and that we would have worked it out."

"Brett, I was so frightened. But you know now, it's all out in the open now. Please, Brett. Do you want me to beg? Will you believe me if I beg?"

"No, Jenna, it's too late. I'm sorry, but it's too late. I just thought you should know what Kendrick had to say before it's all over town and I thought it'd be easier to take hearing it from me. There will probably be some paperwork to tie up and then, well then you can do what you wanted to for the past few months and leave. You won't have me standing in your way."

Tears pooling in her eyes, she softly said, "Brett, please, I love you. Please, don't leave me, don't send me away."

"It's not enough, Jenna." He stood and moved a step away from her. "I'll talk to Belle and ask her to come talk to you. I'm sure you can stay with her and Henry till you decide where you want to go."

Walking away was one of the hardest things Brett Parker had ever done, but he had to. He couldn't let her hurt him, not again. Loving Jenna was one the most painful things he'd ever done.

Jenna had no idea how long she sat in the gazebo, staring ahead with tears rolling down her cheeks. Belle came up the path and put a comforting arm around her. "Come on, Jenna, you'll stay with Henry and me till we sort things out."

"Oh, Belle, I'm sorry, I'm so sorry. How can you even stand to be around me? After all the horrible things I did, how can you ever speak to me?"

"Jenna, you did what you had to in order to survive. Who are we to say we would have done different? Even if he hadn't killed your Papa, what he did to you was beyond comprehension. He's a sick man, a very sick man. And you know, I'm glad you hit him and by time this is all done he may well wish he was dead. Now come on, let me take you home."

"What about Henry? Will he mind?"

"No, if Henry knows what's good for him, he'll welcome you with open arms."

Belle settled Jenna into one of the warm and cozy rooms at her home and went to order a bath and bring some tea. Jenna welcomed the hot water and soaked away not only the grime of the day, she tried to let go some of her worries. Part of her understood why Brett wanted to be done with her, but part of her hurt. She napped a bit after the bath and then only reluctantly went downstairs to dinner.

"Not much work got done in town today, that's for sure." Henry told her. "And I can tell you, that Carlman wasn't liked much when he first got here and he's liked even less now. I don't understand Brett, not a bit. Hope Rick talks some sense into him and soon."

"Yes, Henry, so do I, so do I."

After dinner Jenna begged off talking with the couple. She hadn't really been alone the past few weeks because of Rick having someone around her at all times. She appreciated his concern that Uncle Julian would try to hurt her — and had no doubt he would have if he could. Now, however, she had another, more pressing concern. She hadn't had her monthly time since shortly after she and Brett made love the morning Julian arrived. And who knew what he would do if he found out. He could easily take their child from her. At least a child would be a part of Brett she would always have with her. If she told him and took her home with him she would always wonder if it was because he was in love with her or because of the child. If he even accepted the child. All she knew for certain was she needed to disappear, again and soon, but how? Brett had told her she needed to stay in town until things had been settled with Julian's arrest. Henry told her last night that Uncle Julian would probably be transported back east to stand trial because that's where the crimes occurred. But how soon would that happen? How could she hide her pregnancy, if in fact she was pregnant? And it was becoming more probable that she was, in fact, expecting. It seemed not a morning had gone by she wasn't sick and her clothes were getting a bit snug in the waist.

Waiting till her stomach settled she finally made her way downstairs. At least Belle would think that her delay was more from exhaustion over the past few weeks than anything else. If she thought it odd that Jenna only had some tea and toast for breakfast, she didn't say.

"I was thinking to do a little shopping today. Would you come with me, Jenna?"

"I don't know, Belle . . . I'm still a little tired."

"Are you tired or are you afraid of seeing people?"

"Honestly? How can I face anyone after the past few weeks? They know I lied about my past. They know my husband left me. I can't subject them to me, nor me to them."

"I think you're wrong. Everyone woman in this town understands why you did what you did. And if the men are smart they will support their wives . . . if you get my drift."

"Brett's a good man, Belle. I can't do anything that would embarrass him, I can't. He deserves better than that."

"The man leaves you, sends you away, doesn't even visit you in jail and you don't want him embarrassed? Jenna Parker, Brett Parker can take care of himself just fine. And you know, if you don't come with me, most of the women will be coming out here. Now I do enjoy company, but if they come here getting them to leave in a hurry won't be happening. At least in town you can mosey on sooner rather than later."

Jenna sighed. "I suppose you're right. Alright, I'll come."

Belle had the wagon hitched up and the pair drove the short distance into town. First they stopped in to see Bea who welcomed Jenna with open arms. "I knew you didn't do the things that awful man said. I knew it! He'll rot in hell for what he did to you."

"Thank you, Bea. Your friendship means more to me than I could ever say."

"Care to join us for a bit of shopping?"

"Yes, I think I will."

The trio set off down the street and stopped in the Emporium first. Jenna wanted to look over the baby items, but if she did, Belle and Bea would ask questions or just come to their own conclusions and it wouldn't be long until Brett heard. She wanted Brett, but wouldn't use a child to win him . . . he had to want her for herself and that didn't seem likely to happen.

Feeling a wave of nausea come over her, Jenna excused herself to get some air, hoping the other two women would just think she saw something outside. As she exited the Emporium, Jenna felt something was wrong before she even saw the shadow. All of a sudden she was grabbed from behind, a knife to her neck.

"Just step back with me my dear and everything will be just fine."

Uncle Julian. It was her uncle and he was out of jail!

"Unc..Uncle Julian . . . wha . . .what are you doing out of jail?"

"Shut up, you stupid bitch. Say another word and I'll not only cut out your tongue, I'll take the time to kill that husband of yours. I'll carve him up into pieces in front of you."

As he pulled her back into the alley way next to the

Emporium, she felt moisture in the area where the knife had already bit into her neck. The slimy bounty hunter — Donny, she'd heard his name was Donny — she'd seen with her uncle came up to them and while at first she thought he might have been there to help her, she was quickly disabused of that notion when Julian asked him for the rope. In no time he'd had her gagged, tied and thrown in the back of a wagon. A moment later Julian and the man he called were in the wagon and it was moving.

I wanted to leave . . . but not this way, not with him. Someone, help me, please.

A short distance out of town, Julian climbed in the back and leered down at her. Donny continued driving the wagon further from town. The man didn't seem very bright and maybe she could use that to escape.

It was Julian who truly frightened her. Julian's smile left her wanting to vomit, but the gag kept her from even drawing moisture into her mouth. She felt his hand reach for her collar and in one quick motion, he ripped the bodice of her dress. He wasted no time baring her breasts and grabbing them with his hands. Not the sensuous plumping and caressing she'd experienced with Brett. He squeezed and grabbed and took great pleasure in hurting her while he mauled her breasts.

"Beautiful Jennifer, so beautiful. I hope you like it rough my dear because that is how I intend to give it to you, night after night . . . and if you're lucky, we'll even do it in the daytime as well. And of course you will need to pay for your defection and pay again for giving yourself to that brute first. Your cherry was *mine* and I waited so long to have it. And you just up and gave it to him without another thought. His hands continued their movement, squeezing her breasts, rubbing along her rib cage. There was no doubt in her mind that any minute he was going to rape her and this time she had no way to fight him. Tied hand and foot she could only lay there and endure his touch.

"Will you struggle, dear Jennifer? I must tell you it's so much better when the woman fights or at least pretends to. Your mother did . . . but being as she was my sister I could only really enjoy her struggles as she died. You *did* know that, didn't you my dear?"

He laughed, a sick sound at her wide-eyed shock at his revelation. Surely he didn't kill his own sister?

"Yes, my dear. I met her earlier that fateful day and told her I needed money and she refused to go to your father to get it for me. She told me that she'd already given me all she could and your father refused to give her more for me. I had to show your father that it wasn't nice to refuse me . . . so I killed her . . . choked the life right out of her and then I had to dirty my hands arranging for it to look like a carriage accident."

Jenna's stomach roiled at the look of absolute bliss on his face describing how he'd killed her mother. When he continued, the excitement in his eyes sickened her even further. "Now your father . . . he was still fairly depressed at your mother's death . . . it was easy to convince him it was his fault she died. But when it came down to it, well he didn't trust me, had actually argued with your mother about making me your guardian, but your mother won out . . . and I became your guardian." He sighed, a sound of pure pleasure, as if he had just consumed the finest meals ever prepared. "So, I had to help your father leave this world . . . I had to actually hold the gun in his hand and force it to his head . . . do you have any idea how hard it was to make that look like a suicide?"

When she only stared in shock and despair he told her, "It was difficult Jennifer, very difficult. But we finally got the trigger pulled and then, since you were due home at any time, I had to hurry to straighten things and leave so you wouldn't catch me.

"You know, now that I think of it, I should have killed that erstwhile husband of yours at the outset. Come to think of it, once I get you . . . settled," he laughed and gave her breasts a painful squeeze, "I think I'll lure him to our little play area and kill him. But don't worry, Jennifer . . . I'll make sure you get to watch how nice and slowly I kill him. That bastard popped your cherry, just like that." He snapped his fingers. "It was mine! *Mine!*" He shouted. "He'll pay for that. I swear he'll pay for that."

"Julian?"

She thought perhaps the other man, out of common human decency, would do something to help her, but then he continued, "Julian, you're gonna give me a chance too, aren't ya? Just like you promised, right?"

"Of course, Donny, of course. I'm going to need a lot of help to break her in just right. By time we get to San Francisco she'll know just how to please a man, any man, every man."

The man called Donny laughed, if it could be called that. It was more of a dry cackle that frightened Jenna almost as much as the vile words that spewed from Julian's foul mouth.

"Did I tell you that was where we are going, dear Jennifer? To San Francisco, to those rich gold miners."

"Kin we do it now, Julian, kin we?"

"Later, Donny, we need to get to a safe place where we won't be disturbed. And remember how I told you we could make it really good?"

Donny nodded in the affirmative and cackled again. "Tell me again, Julian, tell me again how it's gonna be."

Julian settled himself so he could keep touching Jenna . . . kneading her breasts, but roughly, nothing like what Brett did when arousing her to the passion they shared. "First, Donny, we're gonna strip her totally naked for us." At the word *strip* he pinched her nipples, hard, painfully. It took all of Jenna's strength not to cry out—knowing that was what he wanted she fought not to give it to him.

"Then, once we have her naked and we've looked our fill to get ourselves nicely aroused, we're going to tie her. There's always more pleasure when the bitches are tied." The wagon's bumpy ride jostled her causing more pain, unable to move away from Julian's odious touching, her wrists and legs growing numb from the bindings, Jenna sought the solace of oblivion. If only she could pass out he'd stop, he'd stop. She held her breath, hoping to hurry that fuzzy state of unknowing.

"Yes, Donny, we're going to tie her arms high above her head and her legs spread wide, real wide and then I'm going to teach you how to use a whip just so . . . not to permanently damage, but to add a thrill to the sex."

"I like that, Julian, I like that idea a lot Julian," Donny faded into the background as Jenna finally succumbed into unconsciousness.

Tom McKendrick stumbled out of the jail, his arm at an odd angle, blood running from his nose, one eye swelling shut. "Help,! Someone help! Someone broke the prisoner out! Someone broke that Carlman fella out."

Men came running from the saloon "I'll get the Sheriff," one called. Another yelled that he'd get Brett.

Belle and Bea had stepped out to see where Jenna had gone and found her purse lying in the dirt by the alleyway, one of her shoes further down.

"He's got Jenna!" Bea's panicked scream was heard throughout the street. "He's got Jenna."

Rick came running towards the women, panic clear on his face. "How do you know?"

"I found her purse here, her shoe, just one shoe down there.

And look, the ground, it looks like a struggle happened here."

He made a quick check of the area and found wagon tracks and hoof prints for what appeared to be two horses. Rick had approached the group and informed them, "Tom's with Doc, looks like he'll be ok."

"What happened to him, Sheriff?" one of the men asked.

"Tom said that bounty hunter, Donny, I think his name is, came in to see Carlman. Next thing Tom knew Donny punched him in the face, made him dizzy enough that he stumbled and Donny grabbed the keys and let Carlman out. Carlman was the one who really beat Tom up. But he's gonna be okay. I'm looking for a few men to come with me to take both of them in. Brett?"

"You know I'm in . . . he took Jenna. It's my fault he took her. If I had stood by her this wouldn't have happened. I should have fought for her the day he came, stayed beside her through the trial and brought her home when it was over. If I'd believed her instead of giving into my hurt pride she'd be here now."

"Jenna?" Rick asked.

"Appears so, Bea says that's her purse and shoe, if she's still alive I doubt she will be for long with him."

About ten men mounted up and headed out, following the trail left by the wagon. Even though Julian had about a half hour lead, the horses were going to make good time catching up. Thing was, in the open range Carlman would see them coming and Brett had no doubt he'd hurt and possibly kill Jenna to try to allude capture.

For the next several hours they tracked the wagon. Rick kept a close eye on his friend and deputy until Brett turned and told him, the ice in his voice palpable, "You forget, my mother's blood runs as strong in my veins as my father's. If she's still alive I'll save her. If he's killed her, he's a dead man."

Orem, one of the men in the party, responded to Brett's statement. "If it was my Cassie I don't think I'd be as calm as you are, Brett. I know you two have had your problems, but she's still your wife and I seen the way you look at her and she looks at you."

"It's not easy, Orem, but I'm glad you and the others are here with me."

Darkness finally began to settle over the country and in the distance the rescue posse saw the wagon pull towards a grove for the night. Brett signed Rick to approach from one side with him and two others crept forward from one side while the others moved in from the other. The only indication of Brett's anger was his sharp intake of breath when he saw how Jenna had been trussed up. Carlman handed her down off the wagon to Donny so that he wouldn't have to untie her legs. Donny held her, making her gag with his foul breath, until Carlman took her again and abruptly dropped her on the ground near an old fire pit. He ordered Donny to get the fire going while he pushed Jenna to the ground. The movement confirmed to Brett that indeed Carlman had torn her blouse from her and even in the faded light he could see the bruises forming. They'd wait till Carlman moved away from Jenna before moving in . . . and in a surprisingly few minutes he did.

Brett cocked his gun as he stepped into the circle. "Hold it right there, Carlman." Before Julian could respond he heard the clicks of several other guns being cocked. He spun on his heel to try to reach Jenna, but slipped on some kind of debris on the ground and fell forward. At the sound of the guns, Donny, who had been sitting on the ground, took out his knife and had it held at the ready. As Carlman fell forward, he landed with a thud on Donny's knife. Within seconds Donny was drenched with Carlman's blood. Even with the life pouring from him Carlman tried to inch forward to do some unspoken harm to Jenna.

"I'll get you, you stupid bitch, if I can't make it so you see that bastard die I can make sure he sees you do."

After hours of holding in her screams during Uncle Julian's abuse, Jenna began to scream. Despite the gag still in her mouth, her panic was clear. In two long strides Brett was at Carlman's side, picked him up with one hand at his neck and the other by the seat of his pants and tossed him to the other side of the campsite where several of the other men took him. Brett got to Jenna's side and knelt to hold her.

"I've got you, sweetheart, I've got you. It's okay, I've got you and I'm not going to let you go, I'm here, sweetheart."

The sound of Jenna's keening tore at his heart. He fumbled to remove the gag while Orem came from behind to untie her hands and feet. Her tears tore at his heart . . . this was his fault. If he had swallowed his pride, if he'd put it aside and taken her home where she belonged, this wouldn't have happened. She would have been safe.

"He's dead." Rick called from where Carlman lay.

"Cheated me out of the pleasure of doing it myself."

"Oh, Brett," Jenna's voice reached him as a raw sob. "He killed my Momma and Papa, he killed them." Her tears flowed freely as her body was wracked with sobs. Brett held her close, whispering softly in her ear while he stroked her back. He rocked her back and forth, trying to sooth her fears.

"How is she?" Rick squatted down beside them, concern evident on his face.

"Alive, but I don't know how bad she's hurt."

"We gotta check her out, Brett, at least to see if anything's broken and then Doc's gotta look at her."

"I know." Still holding her in his arms, he tried to shift her so Rick could check for broken bones.

"Noooo! Brett, please, hold me, please. Don't let me go."

"I won't, darlin', I'm right here . . . but we've got to let Rick check you out, ok? Will you let Rick check you for broken bones?"

"You won't leave me?"

"No, Jenna, I won't, I'll be right here."

"Un..unc . . . Julian . . ."

"He's gone sweetheart, he's gone. He can't hurt you anymore."

She turned her tear-stained face to Rick "I think I'm okay, really."

"We gotta check you, Jenna. If something's broken we gotta know so we don't make it worse, like your ribs, ok?"

She nodded and Rick did a quick check telling her and Brett, "Appears nothing's broken, but I'm sure you'll have some nasty bruises come morning. But you're ok, Jenna, you're gonna be ok."

While Rick helped Jenna and Brett, the others secured Donny and placed Carlman's body in the wagon. All the while Donny babbled on about not knowing what Carlman had really planned and how he didn't really mean to kill the other man. One of the men finally had enough of Donny's ranting and told him if he didn't shut up he'd stick his dirty socks in his mouth. They helped Donny into the wagon and secured him to the side, sitting just a short span from Carlman's body.

As Jenna stood, Brett took his shirt off and wrapped it around her. The men had been polite in not looking her way which helped somewhat to restore her dignity. But it was the scent of Brett's shirt, his scent, that gave her comfort. He'd come for her . . . Brett had come for her. Would he want her? Would he believe her that all Carlman had done was grope her?

"Jenna, unless you want to ride in the wagon, we're gonna

have to mount you with one of us on one of the horses."

She looked up at Brett, trust in her big brown eyes. "Can I ride with you?"

"Of course, darlin', of course." He helped her on to his large roan and mounted behind her. She felt safe, safer than she ever had in her life nestled in his arms. Her back against his powerful chest giving her the reassurance she needed. And maybe, just maybe, he'd want her back. Maybe they could work things out.

He kept the horse to a slow pace so as not to jostle her and was relieved when she fell into an exhausted sleep in his arms. Arriving in town a few hours later they went straight to Doc's so he could check her out. When he refused Brett admittance into the exam room, Brett's look was intimidating, but it was his, "She *is* my wife." that sealed the deal for him.

Doc knew better than to interfere with a married couple. His expression was calm, with appropriate reserve until he palpated her abdomen. The look of utter panic in her eyes silenced anything he thought to say . . . there was no doubt in his mind the woman was pregnant . . . nor did he doubt that she hadn't told her husband.

When the exam was done, Doc lent Jenna a clean shirt. "You seem just fine physically, young lady. If something bothers you, if you hurt or cramp . . . cramp anywhere, you come talk to me. If you need to talk about anything, you know where I am, ok?"

"Yes, thank you." He read in her eyes that her thanks were for more than the exam. It confirmed that she was indeed pregnant and that Brett didn't know.

"You ready to come home, Jenna?"

Brett's question startled her. It was what she hoped, but didn't expect.

"I . . . well I . . ."

Fear clutched at his gut. Not the same fear of earlier when he knew Julian had kidnapped her ... not the fear that she would die by her uncle's hand. No this was a different fear. If he never heard the words that she didn't want him then he could always hope she would change her mind. Doing what he always seemed to do when it came to Jenna, Brett refused to listen to what she had to say and cut her off telling her, "I'll take you to Belle and Henry's. She'll be glad to see you're home and safe."

He took the liberty of picking her up and, at her startled look, explained, "You seem to be missing your shoes, don't want you cutting up or hurting your feet."

Her arms crept around his neck, but she didn't look at him again, not on the horse, not during the ride, not until they arrived at Belle and Henry's and he knocked at the door. When Belle opened the door, she threw her arms around Jenna and pulled her into the house.

"I'll ah ... well I'll come by in the morning to check on her."

"Okay, Brett, we'll be fine." Belle hurried Jenna off to the room she'd been using while Henry offered Brett a drink.

"'Preciate it, Henry, but no thanks, not tonight. I'm tired and I think Jenna will rest easier if I'm not here. I'll be by in the morning."

"Well night then, Brett."

CHAPTER TWENTY-ONE

Brett spent a sleepless night, tossing and turning. When he did sleep his dreams were intermingled with visions of the night he met Jenna, the nights they spent loving each other, and Carlman taking her away and running his dirty hands over her, hurting her, taking her from him.

But then Brett himself had sent her away. It was his own ego, his inability to accept her as she was that caused him to lose her. She turned to him tonight, she clung to him. But when he said they'd go home she didn't want to come with him. Had he hurt her so bad that he'd lost her forever?

He was up and dressed before the sun, warmed some left-over coffee and set out for the Bascoms, his heart in his throat, and prepared to put it in his hand if it would bring Jenna back to him.

Riding into town, Brett went over and over in his mind what he would say to Jenna, how he could convince her to come back to him. He thought back over their relationship and the things that seemed to matter to her, things he could offer her, promises to keep to her, to win her back. Even riding slowly so he could collect and arrange his thoughts — the thoughts that had been his constant companion since he'd left Jenna with the Bascoms the night before, he arrived before he could see any movement in the Bascom household. Finally, seeing Belle descend the stairs, he knocked on the door.

"Brett. What brings you out so early this morning?"

"I need to see Jenna. I need to talk to her."

"I'm not sure, Brett.

"She's my wife, Belle."

Hearing the increasing volume of the short conversation Henry came to the door. "Why, Brett, come on in."

"Henry, no."

"Why not, Belle?"

"I will not allow that man to upset Jenna any more than he already has."

"*This* man is her husband and has every right . . ."

"No he is *not*. That Mr. Carlman said, since she got married under a name that wasn't hers . . ."

"And we all know Carlman was a lair."

"And . . ." she emphasized, glaring at her husband, "*he* told her he wanted a divorce from whatever name she wanted to use. I think the way he behaved is all the information we need to say he'd upset her. And besides, last night she did say she's going to leave with the first transportation out since there is no reason," again she glared at Brett, "to stay here."

"She has every reason . . . she loves me, I know she does and I love her."

The threesome was so engrossed in their conversation no one heard Jenna approach. Brett noticed first and was alarmed at her paleness. Without thought, he pushed past the Bascoms and went to her side. If she wanted to strike him again, so be it. At least it would mean she was reacting to him . . . feeling something towards him even if it was anger. Putting his hands on her shoulders, he held her close, but without touching more than her shoulders. "Jenna, you alright?"

"Am I alright? What do you think? I find out my uncle killed my father *and* my mother. He tricked me into signing papers I would never have signed. He tried to rape me. I thought I'd killed him, then I meet a man who insists I marry him and he promises . . . he *promises* to protect me. I fall in love with him and when my uncle arrives, alive and bent for vengeance, this husband who promised to protect me *believes my uncle!* I try to turn to this same husband and he tells me, no, it's over . . . and the uncle takes me and tries to not only rape me again, but promises to send me into prostitution. Am I all right?"

"Jenna, I was wrong, so wrong. Please talk to me, please talk to me."

She shook her head. "No, Brett I . . ." She had to be strong, just a little longer, she had to be strong and looked up into his face, into his eyes and saw them filled with a combination of love and fear. She loved him. With all her heart she loved him. Could she live her life without him? Deciding that being strong meant hearing what he had to say, she nodded. "All right, I'll listen."

She reached for her coat and walked towards the door.

"Jenna, are you sure?" Belle's concern evident in her voice as well as her eyes.

"Yes, Belle, I'll hear what he has to say."

They walked a short distance away from the house to a wooden bench Belle had in the garden she'd been growing. Jenna sat and looked up at him.

"Jenna, I've been an ass and a fool. I love you. I think I fell in love with you the moment I saw you. Even before we spoke, when I saw you where the bride train had camped for the night, I knew you were the one. You had my heart from that moment on. I wanted to be with you . . . not wanted you, but wanted to *be* with you from that moment on. And I was afraid, so afraid you'd want someone else, that you'd reject me, and I gave into that fear and did whatever I had to, said whatever I had to, to make you my wife. And then . . . and then I betrayed you when I said I would protect you and I didn't. I should have believed you, Jenna, I should have understood and instead I got angry. I let my ego control me and blamed you because you hadn't told me what had happened.

Jenna, it's not your fault. It's been my problem. For so much of my early life I felt left out, not included, different. As a kid, Rick was my only friend."

Seeing her look of compassion, he put his hand out as if to stop her thoughts. "No, I don't want sympathy. It's over, done. I have friends now, good friends. My pop loved my mom. He loved her like I've never seen anyone love before. And she loved him. I've heard the old timers tell me they were a once in a lifetime love, the kind of love I wanted in my marriage and I made the mistake of trying to force us to have that love from the beginning, without giving you a chance to fall in love with me. Some of the kids were friendly, but their parents didn't much care for Indians and especially for a half-breed. When my dad died my mom took me back to the village. There, my mom's tribe, they love children, any children. She remarried and had Wolf. But she made sure I knew about my dad's people and that I could still do things with Rick.

"At first I thought it was because I'm half-Indian that turned you from me, but then when I saw you with Wolf, how friendly and open you were, how warmly you treated him, like a true friend, I knew that wasn't it. And that was a relief. It meant you could care for me for myself. But it also meant that there was something else, something else that was keeping you from me. I felt like I had to make you pay for not trusting me and that was wrong, so wrong because, Jenna, I love you. I do love you. My chest feels like it's going to burst just thinking about you. And when I'm with you, when I hold you and make love to you, it's like that part of me that was missing for so long is there. Jenna, I can't bear to lose you. I will do anything for you to stay. Anything. Just please, give me a chance."

He sat beside her, the pain in his eyes tearing at her heart. "Oh, Brett, I do love you . . . I want to be with you . . ."

Before she could utter another word he took her in an

embrace, his lips meeting hers in a deep kiss. The fervor in her return told him she would stay, she would be his wife and they would have a family and grow old together. Everything was going to be all right. Until . . .

"No, Brett, it's not that easy."

His heart broke, shattered in a million pieces.

"Brett, there's things we need . . . I need to talk about. We never talked about those things. We didn't talk about what I want, what I need."

"Tell me what. Jenna, please give me a chance, what do you need to know?"

"There are things I need to know. Important things."

His normally deep baritone voice cracking, "Tell me."

"Do you like children?"

"Of course . . . yes, I love children."

"Do you want them?"

"Oh, Jenna, yes, I do . . . but if you don't want them . . ."

"I do, Brett, I do . . . but we never talked about children, never talked about having them, raising them."

"We can talk about them now . . . anything you want. Anything, Jenna. Yes, I want them and if you do we'll have as many as you want."

"When?"

"Whenever you want."

"What if . . . what if we had one soon?"

"If you want one soon we'll start now, today, trying to make one and I'll give you as many as you want."

"Are you sure, Brett? You won't resent one or think we have a problem if there is one?"

"No, sweetheart. Never. I promise."

"Then I hope you will understand and not condemn me for not saying anything because, Brett . . . well I needed to know it was me you wanted. Me, for myself. Me, Jenna. Not an image of someone you wanted or . . . or someone else. Just me."

"I do want you, Jenna. Just you . . . and our children."

She drew in a long breath. "Then I need to tell you. I'm pregnant. I'm going to have your baby."

Sheer wonder crossed his handsome features, the longing in his eyes became a warm liquid glow and his smile had never seemed so bright. "You're going to have my baby?"

"Yes."

"When? When, Jenna?" Seeming of its own accord, he slid his hand to her belly, his excitement at the prospect emanating from every part of him.

"From what I can guess, in about seven months."

"Jenna!" He grabbed her, held her tight and gave her a quick, hard kiss.

And then he stopped, his look sobered.

"What, what's wrong?"

"Carlman . . . he didn't hurt you or the baby, you're sure?"

"Yes, Doc checked it out last night. It wasn't easy with you in the room, but he understood, I think he understood, I hadn't said anything yet. But we're fine."

Brett rose from the bench and went down on his knee, taking her hands in his he asked her, "Jennifer Matthews, Jenna Martin, will you make me the happiest man in the world, will you have my children, grow old with me, be my wife?"

"Brett Parker, yes, I will. Whenever you want."

He moved back on to the bench and again took her in a kiss. To Jenna it was the most romantic, most passionate kiss he'd ever given her.

CHAPTER TWENTY-TWO

A week later Jenna and Brett were married again, this time
with no secrets between them. Just to be on the safe side
so that no one could challenge the vows the reverend called
her by not only Jennifer Matthews and Jenna Martin, but also
by Jenna Parker. This time the bride glowed in anticipation as
Rick walked her down the aisle. Her gift to Brett came in the
form of her invitation to his mother's village. Her request that
he include all of his relatives in their life had him do something he'd never thought he'd do . . . it brought tears to his
eyes.

After the day's celebration, Brett brought Jenna home. This
time, at the front door, he stopped, picked her up and carried
her over the threshold . . . and up the stairs to bed. This time
he didn't even pause at the door to the room that had been
hers. He took her right to his room—their room. She caught
the glow of love in his eyes just as he dimmed the lights . . .
not quite all the way . . . just enough to add to the sensual aura
of the room. When he took her to bed the passion they shared
was more than either ever thought possible, but knew that it
would only get better and better.

"Knight, can I see you in my office?"

Morgan Knight groaned. Not that what Humphrey was calling him in about wasn't expected. What with the economy in the tank, even being with Hastings for almost six years, he was still one of the most junior line staff. With its high paying salaries, good benefits and comfy working conditions, Hastings Technological was one of the most sought out companies to work for. No one left the firm and positions were hard to come by. With a fencer's grace, Morgan rose from his chair and headed into Humphrey Hastings' office. The telltale tingle on the backs of his hands told him it wasn't going to be about a raise or an interesting new project. No, it wasn't going to be any kind of good news.

"How's it going, Knight?"

"You tell me, Humphrey."

"That's what I've always liked about you, Knight. You're a straight shooter. What you see is what you get and you don't need a lot of grandstanding."

"I guess."

"This isn't what I want. Hell, I didn't want to let the twenty-three folks before you go, and if I could pick and choose who to keep, you'd be at the top of the list."

"But you can't. Least seniority goes first, I know."

"And that kicks my gut. In five years, you've only taken a vacation day here or there and never once called in sick. You stay late to get critical jobs done and make it in on time the next morning. I couldn't have asked for a better employee."

"Thank you, Humphrey. That and $4.05 will buy me a triple venti latte at Starbucks." Morgan softened the bitter statement with a smile. After all, it wasn't as if Humphrey Hastings wanted to see his business tank.

"Well, there you go. I wish there was a way around the union's rules—"

"I'm not a member."

"Oh no?" That surprised his boss.

"No. They take your money and negotiate away your rights. I'd much prefer a free flowing choice of employees myself. Raises and promotions on merit, not because you've worked some place for x number of years."

"Well now, that's good to know. For future reference I mean."

"So in lieu of the usual goodbye speech, what do you have for me?" Morgan had never been one for emotion for the sake of emotion. Losing his job was bad enough without pretending to care when he really didn't.

"Your final check, vacation payout, severance and COBRA forms. I don't know if you heard when the others left, we pay a thousand a month for every year you worked for us. I know it's not much, however, we don't challenge unemployment. Although . . . with your skills, I'm sure you'll find something else right away. Now, I ah, well don't tell anyone else this, but I worked it out with HR that we'd pick up your medical for the next six months so you won't need to worry about insurance till then and I had them cash out your fifty sick days you had on the books which gets you another six weeks pay."

Morgan looked down at the stack of papers sitting on Hastings' desk. Generally mild mannered and a go-with-the-flow kind of guy, at that moment Morgan was tempted to snag the stack and shred it to bits. Unfortunately, he needed the money. Rent was due next week on both his apartment and the stables. He'd heard stories about people having to give up their pets, but Buster, his big orange cat and Trigger, named after his dad's childhood hero Roy Rogers's horse, were all he had in the world. No how, no way would he give them up.

"Seriously, Knight, as soon as things pick up, you are back on the payroll. I promise."

"Sure, Humphrey, I know. Well, thanks."

"Ah, no need to finish out the day. Just leave your badge and key and, well, ahhhh . . ."

"Don't worry, I saw security when the others left. It would be wrong not to have them at mine."

It took all he had not to rant, rave and rage. Somehow Morgan Knight made it to his desk, packed up six years of personal gear without even a glance at his co-workers and left the building. He'd head out to the stables and take a long, hard ride on Trigger before going home and trying to figure out the rest of his life.

The rest of his life. Just when you think it's all going well, stable, secure and time to plan for the future, you get your ass kicked.

About the Author

From earliest childhood Regan was an avid reader and upon discovering Alexander Dumas and Charles Dickens she was hooked on books that carried the reader away to a different time and place. Preferring the quiet of her room and a good book to spending time with people she traveled far beyond those four walls.

It was while working as a police dispatcher, first for the California Highway Patrol and then her local police department, she began to write fiction, primarily time travels and romantic suspense. In the spring of 2009 she returned to the day job she always liked best, working as a legal secretary. Although, curled up in her bunny slippers with her furfaced children, Missy and Lulu, while writing is one of her most favorite things to do.